PROLOGUE

The sorcerer was angry. Furious. He didn't like to lose, and he had lost this battle: plummeting through the clouds to his death.

Someone weaker might have submitted to his fate, but he'd fallen before and survived. There was, perhaps, one last hope: the sorcerer didn't always take the shape of a man. In his changed form, he might just have enough magic to escape the unescapable. His calmness and patience had always been his strength. He chanted his spell of transformation, over and over. The words came automatically. Time slowed. There, in the icy clouds, he tumbled, turned, and fought for his life with all the magic he knew. His heart hardened and his whole being froze.

He emerged from the clouds floating, not falling, in his changed form. Icy, steely, sharp.

No man could survive this fall, but he could. He had.

Once again, he had beaten the odds. He'd lost everything he'd worked for, but that didn't matter. He could work hard again, build up his power from nothing as he had always done before. Find an isolated place, take control.

This time, there was one difference.

This time, he had paid a heavy price.

This time, there was no changing back.

The Frozen Unicorn

Published in the UK by Scholastic, 2022
Euston House, 24 Eversholt Street, London, NW1 1DB
Scholastic Ireland, 89E Lagan Road, Dublin Industrial Estate,
Glasnevin, Dublin, D11 HP5F

ISBN 978 0702 31167 3

A CIP catalogue record for this book
is available from the British Library.

Printed by CPI Group (UK) Ltd, Croydon, CR0 4YY
Paper made from wood grown in sustainable forests
and other controlled sources.

1 3 5 7 9 10 8 6 4 2

www.scholastic.co.uk

The Frozen Unicorn

BY ALICE HEMMING

SCHOLASTIC

Also by Alice Hemming

The Midnight Unicorn

The Darkest Unicorn

The Cursed Unicorn

The Blazing Unicorn

To Willow and Sonny

MANY YEARS AGO

IN MILLBROOK

CHAPTER ONE

APPLE CAKE AND STORIES

"Tell us about the snow," pleaded Violet.

A cluster of children had gathered in Madam Verger's parlour as they did every afternoon at harvest time. Most of them worked in the orchard, twisting ripe apples from the laden branches and climbing the trees to reach the uppermost fruit. Not Violet. Mother would never have let her climb a tree. Instead, she sat inside sorting the fruit with Madam Verger, a crisp white apron tied over her dress. She placed apples with unbroken skins on the wooden rack for winter storage. Those with bruises and imperfections went into a metal pail ready for the press.

The other children joined them afterwards, cheeks red as the apples from exertion and the autumn wind. Violet removed her apron and perched on the settle so as not to crease her new frock. Most of the children sprawled on the floor near the warmth of the hearth. Madam Verger never sat. She liked to keep moving as she told her stories, and the children always wanted to hear them. Stories of faraway lands, of great journeys and battles. Stories of secret places where the fairy folk lived. Some true stories of her own experiences. Others more fanciful.

On this particular day, they all had one tale on their minds.

"Tell us about the snow!"

They had heard all the tales before, and this one more than most, but it didn't stop them from asking. Again, again. Some stories grew better with retelling. Madam Verger stood by the window, upright and elegant despite her age. She wore an old-fashioned layered white dress that swept the floor, and an embroidered blue scarf at her throat.

"So, you want to hear about that winter. The cruel winter, long ago, when I was a young girl." She paused and walked to a glass cabinet in the corner of the room, which held all manner of trinkets and curiosities. Violet loved that cabinet, and the stories attached to the objects within. A bronze statuette of a child, a shining golden apple and a spindly feathered dart. What would they reveal? But this time, Madam Verger reached for a snow globe containing a wintry scene. A horse or a deer stood in the snowy hills; Violet couldn't quite tell from where she was sitting. Madam Verger shook the glass sphere, and all the children watched, entranced, as the white flakes settled in the clear liquid. She returned it to the cabinet and gazed out of the window as if she could see snow falling outside, too. Then she began, telling the tale the way she always did.

"Snow fell everywhere. Deep, powdery snow, white as a firstborn's blanket, draped across doorsteps, rooftops and vegetable plots until all was white. Millbrook had never known weather like this. At first, the people rejoiced at the proper Wintertide weather. What a time for a holiday! We children tried to make snowballs and snowpeople, but it wasn't the kind of snow that stuck. This snow scattered like flour if you threw it; you'd have been lucky to build a snowman a foot high. Still, it was fine snow for sledging, and for skating."

Madam Verger leaned across the spindly table and cut the spiced apple cake waiting there. She halved it once, then cut through three more times, so there was a slice for everyone. At her nod, eager hands reached forward for their portion. Violet waited until last and took one of the overlooked plates and forks for her slice. Grabbing and gobbling was not for her. What would Mother say if she saw Violet shovelling cake into her mouth the way the village children did?

Madam Verger continued.

"The millpond froze solid. The whole village gathered on that patch of ice. There were little ones barely toddling and folk the age I am now. Even older. All risking broken bones or wet behinds if they fell. Some folk even made skates from cattle bones, and smiles were plentiful those first few days."

Madam Verger stopped for a moment, smiling herself as she remembered. Violet used the opportunity to take a big forkful of cake, enjoying the tang of the apple and the warmth of the cinnamon. She couldn't decide whether she came to Madam Verger's for the stories or the cake. Like the apple and the cinnamon, the two blended together in her mind. She closed her eyes as she ate and tried to picture the Millbrook Madam Verger had described. She could see herself gliding on the millpond in her warmest cloak – the one with snow-white fur around the hood – snowflakes dusting her cheeks.

But one boy, Nicolas, pulled himself up next to Violet on the old settle, interrupting her happy imaginings. "Tell us what happened next, Madam Verger," he said, through a mouthful of cake. "Get to the exciting part."

He sprayed Violet with crumbs as he spoke. She shuffled away, wrinkling her nose until she was in danger of falling off the edge of the settle. Mother insisted on Violet keeping her distance from the village children, because of their not-too-clean clothes.

Madam Verger moved her long white plait over one shoulder and continued.

"The truth is, the exciting part didn't feel exciting at the time. That snow: the pretty, thrilling snow, soon changed. It kept on falling, until it was well past our knees. Then it hardened and became icy. The winds howled and buffed it so smooth it became treacherous to walk upon, so we retreated into our homes. Everyone had supplies set aside for the winter, but they didn't last for ever. This was a crueller winter than we'd ever known. Our prosperous community was thrown into starvation. We felt someone must have wished it upon us—"

"What about the cypress wreaths?" Nicolas was practically jumping up and down in his seat now. Violet sighed. She didn't like this part of the story as much as he did – it was sad.

Madam Verger looked sad too, staring off into the distance as she remembered.

"As Wintertide approached, things looked bleaker than ever. Then, for a time, things began to look more positive. One or two families in need received mysterious bundles of gifts and food."

"What was in the bundles?" asked a little girl whose name Violet didn't know, eyes wide.

"Blankets, clothing, oats – all the things a family needs to get through the winter."

"Apple cake?" asked the girl hopefully, and the others laughed and shushed her, wanting to get on with the story.

"Perhaps apple cake," replied Madam Verger. "But whatever else was in the bundles, they all came with a cypress wreath to hang on the door. And for a time, the faces of those families lost that pinched, gaunt look, and everyone began to welcome the upcoming festivities."

"Then the people started going missing," Nicolas said loudly. This time, Violet was the one who shushed. She preferred hearing the story from Madam Verger.

"Yes, they did. The first one was a man called Downing. A kind man – gentle – who always put his family first. He disappeared just after his family received a mystery bundle. Vanished into the snow. It was presumed he'd met his death out in the forest and that when the snow melted, his body would be revealed, but it never was."

Nicolas grinned and elbowed Violet at the mention of dead bodies, but she ignored him and listened only to Madam Verger.

"That was the way it went, that cruel winter. We began to dread those cypress wreaths. Every time one appeared on a door, that family would briefly flourish – as if by magic – and then within days, they would lose one of their own."

One of the youngest, Billy, stared, waiting for more. It might have been the first time he'd heard this story. "Where did they go? The missing people?"

Madam Verger swept some cake crumbs from the table into the palm of her hand. "They were never found," she said, her voice matter of fact.

"Who took them?" asked Nicolas.

Violet sighed at the constant questions. They had heard this story countless times. Did they really expect the ending to be any different? The people disappeared, the snow melted, life continued as before and they never found the missing folk. Yet Madam Verger had a habit of giving them an extra titbit of information each time she told the story. A name or a detail they recognized from the village was enough to fire up their imaginations all over again.

And this time, Madam Verger reached back into the cabinet and took out the snow globe once again. She shook it vigorously, then crouched down in front of Violet and Nicolas, holding it out so all the children could see. The room fell silent as they watched the white flakes fall.

The little model in the wintry scene was revealed to them all. It wasn't a deer or a horse at all, but a beautiful white unicorn.

"Unicorns," whispered Madam Verger, her pale eyes fixed on Violet. "Their outward beauty may hide an inner evil."

"Unicorns?" said Violet and Nicolas, almost together. Unicorns had never been a part of this story before.

Madam Verger nodded slowly and continued speaking in her natural storyteller's voice. "That winter, just before the snow came, I spotted a unicorn on the hillside outside Millbrook. And again, after the cruel weather subsided. I believe the creature brought misfortune to our village for reasons we cannot know, then lifted its own spell."

Violet turned to look at Nicolas and his mouth gaped open like her own.

Before they could gather themselves and begin an onslaught of questions, Madam Verger clapped her hands together.

"That's enough stories for one afternoon. You children have homes to go to, and I have chores to get on with."

"Please tell us the rest, Madam Verger!" shouted one of the little ones, but she shook her head.

"Next time, children."

She paid no heed to the complaints and pleas to hear more, and chivvied them all up and out of the house, closing the door without ceremony.

The children began to retrieve their muddy shoes from where they'd discarded them in an untidy pile under the porch to the left of Madam Verger's door. Violet's new fur-lined boots were paired neatly together on the right-hand side. She didn't want them to get mixed up with the others and end up on the feet of one of the village children.

She picked them up and, avoiding the snatching group, sat on the edge of the porch steps, pulling each boot on slowly while she waited for the other children to leave. The truth was, this was the first time she'd worn them and she had no idea how to lace them up. She tugged at one of the laces in an attempt to look busy, but somehow managed to unthread the whole thing. She bunched it up in her palm and looked out into the orchard.

Most of the children scattered in pairs or threes, older children dragging younger siblings by the hand. Violet watched them go, wondering what it would be like to be part of a big family. Never lonely, she guessed.

Nicolas remained on the porch, shoving his feet into a pair of shoes that looked a few sizes too big. Hand-me-downs from his father, perhaps. He stared at Violet and she left her boots alone for a moment and pretended she was watching a greenfinch on one of the apple trees. Why didn't he leave, like the others?

After a moment, he said, "D'you want me to do them laces?"

Violet's cheeks flushed pink. He had known she wasn't really watching the bird. "No thank you," she said primly, but he smiled and knelt down in front of her.

"It's no problem," he said. "I do it for the littl'uns at home all the time." This time, she didn't protest, and handed him the loose lace. He threaded it expertly through the eyelets of her left boot and pulled the ends tight. His head was close to her own and he didn't smell too bad after all. Woodsmoke and Madam Verger's apple cake.

"Who did them up this morning?" he asked, tying a deft bow.

"Meg," she replied, not explaining that Meg was her maid.

"Ah," he said, smiling again, and she wondered what he thought of her. Violet Reddmene: a girl who required help to put on her own boots. But if he thought it, he didn't mention it, and she was grateful.

When he'd tied the second bow, he sat next to her on the steps, and she didn't edge away.

"D'you believe it?" he asked.

Violet knew straight away he was talking about the unicorn.

She wasn't sure, herself. She believed in the unicorn part. Once or twice, on a misty day, out in the woods, she had almost convinced herself she had passed one. But, "I'm not sure I believe that magical creatures like unicorns would wish harm on people. Do you?"

He grinned. "Bad unicorns? Yeah! I reckon they're like people. Some good, some bad, some in between."

He stood and jumped from the porch step. "Bye, then!" he said, and scampered off in the direction of the village, shoe heels flapping. It was only then she realized he had no laces in his own shoes.

"Thank you!" called Violet a few seconds later, although she wasn't sure he heard. She stood, smoothed down her dress, buttoned her coat, and headed the other way, in the direction of home: Millbrook Manor itself.

SEVEN YEARS LATER

IN MILLBROOK

CHAPTER TWO

BASKETS OF KINDNESS

It was early winter. Bare trees stood out against a sky white with clouds. The ground was hard, and Violet's feet rustled the crisp leaves. She balanced a basket in the crook of one elbow and carried another in each hand. The cold nipped at her fingers through her soft gloves, but she tried not to mind. A least she *had* gloves, unlike others from the village. That was what Father said.

The windows of Madam Verger's house glowed fuzzy orange with candlelight, warm and inviting. Violet did love the orchard house. It felt cosy despite being at least three times as big as most other houses in the village (not the manor, of course). She'd continued to visit there since childhood and was tempted to pop in now, for a small slice of apple cake and a bigger slice of story. But the stories (and the cake) would wait. She had packages to deliver. Packages that would help the people of Millbrook over the coming months. Firelighters, cake, slices of sausage in waxed paper, jugs of cream and jars of preserves. Her father was encouraging her to try and think of other people. Apparently, in the village, not even a mile from her comfortable manor house, the children lived a different existence to her own. Father thought Violet should go and see this for herself.

She strode past the orchard without looking back and took the path winding down to the village, stepping gingerly around the puddles. Her finest velvet cloak swung attractively as she walked. Father had suggested something more practical, but Violet had insisted and Mother had agreed. The bottle-green cloak was thick, warm and perfect for frosty days like these. If its fur trim contrasted becomingly with the dark waves of her hair, then this was just an additional plus point.

The idea of bestowing exciting presents on those less fortunate was quite appealing. She smiled as she thought how pleased the villagers would be. Whoever knew doing something so tiresome would make one feel so good? Her thoughts drifted away as she imagined what it would be like. The little children might be shy at first, but then their eyes would grow wide as they peeked inside the baskets at the stuffed dates and marzipan fruits she'd packed for them. One might ask to touch the soft velvet of her cloak. She'd let them, of course, and might even sing a song or tell a story while she was there. She didn't know any small children, but she remembered being one herself. They would listen with the same rapt attention she'd shown Madam Verger when she was a child.

Violet was so caught up in picturing the scene that she forgot to pay attention to where she was putting her feet. The toe of her boot caught on something – a stone or a bump in the path – and she went flying forwards.

She landed on her knees, both hands palm-down in the puddles. The baskets she'd been carrying in her hands fell on their sides, the contents tipping out. The third basket remained at her elbow. In fact, her whole elbow was now contained within the basket.

"Oh!" she cried, and then, "No, no, no!" as a large orange rolled slowly down the path in the direction of another puddle, arriving with a muddy splash. As she tried to right herself without dropping anything else, she caught sight of two large pairs of eyes, peeping out at her from behind a nearby tree.

Two children, no older than six years, were gazing at her silently. Siblings by the looks of things, twins even, hand-in-hand. Her shouts had probably frightened them. She attempted a smile, despite her sodden skirt and the smarting pain in her palms and wrists.

"Hello, little ones," she said, in a soft voice, so as not to alarm them further. "Don't be afraid. Will you help me out of this puddle? And pick up my things? I'm sure I'll be able to find some marzipan treats for you if you do."

At this, the children exchanged a glance.

Violet smiled and tried to untangle her arm from the basket, without getting more mud over everything. "That's right, the marzipan's in that basket over there." She nodded to the furthest one, lying on its side. "You may have a piece if you pick up those oranges first... No, don't do that!"

The children seemed to have heard little else after she mentioned the marzipan. They threw everything else from the basket, flinging packages and bundles to the ground, in their search for the marzipan. They found the tin in seconds and opened it, giggling together as they stuffed chunks of the sweetmeats into their mouths.

"No!" protested Violet. "Not all of it! There is a little there for everyone." Surrendering her velvet cloak to the mud, she struggled to an upright position, but the children had already gone: vanished into the woods, leaving the empty tin upturned on the path behind them.

"Oh, what a mess!" cried Violet. Now, not only was her skirt ruined, and her new cloak spattered with mud, but all the carefully packed gifts were in disarray around her. Tears pricked at her eyes. All she could do was pick her way through the mess and retrieve anything that still looked edible.

She removed the glove from her right hand and, with chilly fingertips, plucked the orange from the puddle. She wiped it with her handkerchief and examined it. The orange was thick-skinned. It would survive.

"You all right?"

The voice, loud behind her, made Violet jump. She turned, cheeks flaming, to see a boy about her age pick up her basket and brush it off. He looked like one of the lads from the village and was presentable enough. Unlikely he was looking for marzipan to steal. Besides, he was handing the basket back to her with a sympathetic smile. He carried a bundle of thin branches under one arm and had dark grey eyes and messy hair that flopped over his forehead under his cap.

Violet was suddenly only too aware of her own dishevelled

appearance. She started to replace her glove, but it was sodden and brown so she held it limply. A wet globule of mud dropped to the ground.

"I fell and while I was incapacitated, some horrible, greedy children stole my marzipan."

The boy raised an eyebrow and she felt a little bad for calling the children horrible.

"I would have given them a piece. Just not all of it," she explained, taking the basket and placing the orange back inside.

She supposed she should give him something. "I'm afraid I have no money on my person, but if you call into the manor later, my mother and father would be happy to give you a few coins for your trouble."

He raised his other eyebrow and smiled. "I don't need paying," he said, picking up a few more stray packages and stashing them neatly away. "I'd help anyone who took a tumble, not just a lady of the manor."

His kindness touched her and tears welled in her eyes. She swallowed and picked up the rest of the items with him in silence.

There wasn't too much damage after all, and it only took a couple of minutes for them to pack it all away. "You going to the village?" he asked when they'd finished. "I'm heading that way."

Violet shook her head and gazed forlornly at her cloak. "I should return to the manor and change out of these muddy clothes."

He smiled. "No one in the village will give your clothes a second glance, but if it bothers you, you could always turn your cloak inside out. That's what I'd do. Then at least your top half would be presentable."

"Turn it inside out?" Violet looked down at the stained velvet. She bit her lip, hesitating. Why not? Mother had visitors back at the manor and would be inside all afternoon. She would never know. Violet stuffed the dirty gloves into her pockets, then removed the garment, which luckily wasn't soaked through, just speckled with mud. She shivered slightly as she put it back on the other way. The dark brown lining wasn't as fetching as the green, and the fur trim was hidden, but it was clean, at least.

"Ready now?"

Violet nodded gratefully and they began walking side by side down the path. He didn't offer to carry any of her baskets, but then his hands were quite full with his own bundle. This time, she watched where she stepped.

After a few moments he stopped and turned his gaze to her. "You don't recognize me, do you?"

Recognize him? Why would she recognize him? She rarely went

down to the village, and if she did, she avoided the young people, who were usually in a group, laughing and joking with one another.

But now she really looked, there was something familiar about him. The messy hair, the smattering of freckles and the easy, wide smile. She mentally subtracted a few years and a few inches of height. His shoes fitted him perfectly, but other than that, he hadn't changed much. She couldn't believe she hadn't spotted it before.

"You're Nicolas!"

NICOLAS

He nodded.

It *was* Nicolas. The little boy she used to try not to get too close to at Madam Verger's house. How had she not noticed? She wondered briefly if he still smelled of woodsmoke and apple cake, and resisted the urge to move closer to find out. The heat rose in her cheeks and she hoped she wasn't blushing.

Violet remembered how the other children had gradually stopped coming to hear Madam Verger's stories, and had always wondered why. She'd never tired of the tales, and still visited the orchard house every week.

"You stopped coming to Madam Verger's," she said, distracting herself. "Did you begin to find her stories too childish?"

"I'm sure I'd still enjoy 'em, given half a chance, but I had to work. We all did. Not much money in apple-picking."

"Of course," said Violet, definitely blushing now. She couldn't imagine having to work at such a young age, and wondered if he thought her dreadfully lazy.

They began walking again.

"Where are you heading?" asked Nicolas, after a pause.

"I'm not sure exactly. Father asked me to hand out these packages to those who might need a little extra over the cold months. I don't often head down to the village, so I have no idea where to start."

Nicolas smiled. "You can start at my house, if you like."

THE EVERGREENS

Nicolas and Violet continued down the hill, past Millbrook's village hall and over the arched stone bridge to the village. Nicolas's house was one of the first they reached. It was quaint and pretty: a single-storey, cruck-framed cottage with pinkish walls and a low thatched roof. It stood on its own, surrounded by a woven willow fence that contained a few pigs and a couple of geese. And, Violet noted, it was very small. Back at the manor, Oates the gardener lived alone in a similar-sized house within the grounds, whereas from the sound of conversation within, this one must contain Nicolas's entire family.

The door stood wide open despite the cold, and they walked in without announcing themselves. The cottage was dark with just one small window letting in the weak winter sun, but it was full of children, chatter and noise. A wall of heat hit Violet straight away from the fire burning in the hearth. Two children sat at the scrubbed table with their father, and another younger pair were playing in the corner. At the hearth, a woman in a checked skirt appeared to be half-climbing into a huge pot as she stirred.

Nicolas stamped his boots on the mat and the woman called out:

"Nicolas, is that you? Can you give those scraps in the pail by the door to the pigs? Then you can come in and get warm."

"In a minute, Ma," he said, with a smile. "We have company."

At the mention of company, his mother stood up, face red from the heat, looking a little flustered. When she saw Violet, her expression changed to a look of horror. "Why, Mistress Reddmene! You've rather caught me by surprise. Dear, oh dear, look at the state of me. Look at the state of all of us!"

Madam Evergreen rubbed her hands on her stained apron, then untied it and used it as a flannel on the sticky face of the nearest child. She appeared not to have noticed the bottom few inches of Violet's dress were soaked in puddle water.

Violet felt awful to have walked in unannounced, interrupting their family time.

"Call me Violet, please. And don't go to any trouble on my account!" She took a step back to avoid a goose wandering in from outside. How awful to have a bird flapping into the house whenever it pleased! Nicolas chased it out and it waddled off comically. "I won't stay long. I've just bought you some things . . . for Wintertide. . ."

Violet held out one of the baskets, at a loss to explain the gifts without drawing attention to the fact the family had a lot less than she did.

"Do you hear that, everyone?" said Nicolas's mother, taking the basket. "Miss Violet has brought us the Wintertide parcel from the manor." She turned to Violet. "Your father normally brings these down himself. Is he well?"

"Yes, he—"

"I suppose you are taking on some of his duties now you are. . . How old are you now, Miss Violet? No . . . don't tell me . . . you're sixteen summers, same as my Nicolas?"

"Yes, that's right—"

"And pretty as a picture. But then, you always were. I remember when you were children, you all used to go to that strange woman's house up by the orchard and listen to her stories—"

This time, it was Nicolas who interrupted. "Ma! Give poor Violet a chance to breathe. She's only just stepped inside."

"Of course, you're right. Let me put your kind gifts away and you can meet the rest of the family. Nicolas! Where are your manners? Introduce Miss Violet."

Nicolas obeyed with a smile, pointing out his family members.

"My father, Jed," he said.

The quiet man at the table removed his cap in greeting, giving a wide smile like his son's. "Miss Violet. It's a pleasure."

"You've already met the twins," said Nicolas. He pointed to the pair playing marbles in the corner. "Caty and Benjamin. Trouble, the pair of them."

They looked up, giggling together, and she recognized

their innocent-looking eyes: it was the children who'd taken the marzipan! Her cheeks grew pink as she remembered her outrage. She'd called them horrible. And greedy. In front of Nicolas. Seeing them here now, they didn't look like greedy children. Hungry, perhaps, but not greedy.

Nicolas didn't seem to hold it against her, though. He was smiling as he introduced his other siblings.

"This is Cora and Matty helping my father. Here y'go, Pa."

Nicolas deposited his bundle of branches by the table. The older two children sat there with Mister Evergreen, weaving baskets. Matty broke the twigs into similar-sized lengths, which he passed to his sister and father, who worked on a basket each. The children waved shyly.

Caty and Benjamin's game brought them under the table and under their older brother's and sister's feet. Cora and Matty swung their feet violently in response, which led to screeching from the younger two. It was all so much noisier than Violet was used to as an only child, but she liked it.

Nicolas's mother continued unpacking the basket, every so often throwing out a comment about the contents. "Ooh, look at these beeswax candles," she said. "They'll smell lovely, won't they, Jed?"

Nicolas's father nodded.

"There are a couple of items in there which should go in the cold pantry," said Violet. "A block of butter and some cream."

The twins began giggling again and Caty repeated, "the *cold* pantry," in an imitation of a well-to-do voice.

Nicolas's mother gave them a stern look. "Don't mind them, Miss Violet. They're not used to visitors from the manor."

"We don't have a cold pantry," explained Nicolas. "Or any other sort of pantry."

Violet looked around her. A doorway led through to a sleeping area, but it seemed most activities took place in this one space, which was roughly the size of Violet's dining room. A ham and some leeks hung from the rafters, but she didn't know where they stored the rest. Outside, perhaps, to keep it cool. No cold pantry, of course.

She wasn't sure what to say.

Luckily, Nicolas's mother, still unwrapping the food in the parcel, had plenty to say.

"Ooh, have a sniff of this fruit cake, Jed."

Mister Evergreen obeyed. "Mmm, smells good. Real brandy in there, I'd wager."

"We'll enjoy that." Madam Evergreen turned to Violet, holding aloft the cake in its paper wrapper like a prize piglet. "Won't you stay for a little while and have a slice, Miss Violet?"

Violet couldn't possibly stay and eat the cake she'd just given to them.

"That's very kind of you, but I must deliver the rest of these parcels."

"Of course, dear, we understand."

"Let me be your guide," said Nicolas. "I know the households in real need, and the ones who might steal your marzipan."

Violet smiled at the comment. "Only if you're sure."

"What a good idea!" His mother beamed. "Take her to the Campbells and the Kemps. But hold back a few things for Madam Tait as well. . ."

"It's all right, Ma, I know where to go," said Nicolas, ushering Violet outside again as she waved goodbye to the children. Then they were outside in the cold and the quiet, and it was just the two of them once again.

"Ma enjoyed your visit," said Nicolas, breaking the silence.

"Oh, I'm sure she was just being polite," said Violet, secretly hoping he was right.

"Believe me, you'd know about it if Ma didn't like you. She has her own opinions on everything and everyone."

Violet hoped Nicolas was right and they did like her. She rather hoped Nicolas did, too.

THE VILLAGE BELOW

Nicolas took her to all the households his mother had suggested. At each one, Violet grew increasingly dismayed at what she saw. These people had so little compared to her. Compared to anyone. At the Kemp's cottage, one of the children had a hacking cough, and wind whistled through a hole in the roof.

Nicolas peered up at it. "That just needs patching," he said.

The mother, nursing an infant, shrugged. "Got no straw."

When they left, Violet said to Nicolas, "I'm sure we can bring some straw, but who'd do the repairs?"

Nicolas smiled. "I'll do it. Or anyone will. We look after each other around here."

"So you mend roofs?" Violet thought aloud. "I thought your family were weavers."

Nicolas laughed at that. "Nah, we all do a bit of everything in the village. Mainly we work in the fields, but in the colder months there's less to do outside so we might weave a basket or two, or fix up our houses."

Violet nodded, taking it all in. She'd seen the villagers out in the fields, of course, and enjoyed the harvest celebrations, but never considered what they did in the depths of winter. In all honesty, she'd never given the villagers much thought at all.

Although her fingers were pink with cold, she was glad she had no gloves and that the ordinary lining of her cloak was on display. The rich green velvet would have felt too showy amongst the browns and greys the villagers wore.

After visiting the last house, Violet showed Nicolas the empty baskets. "I have no more parcels."

"Oh." Nicolas stared at the row of cottages, many in disrepair. "There are so many other families in need."

"There are more parcels up at the manor, but my father will deliver those with the horse and cart tomorrow."

"That's a shame," said Nicolas. "Folk enjoyed meeting you."

"No," she said. "They all like you, not me. You make them laugh. People don't, as a rule."

"They don't what?"

"They don't tend to like me."

Nicolas furrowed his eyebrows.

"Not that I mind," she added hurriedly, worried she was revealing too much of herself. "I'm used to being on my own."

Nicolas smiled. "I don't know what you're talking about. Everyone today liked you. And before you think it, or say it, it wasn't just because you were bringing them things."

Violet blushed. He'd read her thoughts.

"No," he continued, "it's cos you relaxed in their company and showed a little bit of the real you – not the uptight girl from the manor. I thought you enjoyed meeting them too."

Violet smiled. She *had* rather enjoyed meeting them, and spending the time with Nicolas.

"Perhaps I could bring some of the parcels tomorrow," she said, spontaneously. "I'm sure my father wouldn't mind."

Nicolas smiled again, and his eyes crinkled so much they nearly disappeared. "They'd like that."

She wondered if he meant *he'd* like that, and the thought made her blush again. She inwardly cursed her pale skin that reddened so easily.

They walked back in the direction of the manor, and when they reached his house, she stopped, ready to say her goodbyes. But Nicolas kept on walking. "I may as well walk home with you. Ma would be cross if I let you go on your own."

Violet laughed. "I can well believe it."

Nicolas escorted her out of the village and over the arched stone bridge. After the bridge, the path forked. One way, the path they'd taken that morning led up past Millbrook Hall, the orchard and Madam Verger's house, all the way to the manor. The other path wound around the millpond.

Nicolas stopped, removing his cap and running his fingers through his hair.

"I don't s'pose you fancy a stroll up the hill?"

A stroll. Her shoulders ached from carrying the baskets, her hands were numb from the cold, and her feet still hadn't dried since her tumble in the puddle. Besides, she knew her mother wouldn't approve.

"Mother did tell me I was to come home by the main path. . ."

"Come on, where's your sense of adventure?" urged Nicolas. "It would be a shame to miss the view on a lovely day."

A lovely day? Violet didn't associate cold winter afternoons with loveliness. Still, it was true the millpond she'd known all her life had never looked more beautiful. The trees were bare of leaves and stark against the grey sky, but their reflections rippled attractively in the water. Two geese glided past, looking much more graceful than the one in Nicolas's cottage. And she didn't feel ready to say goodbye to Nicolas yet. She took a deep breath.

"A walk would be lovely, thank you."

He smiled. "Can we stop here a minute first? I never pass the millpond without skimming a stone. My record is thirteen skips."

He said this proudly, although Violet didn't have a clue what he was talking about. It must have shown on her face, because he laughed.

"Don't tell me you've never skimmed a stone before, Lady of the Manor?"

She lowered her eyes and shook her head.

"Come on, first step is to find a good stone. Round and smooth with a flattish bottom."

She put her baskets down and began to search the sparse grass at the water's edge. She rejected a couple of sharp-sided stones and found a speckled grey pebble of the right shape.

"Will this do?"

Nicolas was crouching down nearer the water's edge, a small collection of stones already held in his hand. He looked up and flicked his dark hair out of his eyes with a backwards tilt of the head. "Yep, perfect."

He stood up.

"I'll show you first. Hold the stone like this, curled in your forefinger, then crouch a little and let it fly, parallel to the water. Like this—"

The stone flew out across the pond, thankfully in the opposite direction to the geese. It bounced magically on the surface of the water, once, twice, three times, before sinking into the depths below.

"Like magic!" cried Violet.

He shrugged. "Not a particularly good effort. You must make me nervous."

Before she could blush again, he stood back and gently pushed her forward. "Your turn!"

Violet tried with her stone and the rest of Nicolas's. Even after a few attempts, her stones span and tumbled and plopped into the water without skipping at all.

"You just need practice," said Nicolas. "No one can ever do it the first time."

But Violet wasn't so sure. She suspected she didn't hold the right kind of magic in her fingers. "Shall we carry on to the hill?" she suggested, and they picked up the baskets and walked on.

As they walked past the mill, the old wooden wheel was turning and the water was rushing so loudly that conversation was impossible. They continued along the path a little way, then Nicolas turned to his left and began climbing up the grassy bank. It was steep, but it looked as though many people had taken the same route, and a path was trodden into the hillside.

"Not far now." He checked she was following, and she tried not to look quite as out of breath as she felt.

Then, when the top of the slope was in sight, Nicolas turned and grinned again. "Nearly there – just one more small climb to go!"

Violet clutched her side. She was getting a stitch. "What do you mean, another climb?"

"Just to the top of the tower." He pointed and Violet could make out what looked like a pile of stones. She had a feeling she might have glimpsed it before but had assumed it was just a shepherd's hut or similar.

"What is it?"

"The ruins of an old watchtower, with the best views of Millbrook."

Violet was beginning to think that this walk up the hill might not have been a good idea after all. She turned and looked back down at the path they'd taken. She could see the tops of the trees and part of the millpond below.

"Do you know, it's rather pretty from here. I'm not sure we need to go any further."

Nicolas laughed.

"Come on, it's barely a climb at all, just a few steps and a small leap! The view's worth it – promise."

Violet sighed. A small leap sounded daunting. Still, she followed Nicolas right up to the top of the hill and towards the ruins. The structure had obviously once been a square-sided tower, but had lost most of its top half and two of its sides so that just two facing corners remained, one taller than the other. At its tallest point it was about twice as high as Violet.

"Are you sure this is safe?" asked Violet.

"I've been coming up here for years and I haven't broken anything yet!"

Nicolas stepped over a couple of layers of stone into the ruins, helping Violet do the same. A dozen or so steps were left inside the tower, and they followed those up to one corner of the building, where some of the stone flooring was intact.

In one easy motion, Nicolas jumped across a gap to the remains of the floor in the other corner and held out his hand to her.

"It's not even really a jump – just a big step. Trust me," he said, his brown eyes very wide.

Violet looked. He was right, it wasn't very wide. Without even picking up the hem of her still-muddy dress, she took a giant step, reaching forward for his hand.

She made it across but wobbled when she landed, and half fell, very clumsily, into Nicolas. He helped her to her feet.

"That's the second time today I've picked you up after a tumble," he said. "At some point, you're going to either have to stop falling over, or pick yourself up!"

His eyes sparkled, and she could tell he was only joking, but she still felt cross and pulled away.

"I'm perfectly fine, thank you. Please continue."

He nipped nimbly up another very small flight of stairs. Violet followed, and there they were, at the very top of the tower, as promised. Nicolas removed his cap, and stood with his arms wide, the breeze ruffling his black hair.

"Isn't it amazing?"

Violet gaped. Nicolas hadn't exaggerated the view. She could see the whole of Millbrook below: the mill and the millpond, looking smooth as glass, the village behind with the people like little specks. And her own home: the manor house, with its well-kept grounds and trout pond, taking up as much space as the whole of the village. She'd never truly understood before quite how much her family had.

Nicolas looked behind him, into the hills. "I always think, if I were to see Madam Verger's unicorn, it would be up here."

Violet smiled at the memory of their childhood stories. She had once taken every word to be the absolute truth, but she wasn't sure she believed in such things any more. Mother said there were no unicorns left in these parts, that they'd died out long ago. "Do you think what Madam Verger told us was true?"

Nicolas shrugged. "Don't see why not. She told us about trolls and other fairy folk too, and I know that they exist. I've seen fairies for myself."

Violet raised her eyebrows sceptically. "Really? Where?"

"Out in the woods. At daybreak, before anyone else was about. There were just four or five playing together, tiny little things, but they scattered when they caught sight of me."

Violet didn't know what to say. Was he speaking honestly, or teasing her? Maybe he thought he'd seen them but was mistaken.

"I did see them," Nicolas insisted in response to her silence. "I reckon there are loads of creatures out there that hide away from people. They probably keep to the wild, unspoilt places."

They stared out at the view together.

There was so much world out there to explore. Maybe Nicolas had seen fairies. Perhaps unicorns did frolic in the woods. Violet might never know.

"I've never seen Millbrook from up above," she said.

Nicolas grinned. "You're telling me that you, Lady of the Manor, have lived your whole sixteen years in Millbrook and you've never once been up the hill and looked down at the millpond?"

Violet shook her head. Nicolas would be surprised at how little she knew of her local area. She tended to keep to the manor grounds for her daily exercise. If she and her mother travelled further afield, to visit relatives or acquaintances, then they took a carriage. It was so different to Nicolas's life – she couldn't expect him to understand.

"I don't actually like it when you call me 'Lady of the Manor'. It's not my fault I've never skimmed a stone or climbed this hill, let alone the watchtower."

He laughed again. "Sorry. I won't call you that any more. Still, it must have been nice growing up the way you have. I bet you've done lots of things I haven't."

"Like what?"

"Like ... I don't know... Drink from a silver tea service or dine with royalty—"

"—Dine with royalty? I've never done that!"

"Well, how should I know what you have or haven't done? I can't imagine what goes on at Millbrook Manor!"

There was a moment's silence before Nicolas spoke again.

"You've changed since we were children."

She widened her eyes. "How?"

"You used to think you were better than us."

"I didn't!" But Violet flushed pink; she knew it was true. She paused. "I have changed. At least . . . I'm trying to change."

"I could tell that today. But I hope you don't mind me saying: the only way to *really* change is to do different things."

"What do you mean?" The wind whipped her hair in front of her face and she pushed it back.

"If you stay here in Millbrook, you will always be the girl from the manor house who thinks herself better than the rest of us. If you really want to change, then you need to go out into the world and have some adventures. Stand on your own two feet. Make some mistakes. Find out what you're capable of. That's what I'm planning to do, as soon as I can."

Violet smiled and tried to imagine herself setting out on a great adventure. It was a nice idea, but not something that would ever actually happen. Perhaps for Nicolas. Perhaps for any other young person in the village, but not for her. She gazed wistfully over at the manor house. No, her adventures would be confined to comfortable coaches and other people's drawing rooms. But she didn't want to talk about that now. She wanted to enjoy the moment with Nicolas.

"I suppose you've climbed up here with many different girls," she said, aiming for a teasing tone, but it came out more like an accusation.

Now it was Nicolas's turn to blush. "I don't know about that," he said.

But Violet didn't mind. Right now, he'd chosen to be there with her and it felt good. She wanted to shout it out from the top of the tower, although she didn't, of course. Whatever would Mother have said?

CHAPTER THREE

APPROACHING WINTERTIDE

The days grew colder in Millbrook. Each morning brought a white sheen of frost on the fallen leaves. People drew mufflers up to their noses and their hats down to their brows. But the bite in the air didn't put Violet off visiting the village. She told Father there was no need for him to deliver the rest of the parcels: she would do it herself.

On every trip, she found some new need. She brought straw to the Kemps, and goose fat to put in poultices for their nasty chest colds. These were all small things for those at the manor, but meant a lot to those in need. She even began to knit a pair of mittens and matching scarf for Madam Tait, from the softest, most expensive wool she could find. Knitting was not her strongest skill, but the wool was thick and warm. A few small holes would make no difference.

"You might even get them finished by next Wintertide," said her father, with a wink.

Both her parents were surprised and a little amused at her sudden charitable urges. Violet could see why, but her trips to the village had opened her eyes to what was going on under her nose. Besides, if she was honest with herself, there was another reason for her visits to the village; one which had a wide smile and crinkly eyes and was particularly good at skimming stones.

The villagers did most of their work in the mornings, so she timed her visits for the early afternoons when they were free to talk. The route home always took her past Nicolas's house. If he wasn't home, then Madam Evergreen invited her in for a quick chat and to warm her chilled body by the fire. But on some days when she walked past, he might be repairing the cottage or feeding the animals. On those days he would wave and ask, "Are you heading home?" and Violet would nod.

"D'you mind if I walk with you awhile? Could do with stretching my legs while there are some hours of daylight left."

He would always find an excuse to accompany her and Violet would always accept.

"Of course," she would say casually, as her heart skipped joyful beats.

On most days, they walked away from the village and over the bridge, taking the usual path past the millpond. But sometimes they explored different areas. Once, they carried on through the hills as if they were heading far away from Millbrook. Another time, they floated stick-boats along the stream to the south of the village. Yet they never went up to the manor grounds. Violet didn't suggest it and Nicolas didn't ask.

On one rainy day, Nicolas suggested they explore the woods, where it was more sheltered. The forest floor was carpeted with deep orange leaves. Shallow puddles shone in the winter afternoon light. A single blackbird boldly hopped across their path, stopping to watch them for a moment before flying away.

"It's so quiet here." All Violet could hear was the light patter of rain on the leaves and their own footsteps.

"Quieter than usual," said Nicolas. "Usually at this time of year there'll be someone up from the village hunting and foraging. Your father doesn't mind what we take from here if we catch it ourselves."

Violet felt strangely proud of these woods that belonged to

them, and which they shared with everyone else in the village. "What do you catch?"

"You know, the usual: game birds, hedgehogs, squirrels."

Violet wrinkled her nose involuntarily at the thought of eating hedgehog or squirrel. She imagined her mother's face if Cook were to put roast squirrel on the menu for dinner one day.

Nicolas must have caught her expression. "We're not too proud to eat whatever fills our bellies."

"Of course!" said Violet hurriedly, before attempting to change the subject. "It's such a pretty spot. Is this where you saw the fairies?"

"Yes!" said Nicolas, the squirrel immediately forgotten. "They were playing just over there. No hope of seeing any today, though."

"They will have heard us coming," agreed Violet, who still wasn't sure if she believed these tales.

There was a pause.

"If you think it pretty now, then you should see it in the spring, when the wild violets are in flower," said Nicolas. "The colour and the scent are something else. It always makes me think of the flower song."

"*Don't forget the violet, the sweetest of them all,*" sang Violet, who had learned all the words as a little girl.

"Ah yes, Sweet Violet. We should come and see."

Violet blushed, although she knew he was just naming the flower.

"I'd like that," she said.

Nicolas grinned and picked up some pine cones from the forest floor. He juggled them expertly and she laughed when they all came falling down.

"If m'lady wants to see the violets, then I'll come here every day to check when they're in flower. I'll bring the first bloom to you."

They both laughed at the same time.

Violet knew it was silly, but still felt a rush of pleasure. Nicolas wanted to bring her flowers!

There was a moment's silence, where they stood, face-to-face. Violet hoped he might kiss her, but the moment was broken by the sudden loud cries of some geese flying overhead. He turned away briefly, and when he turned back, Violet knew she couldn't let the moment go. She leaned forward boldly and kissed him on the lips.

Nicolas flicked back the hair from his forehead and smiled.

"That was nice," he said.

Violet felt suddenly flustered and unsure how to behave. She lowered her head, cheeks pink and turned back to the path. "We'd better be heading back now, before Mother begins to wonder where I am."

As they made their way out of the woods and back into the light rain, Violet's heart drummed. He had liked her kiss! He'd said it was nice. And he wanted them to return here in the spring, which meant he hoped they would still be spending time together then.

But they had a whole winter to get through first, and Violet had other pressing matters on her mind.

"Will you be attending the Wintertide Dance tomorrow?" Violet tried to make the question sound spontaneous, even though she had thought about it every day for the past few weeks.

Nicolas kept his eyes to the ground, kicking through the fallen leaves, and Violet couldn't gauge his reaction.

"I'm sure my family will be there. Ma loves those dances. They are the highlight of her year."

Violet felt warm at that thought. Her family hosted the dance every Wintertide as a gift to the villagers. No expense was spared with the food and decorations, and the villagers did seem to enjoy the party. Still, Nicolas hadn't answered the question.

"What about you?" persisted Violet. "Will you go with them?" Now that she thought about it, she couldn't remember having seen Nicolas at any of the dances since they were children.

Nicolas still didn't meet her eye. He picked up another pine cone, which he dropped and kicked into the brambles. "Nah, it's not really my sort of thing."

"Oh, but you must come!" Violet forgot she'd been pretending to be unconcerned. "The hall looks so wonderful when it's decorated. Everyone wears their finest clothes and, with just a week to go, it marks the beginning of Wintertide."

He smiled but said nothing.

"And the dancing!" continued Violet. "We have the same players each year. They get *everyone* dancing and it's such glorious fun! Won't you come, please, Nicolas?"

Nicolas sighed good-naturedly.

"Very well, I'll come. But I won't dance."

"Wonderful!" Violet smiled. That was enough for her for now. And by the following evening he would surely have changed his mind about the dancing.

DREAMING OF DANCING

The next morning, Violet couldn't resist a quick peek at the hall which would be the setting for the Wintertide Dance. Millbrook

Hall stood near to the bridge at the edge of the village. It sounded grand but was really little more than a swept-out barn. The servants, however, had been busy for days and the place had never looked better.

Her footsteps echoed on the wooden floor as she took a few paces into the room. She breathed in the scent of the fresh pine boughs, which hung from the beams. Sprigs of holly adorned the tables. New white candles were ready in their candlesticks, waiting for their chance to fill the room with flickering light.

Violet planned to wear a dark purple dress befitting her name, cinched in at the waist and flowing to the floor. It was elegant and becoming. Heads would turn when she walked into the room.

She would sit at the main table at the back of the hall with her mother, father, and a select few guests. Stretching the full length of the hall, on either side, were more tables where the villagers would sit. A band would play merry tunes behind them, and the central space would remain free for after-dinner dancing. Violet's pulse quickened when she thought of all those twirling bodies. According to Millbrook tradition, the manor family always started proceedings by inviting one of the villagers to dance.

Her mother always danced with Oates the gardener, who was getting on in years but as sprightly as ever. Her father asked whoever was on the nearest chair at the nearest table. This often resulted in a good-natured scramble between the women in the village. As for Violet, in previous years, her parents had picked one of the youngest guests for her to dance with. But this year was special. Now aged sixteen, she was free to choose her own dance partner. She closed her eyes and pictured how she would hold out her hand to Nicolas. He had said he wouldn't dance, but he would change his mind and rise to meet her with a smile, one hand clutching hers and the other circling her waist.

She didn't know if he was a good dancer, but it didn't matter; his cheek would be close to hers and they would instinctively move together.

Perhaps there would be more than one dance. Perhaps they would dance together all evening, maybe even snatch a kiss when her parents weren't looking. Whispers would travel up and down the long tables about them. The boy from the village and the girl from the manor. So different, and yet so perfect for each other.

A cold wind whistled in from outside, blowing the door to the hall suddenly shut. Violet jumped at the sound. It was time she went home for her luncheon.

Her boot heels clicked back across the floor as she headed to the door. Seven hours to go before she would be back here, surrounded by guests. She wasn't sure exactly what she was going to do in that time, but she knew they would be the longest seven hours of her life.

THE WINTERTIDE DANCE

The hours somehow passed and Violet found herself back in the hall, which was even more beautiful now it was filled with people in colourful outfits. Her dress fitted perfectly, and she'd even dabbed some sweet violet-perfumed oil at her wrists.

She sat at the top table and Nicolas was at the other end of the hall, seated near the doors. She'd seen him come in and take a seat with his family, and she thought he'd smiled briefly at her, but she'd lost sight of him since. To catch his attention, she would have to stand up on tiptoes and wave; inappropriate behaviour for anyone, let alone one of the manor family. So she sipped her soup and sliced her potatoes and tried to make conversation, all the while thinking of the dance.

On her left was a friend of her parents: an elderly gentleman whose hand shook as he ate. He was nice enough to chat to and they exchanged pleasantries.

"Who will be your lucky dance partner this evening, Miss Violet?" he asked during the main course.

Violet looked down at her beetroot, suspecting she might now match it in colour. "Oh, I don't know. One of our younger guests, I should imagine."

Violet declined dessert and took little sips of elderberry cordial as she listened to the music and waited for the dancing to begin.

Throughout dinner, the band had been playing slow tunes to blend into the background. But as the dishes were cleared away, the fiddle player struck up a jaunty rhythm and the band leader shouted so he could be heard above the hum of conversation.

"Now it's time ... for the dancing! Who will be first to take to the floor?"

They all knew it would be her father, and he didn't disappoint. He stood back from the table with a flourish, threw his napkin down to his plate, and raised one hand in the air. "I will lead the dancing tonight!" The villagers laughed.

He gazed up and down the hall, as if making a decision, then offered his hand to the woman in the nearest seat, as he always did. "Madam Morrell, may I have this dance?"

Madam Morrell acted surprised, although she'd arrived early to reserve that particular seat. She fluttered one hand over her heart and laughed with her dining companions, then jumped up to join Violet's father in a lively jig. The villagers clapped along in time to the music, as Violet's mother followed with old Oates.

Then it was Violet's turn.

She rose to her feet and made her way around the top table, keenly aware the villagers would be admiring her dress in all its beauty. She was glad she hadn't speckled the bodice with soup. All eyes were on her, everyone wondering who her dance partner would be.

She weaved between the two couples dancing and walked down the length of the hall, her silk slippers feeling dainty and light on the wooden boards. She knew where Nicolas was sitting, and when she reached his table, all the family were there, smiling up at her, although Nicolas himself was examining the tablecloth in front of him.

Everyone could now see Nicolas was her chosen one. She smiled at him, willing him to look up and meet her gaze. This was their moment; the one she'd been waiting for.

He did look up eventually, but she was surprised to see his usual warmth and humour absent from his eyes. And, unless she was mistaken, he was shaking his head. It was a tiny, almost imperceptible movement, but it was a shake of the head. Didn't he want to dance with her? Of course that's what he'd said, but he'd never explained why. Perhaps he had two left feet. Still, she was here now. He *had* to dance with her. Violet flushed and held out her hand with a wobbly smile. "Nicolas Evergreen, may I have this dance?"

He shook his head again, more obviously this time. His mother frowned at him, a deep crease between her brows, and nudged his arm. But Nicolas looked her straight in the eye.

"No," he said. "I'm sorry, Violet, but no."

THE BAND PLAYED ON

No. That was what Nicolas said, blatantly, and with no excuse offered. Violet blinked, her dancing dreams disappearing in one instant. The fiddler played on. Her parents continued to dance. Violet stared at Nicolas, surprise and humiliation flaming in her cheeks. She didn't know if anyone else in the hall had heard the exchange, but now she had to do something – find a new dance partner – and she didn't know who.

Nicolas's mother narrowed her eyes at her eldest son, but it was his father who came to Violet's aid. "Son, you're a fool," he declared, jovially. He turned to Violet. "Mistress Violet, may I stand in for my son on this occasion?"

Violet nodded, unable to form any words. She gratefully held out her arm to Mister Evergreen. A smattering of applause broke out around the hall, although Violet sensed the confusion of those who'd missed her exchange with Nicolas. They must have been wondering why the girl from the manor had chosen to dance with Mister Evergreen when she could have had her pick of anyone in the room.

She was confused enough herself. In all her dreaming she hadn't once stopped to consider Nicolas might refuse. Had anyone in the history of the Millbrook Wintertide Dance ever refused a first dance? She doubted it.

Nicolas's father was an experienced dancer and her feet moved automatically in time with his. He didn't speak to her, just smiled kindly and nodded in time to the music. Violet concentrated on not crying. As her body spun around the dancefloor, questions spun in her mind. Why had Nicolas turned her down? Did he like her at all? Or had he just been enduring her presence? All those afternoon walks and evening talks by the millpond – did they count for nothing? She'd been the one to kiss Nicolas. She'd invited him to the dance. Perhaps he'd just been trying to think of excuses to get away from her the whole time.

When the tune finished, Mister Evergreen bowed his head towards her. "Thank you, Mistress Violet, it was an honour."

The floor filled with couples ready for the next dance and Violet was surrounded by little children hoping now was their chance. She was grateful for the distraction from her thoughts of Nicolas. She twirled one child after the other until she was dizzy. These children in their best clothes, patched and spruced up for the occasion, wouldn't ask awkward questions, or any questions at all. Violet could pretend this Wintertide dance was the same as any other, even if her heart was breaking.

COLD FEET IN SATIN SLIPPERS

Violet stayed until the end. She saw Nicolas three times, and on each occasion he was dancing with a different girl from the village. Girls with simple frocks but pretty faces. He was dancing really quite expertly, which put paid to the idea he had two left feet. Her stomach felt like a stone.

She couldn't feign illness and leave early, as her mother could always detect a lie and would only ask questions later. So she carried on dancing with the children and making minimal conversation with the adults. She kept her thoughts to herself and her gaze focused on those immediately around her. That way, she was able to avoid catching sight of Nicolas for the rest of the evening.

As soon as people began to drift from the hall, Violet knew it would be acceptable for her to leave. She approached her mother. "Mother, I'm desperately tired." She yawned discreetly behind her hand. "Those children have worn me out! Would you mind terribly if I made my way home now?"

Her mother, flushed from the dancing and the wine, reached a gloved hand to her daughter's cheek. "You do look tired, my darling. Will you be all right going home on your own?"

Violet laughed lightly for the benefit of her mother. "It's a ten-minute walk, and I go straight past Madam Verger's house. Besides, half the village is out this evening. If anything worried me, I would shout and a dozen people would come to my assistance."

Her mother agreed, and Violet put on her velvet cloak. She left the hall, shivering as the cold air hit her. Snow was starting to fall. Violet always dreamed of snow at Wintertide and would normally have been thrilled at the timing, but not this evening. She pulled up the hood of her cloak as sizeable snowflakes swirled in the air, whirling around like the little ones she'd been swinging on the dancefloor. Her feet in their silken slippers were immediately freezing cold; she would have to hurry home.

She took the main path up the hill to the manor. She'd told her mother half the village would be out here, and it was true, but they were all heading in the opposite direction, towards the village. Violet was on her own.

As she passed Madam Verger's house, she could see a line of light peeping out from around the edges of the closed shutters. Violet hadn't paid a visit there since she and Nicolas had started meeting so regularly, and she felt a pang of guilt. Sometimes Madam Verger went away to visit a cousin near Essendor, but she was clearly home now. Madam Verger never attended the Wintertide dance. Violet had asked her once, years ago, if she would be going, but she'd shaken her head and smiled. *"Dancing is for young people,"* she'd said. *"At my age, I might sing a little as I rock in my chair, but I only ever dance in my memories."* Violet found it comforting to know she was there now, rocking and singing, perhaps.

As the path to the manor grew steeper, Violet's pace slowed, and her sadness about Nicolas began to give way to a slow, boiling anger. He'd been the one to suggest their afternoon walks. He'd suggested they might return to the woods in the spring, and yet he'd refused her company tonight in favour of those other girls. Well, they'd taken their last walk together. She would stay up at the manor for the rest of the winter. She would resume her regular visits to Madam Verger, but she wouldn't visit the village any more. She would forget all about Nicolas Evergreen as he had quite clearly forgotten all about her.

THE QUARREL

"Violet! Wait!"

She recognized the voice and turned to see Nicolas standing a few yards down the hill, not far from the spot where he'd helped her pick up her baskets just a few weeks before. He was breathless and looked as though he'd run from the hall. Snowflakes landed in his ruffled hair.

She had nothing to say to him. She turned away and continued her slow progression up the hill.

"Please wait. I want to talk to you."

Violet swung around again.

"No! You didn't want to dance with me and now I don't want to talk to you."

She knew she sounded like a child, but she didn't care. Did he really think he could humiliate her like that in front of everyone and then speak to her as if nothing had changed? She kept walking. The manor was now in sight through the trees: a picturesque building with pointed gables and black beams. Home. It was a welcome sight that evening.

He ran up the hill until he was by her side. His cheeks were red and so were the tips of his ears. "I didn't want this to happen. I tried to warn you not to ask me."

"You didn't warn me until I was standing in front of your table with all eyes in my direction!" Violet tried to keep her voice steady as she relived the humiliation.

There was a pause. She blinked back tears.

"I told you I didn't want to dance."

"And yet you didn't seem to be quite so firm with those scruffy girls in moth-eaten dresses from the village."

He raised his eyebrows and she sighed. She didn't really mean what she said about their clothes, but she couldn't understand why he picked them over her. "I thought you didn't want to dance because you were an awkward dancer, but clearly you just didn't want to dance with me."

Nicolas sighed. "You've got the wrong idea altogether, Violet. Remember, I didn't even want to come this evening, but you forced me to."

"*Forced* you to?" Violet spat the words. "I asked you. I told you it would be fun. And it looks as though you did have fun, just not with me!"

"I do want to dance with you," he said.

Violet couldn't believe what she was hearing. "It didn't look like that earlier this evening."

"I do want to dance with you," repeated Nicolas. "But not like that. I don't want you to ask me out of charity, or to provide amusement for your noble friends."

Amusement? Charity? He wouldn't say that if he knew how she'd been feeling; how much she'd been looking forward to the dance. "That's not why I asked you. No one would ever think that—"

"They would!" Nicolas raised his voice, and Violet thought she saw the shutters of Madam Verger's house open for a moment. She shushed Nicolas, not wanting to disturb the old woman, who was probably going to bed for the evening. "They would," repeated Nicolas at a lower volume. "You've seen the way everyone laughs when your mother dances with Oates: the Lady of the Manor deigning to partner the gardener. You and I would be like that."

Violet shook her head and strode away, taking the biggest paces her dress and slippers would allow. She couldn't understand what he was saying. He liked her but didn't want to be seen dancing with her in public? It didn't make any sense.

When they reached the edge of the manor grounds, she hung back, not wanting to walk along the path with Nicolas. They would be obvious to everyone, and the servants' tongues would begin to wag. "I suspect you're saying these things as an excuse, when the truth is you're embarrassed to be seen with the uptight girl from the manor in front of your friends."

Nicolas sighed and ran a hand through his hair. "No, you have it all wrong. You're the one who's embarrassed of me. You've stopped now, haven't you, rather than let anyone see us together in your grounds?"

That was true, but not in the way he thought. "I—"

"Look at where you live! You are used to such luxury, whereas I have nothing. One day, I will go far away from here and make my fortune. Then I will come back and then I will dance with you."

How dare he! It wasn't Violet's fault she lived in a big house, or that she'd grown up differently to him. It felt as though he was punishing her for things beyond her control, and she had the sudden desire to punish him in the same way.

"You can forget dancing with me, for I shan't ask again. I

shan't speak to you or come near you. You can forget we were ever friends."

He put his hand lightly on her arm but she shook it away. "Please, Violet," he said. "Let's take a walk by the millpond tomorrow and talk about this. . ."

She narrowed her eyes and he trailed off.

"This conversation is over." She wrapped her shawl more tightly around her and marched along the path towards the manor, head held high. Behind her, she could hear him calling her name, but she didn't look back. She wanted nothing more to do with him.

CHAPTER FOUR

A NEW MORNING

In the morning, everything looked and felt different.

From Violet's seat at the breakfast table, she had a good view across the manor grounds, which were pure, level and white from the night's heavy snowfall. Caps of snow covered each carefully pruned bush, like thick cream on a pudding. Not a single footstep sullied the picture. The beginnings of a straight channel led from the main entrance, dug by Oates, who was following the line of the path beneath. Violet's heart fluttered with excitement. She couldn't remember having seen snow as deep as this before; it was like something out of one of Madam Verger's stories. She wanted to be out in it, building a snowman and having fun, and she could think of only one person she wanted to share it with.

Cook had provided a big breakfast to help replenish their energy after the previous night's dancing. Violet had slept late, heavy snowfall cushioning the usual alarm calls from the manor grounds. She was still up earlier than her parents, and without the critical eye of her mother upon her, Violet piled her plate high. She began with her egg, tapping it vigorously with a silver spoon and removing the top, the inside as white and unspoiled as the snow. She dipped in a buttered bread soldier and took a large bite.

She wanted to see Nicolas. After a good night's sleep, she began to see things from his perspective, and could see that she'd spoken too hastily. After all, he'd tried to apologize. She did lead a privileged life. She knew nothing of the world outside the manor, but she was trying to educate herself, and no one could ask for more than that, could they?

Violet worked her way through fourteen egg-dipped soldiers, punctuating each mouthful with a swig of sweet tea, and feeling happier with every bite. She moved on to a dish of stewed prunes and then took another slice of bread, which she spread thickly with cherry jam. Delicious. She would take some of the leftovers to Nicolas's family. Then perhaps they would go for the walk he'd suggested. She would apologize. They could talk things through. One argument didn't have to ruin things for ever.

WINTER WONDERLAND

Violet packed a basket with items from the breakfast table: boiled eggs from the tureen, some fruit bread, a good pat of butter and the whole crock of cherry jam, of which plenty remained. Enough for a meal for a hungry family, but not so much that her parents would notice.

She put on some warm outer clothes and sturdy boots and left the house. Outside, she raised a hand to shield her eyes from the brilliant sun. The snow wouldn't last long if it continued to shine so brightly.

Oates's shovelled channel extended halfway across the garden. Violet had a strong urge to run through the untouched white part. She didn't, of course – such behaviour was for children – and kept to the freshly exposed footpath. Oates saw her approaching and stopped shovelling for a moment, hand on the small of his back. "Mistress Violet! I didn't expect any of the family out and about yet after last night's festivities. If you don't mind waiting a few more minutes, then I'll have this path cleared for you."

Violet smiled. "That's not necessary, Oates. I am heading to the village anyway and I'll no doubt encounter more snow along the way.

The gardener looked aghast at the thought. "I'm sure one of the young footmen will accompany you—"

"Thank you, but I promise I am quite capable. These boots are sturdy enough." To prove it, she took a great step into the uncleared section, enjoying the satisfying squeak of squashed snow beneath her heel. She continued, lifting her knees high and taking giant steps. Her long woollen dress made it challenging, but the snow was powdery enough to brush off the hem. Oates watched her take a few steps then went back to his work with a baffled shake of his head.

Violet made her way out of the manor grounds and down the path to the village. When she passed Madam Verger's house, she thought she saw a figure at the window. She raised a hand in a half wave in case, but couldn't be sure. She vowed to pop in on the way back up the hill, to see if the old lady needed anything in this cold weather.

She felt like one of the people of yesteryear from Madam Verger's stories. If this weather continued, then perhaps the millpond would freeze. Perhaps, even if Nicolas wouldn't dance with her, he might be persuaded to take her arm and skate. They would mingle with the other villagers and no one would gossip about them.

As if in answer to her thoughts, a sudden flurry of snow began, falling thick and fast as she neared the village. She smiled and held out her gloved hand, enjoying the sight of the giant snowflakes resting on the wool.

Violet walked over the bridge and turned the corner to Nicolas's house: a familiar route to her now. But as she got closer, she hesitated, butterflies rising in her stomach. She hoped this was a good idea. What if Nicolas wouldn't talk to her? But she wouldn't find out by walking away, so she pressed on.

When she was a few yards away, she stopped. Something was different about the cottage. Not just the snow, although their roof had the same white covering as every other house in Millbrook. Not the tiny snowman outside with coal for eyes and twigs for arms. No, it was something else. Hanging on the door. Some attractive green boughs twisted into a circle and decorated with pine cones and a deep red bow. A cypress wreath.

A CYPRESS WREATH

Violet stood in front of Nicolas's door, heart beating wildly as she remembered Madam Verger's tale. But a cypress wreath could mean anything, couldn't it? Nicolas's mother had probably made it herself as a cheery Wintertide decoration. There was no reason to think it was a bad sign. Missing people taken by a unicorn? It had all happened so long ago, if at all. There were no unicorns in Millbrook now.

A path to the front door had already been cleared through the snow and Violet walked along it, eyes still on the wreath. Before she could pluck up the courage to knock at the door, it swung open, nearly knocking her off her feet. It was Madam Evergreen, looking warm and rosy as ever, and somewhat surprised. "Oh, Miss Violet, you gave me a shock! I was just going outside to empty this ashpan." She put the pan down beside her and brushed her hands together. "Dearie me, where are my manners? You must come in from the cold."

Violet walked into their house and gazed around.

The whole family, apart from Nicolas, were sitting around the table, with smiles on their faces and a wicker box of food in front of them. She looked behind them, into the next room, to see if Nicolas was there, but he didn't seem to be at home. She thought again of the cypress wreath on the door. Where was Nicolas?

"Will you join us?" asked his father, gesturing to the little ones to make room on the bench for Violet.

"Oh no. . ." Violet blushed as she remembered how he'd taken pity on her the night before after his son's rejection. She wondered if she appeared desperate by coming here after being turned down so publicly. She realized they were waiting for her to explain her presence, and she found her voice.

"I brought some breakfast things." She placed the basket on the table and the youngest lifted up the cloth to peek inside. "It's not much, but I thought it's nice to have a warm breakfast as Wintertide approaches, especially after all the dancing last night."

"Breakfast things?" Nicolas's mother rubbed at her chin. "But, my dear, you already gave us so much." She gestured to the hamper on the table.

Violet stared at the food spilling out of the hamper. Smoked ham, fruit and bread. A boiled pudding wrapped in muslin. She swallowed as Madam Verger's words from her childhood came back to her.

"We began to dread those cypress wreaths. Every time one appeared on a door, that family would briefly flourish – as if by magic – and then within days, they would lose one of their own."

"But Madam Evergreen," Violet said slowly, "this food didn't come from the manor. Can you please tell me who delivered it?"

Nicolas's mother rubbed at her chin again. "Oh, I'm sorry for the misunderstanding, Miss Violet. I rather assumed... The little ones found it on the doorstep this morning, they said, along with the cypress wreath and all this lovely Wintertide snow. It made their day, I can tell you."

Snow like they hadn't seen for years, a mysterious package of food to see the family through hard times, and a cypress wreath hanging on the door. The winter curse. It was the only explanation. And if it was, then that meant someone from this house was going to go missing. Or was already gone.

Madam Evergreen picked up the box of food and turned it this way and that. She tipped the rest of the contents on to the table to the delight of the twins, who dived straight into the heap to explore. "There's no note outside the box or within. If it didn't come from the manor, then who could have sent it?"

Panic rose within Violet.

She hardly dared ask. "Wh-where is Nicolas this morning?" she whispered.

Madam Evergreen clucked her tongue. "Well, I haven't seen him since the dance last night. He ran out of the hall before we all left..."

To chase after you, Madam Evergreen didn't say, but Violet felt certain that's what she meant.

"We all turned into bed as soon as we got home. Worn out from the dancing, we were. I couldn't tell you what time he got in. He usually makes his bed up in here." Madam Evergreen gestured to a sheet strung up to one side of her, which sectioned off part of the room as his sleeping area.

Violet took in the information but didn't reply, thoughts of curses and unicorns swirling in her mind.

Madam Evergreen continued. "If you don't mind me saying, I rather thought he might have come after you. I thought you might have some things to discuss after the dance."

Violet flushed. She didn't know how to reply. Would Nicolas's mother be angry with her if she knew Violet had shouted at her son and sent him off without a word of forgiveness? "I... We..."

Madam Evergreen began stacking all the food back in the box, although Violet noticed the twins each managed to pocket a barley twist. "When he wasn't here this morning, I wondered if the two of you might have been taking a snowy walk together. But no. Here you are, with your basket." She shook her head in confusion. "It's all a bit odd, come to think of it."

Violet closed her eyes for a second. How was she going to explain this to his mother?

When she spoke, her voice came out croaky and panicked. She put a hand on the older woman's arm. "Madam Evergreen, I think Nicolas ... might have ... gone."

"Gone? What do you mean, my dear?"

Nicolas's father stood up from the table and moved towards his wife, putting a comforting arm around her.

"Gone where?"

Violet began to cry, tears running down her cheeks. She explained what was worrying her, taking big gulps of air between sentences. She told them everything. About the argument she'd had with Nicolas and about the history of the winter curse. How it all fitted. But Nicolas's family still didn't believe her, not really. She could tell from their sideways glances at each other.

"They're just stories, Miss Violet. That woman up at the orchard has always been a little odd. She didn't even live here when she was a girl. She was already getting on in years when she took over the orchard. You shouldn't take her tales so seriously."

Violet shook her head slowly. Was Madam Evergreen right? Was Violet upsetting herself over a mere story? Perhaps, but in her heart she felt that there was more to it. And if it was just a story, then where was Nicolas?

Madam Evergreen handed Violet a handkerchief. "Look, my Nicolas can be a proud boy. Stubborn, sometimes. Like his father." Madam Evergreen directed a pointed look at her husband. "In all likelihood, he has taken himself off somewhere after your little quarrel. It will blow over, believe you me."

She patted Violet's hand and Violet smiled weakly in thanks. She'd stopped crying now, but her eyes still stung and she guessed her face was red and puffy.

"I know it sounds ridiculous, but it is all happening exactly as it did all those years ago – the cypress wreath on the door and the unexpected gifts, and now he's gone—"

"Calm down, Miss Violet." Nicolas's father patted her shoulder. "He's probably out searching for firewood. He won't have gone far. Come on, let's have a look."

He ushered them out, leaving the twins free to munch on their stolen sweets. Violet frantically wiped at her tears with the handkerchief as Madam Evergreen called for her son. "Nicolas! Are you out here somewhere?"

A young man from the village, one of the group Violet had sometimes seen with Nicolas, passed by. He eyed them with surprise and Madam Evergreen called out to him: "Jonas, have you seen Nicolas this morning?"

"No, Ma'am," he said, tipping his cap. "Not since the dance last night."

Nicolas's father strode off in the direction of the woods, calling out in his deeper voice, shouting every syllable: "Ni-co-las!"

Violet ran off towards the mill bridge, calling to him as well. "Nicolas? Nicolas?" every shout a question. She shouted his name into the sky. She leaned over the bridge and shouted it into the water. The shouting made her feel better, as if she were doing something to help. But she knew Nicolas wasn't going to reply. Nicolas had gone.

HIGH ON THE HILL

There was simply no sign of him. Not even footsteps in the snow. But it was no use trying to convince the Evergreens. She left the basket of provisions on the table with their other, unexplained gift, and said her goodbyes.

"If he returns, you will inform me, won't you?" she asked.

"Of course, although I suspect he'll come to apologize himself for giving you a scare, as soon as he's cooled down."

Violet nodded and left, taking the familiar path home, alone. The snow was no longer picturesque, just cold and frustrating. She hoped the Evergreens were right, but there was a weight of dread in her chest telling her they couldn't be. Nicolas had been taken, like those people long ago.

The morning sun had vanished, and more thick snow was falling, as it had the night before. The indentations left by her boots had been filled with fresh snow, and so many flakes swirled in the air that the sky itself was a greyish white. The satisfaction of making new footprints, and her wonder at the changed landscape, had gone.

As she made her way up the hill, she took enormous steps, not caring any more if her dress became soaked though. All Violet wanted now was to be back at the manor, by a blazing fire, with dry toes. She kept her head down and her gaze a few feet in front of her.

But then she heard a faraway, unfamiliar sound like a bray, and she turned to look in its direction. A few black birds scattered in the pallid sky and she squinted into the distance, hand over her eyes to stop the snow obscuring her line of vision. There, on the horizon, in the Millbrook Hills, right where she'd stood with Nicolas that day, was a magnificent unicorn.

THE UNICORN

Violet stood open-mouthed, hardly able to believe the sight before her. Although she'd suspected the unicorn was to blame for Nicolas's disappearance, she had never expected to actually *see* the creature.

And what a creature it was. Its shining white form was distinct against the dark tree trunks. It was pure white, whiter even than the blue-tinged snow, but its tail, mane and horn were all black. Even at this distance, Violet could see it was a well-proportioned, powerful creature with thick, muscled limbs. And it was looking directly at her.

Despite the cold, her heart felt warm, and Violet had a sudden desire to run towards the unicorn and throw her arms around it. But then she reminded herself of the significance of this creature – why it had come to Millbrook. The unicorn had taken Nicolas! What had Madam Verger told her since childhood?

"Unicorns... Their outward beauty may hide an inner evil."

The creature began to gallop down the slope of the hill towards Violet, and the sudden movement shocked her from her daydream. It was coming for her! She had to get away. She would never make it home in time. The unicorn would be much faster than her uphill. And it was too far back to Nicolas's house.

Madam Verger.

Violet could be at the orchard house in minutes, and if anyone would understand, Madam Verger would. Violet turned, her feet sinking deep into the freshly fallen snow as she sprinted away. At the cottage, she hammered on the front door, forgetting everything she'd ever been taught about etiquette. She glanced behind her, to see if the unicorn was close, but there was nothing: only the path, the trees and the snow.

When Madam Verger opened the door, it was such a relief, Violet nearly fell into her house. She didn't worry about the snow from her boots melting on to the rug – she just wanted to be safe. If Madam Verger was surprised by this urgency, she didn't show it. She welcomed her inside and closed the door firmly behind her. "Come in out of that cruel weather."

As Madam Verger took Violet's cloak, Violet noticed she wasn't wearing her usual scarf. Her neck, though wrinkled, was long and elegant, but Violet's gaze was instantly drawn to a pink circular scar on its right-hand side. It was raised and puckered like a star, as if something had punctured her there. Violet realized she was staring, and checked herself, but Madam Verger just took a scarf from a nearby hook, and wound it slowly around her neck.

She led Violet through to the parlour and settled her in a low chair next to the hearth without asking any questions. She placed Violet's boots next to the fire and hung her stockings there too, so they could drip dry. She brought out a blanket, a pair of fur slippers, which Violet's bare feet slid into gratefully, and a cup of something warm and sweet. Only then, when she was comfortable, did Madam Verger speak.

"Tell me what's upset you, my child."

In a rush, Violet's words poured out and she told Madam Verger about the wreath on the door, Nicolas's disappearance and the unicorn on the hill.

Madam Verger listened sympathetically but seemed unsurprised by any of it.

"I knew when I woke up this morning that this was no ordinary winter." She moved to stand in her usual place at the window. "The snow is coming thick and fast and the air feels like it did back then," she said, breathing in deeply as if to sample it. "The Frozen Unicorn has returned, and once again, he has taken one of Millbrook's finest."

It was such a relief to hear this confirmed, rather than the confused, pitying faces of the Evergreens, that tears welled up in Violet's eyes again. These were not stories or legends. She had not imagined the unicorn. He was real. Which meant Nicolas really had gone.

"We cannot let the creature get away with it this time," Madam Verger said in a calm, matter-of-fact voice. Violet hadn't for a moment considered there might be something they could actually do about the situation. She had come here for a safe haven, for understanding – not for a solution. But now she was filled with hope. Perhaps they could actually find Nicolas. She sat up in her chair, the blanket falling from her shoulders.

"I don't understand. How can we stop the unicorn if we don't know where it comes from, or why it takes people?"

Madam Verger continued to stare out of the window for so long Violet wasn't sure if she was going to reply, or even if she'd heard the question. But then she opened the door of the glass cabinet in the corner of the room and took something from the top shelf. She came and sat next to Violet. "What if we did know where to find the unicorn? What if it was possible to go there – to find Nicolas?"

Violet flushed, eyes bright. "Well, of course – I'd do anything . . . go anywhere. . ."

Madam Verger raised both eyebrows high as if she didn't quite believe Violet. She held up the trinket she'd taken from the cabinet, which at first glance looked like a glass ball. Madam Verger shook it so it filled with white. The snow globe.

Violet remembered it from her childhood. She watched, mesmerized, as the white flakes slowly settled in the tiny spherical world.

She forgot that moments ago she'd been cursing the snow. Now she was once again gripped by the romance of it all.

The white flakes fell and the tiny unicorn was revealed, standing alone in a snowy, hilly landscape.

"You must go to the Far North," said Madam Verger.

THE FAR NORTH

"The Far North," whispered Violet, immediately feeling chilly and drawing the blanket around her. People only ever spoke of the place when the weather was bad: *this wind is bitter – it must have come down from the Far North.* All Violet knew about the place was that it was cold, desolate and many miles from Millbrook.

"From where else could the unicorn have brought such a cruel winter?" Madam Verger stared intently at Violet.

Violet nodded slowly. "I suppose it all makes sense." The Far North was the only place where this sort of relentless snow could come from, and the only place where a unicorn could remain hidden for years. It was also the kind of place where a person could vanish, never to be seen again.

"The Frozen Unicorn has an Ice Fortress. A cold, lonely place at the edge of the world, which no one would find by accident. Thick walls of ice; dark chambers within. Imagine being locked away in a place like that."

Violet imagined, and a tear slid down her cheek. Imprisoned all alone, in a strange, cold place. It would be unbearable. They couldn't allow it. Violet had never heard of a person travelling to the Far North, but there must be a way. Her father would surely see to it.

"So how will we get Nicolas back? And all the other people? Perhaps if Father organized a search party, and we asked all the strongest men in the village. . .?"

"No," said Madam Verger quietly, playing with the end of her plait. Violet wondered briefly what colour the old woman's hair had been in her youth. She couldn't imagine what she'd looked like when she was younger, although her high cheekbones suggested she'd always been striking.

"There is so much you don't understand. The unicorn has great magic and can stay hidden in plain sight. He would sense an army of people approaching. Also, the Far North is not an easy place to get to: one must cross a rocky mountain range impassable for a coach or horse. There are ways, which I can explain, but these are much easier for a solo traveller. I am afraid that whoever wants to find Nicolas must travel on her own."

"On her own?" Something about Madam Verger's expression made Violet think she wasn't talking about just anyone. "You don't mean to suggest that *I* should go to rescue Nicolas and all those other people?"

Madam Verger sat in the chair nearest to Violet and drew it close, so Violet could see the flecks of yellow in her irises. "I don't just think it, child, I know it. But only Nicolas. The other people will be long gone now. They vanished when I was a small child and now I am a very old woman. No person would live long in conditions like that. No, it is only Nicolas, and I must be frank: he is unlikely to last long."

"H-h-how long?"

"A few days? A week?"

Violet gasped and put her hands to her mouth. "Oh, I couldn't bear it if anything happened to him!"

Madam Verger nodded. "I realize that, but all is not lost. You can find him. You are the only one who can free him from his prison and bring him home."

Violet almost laughed with surprise, although Madam Verger's expression was serious. She thought of the look on the gardener's face when he saw she was planning to walk into the village without any assistance. She didn't know how to do anything on her own, let alone travel to the Far North to defeat an evil unicorn.

"Madam Verger, I know nothing of the world. I wouldn't know how to find my way, or to fight a foe. And if the unicorn has magic powers. . ."

"All of this is true, yet you have a far greater power. Something that will keep you warm in the bleakest conditions, make you strong when you are weak. Something that will bring Nicolas back to you."

"A power? I have no power."

"Ah, but that's where you're wrong. You have the power of True Love."

TRUE LOVE

Violet's cheeks grew hot. Was the way she felt about Nicolas really that obvious?

Madam Verger seemed to sense her discomfort.

"You forget I am an old woman, who has lived through many years and seen many things. I know True Love when I see it. It has been clear to me since the two of you were children that your destinies are entwined."

Violet wasn't sure about that. She thought of how she'd edged away from Nicolas on this very settle all those years ago. Nine-year-old Violet would have been most unimpressed by the idea of entwined destinies. Her cheeks grew even pinker.

"I'm not sure. We argued after the dance last night and I was worried he would never want to see me again. I went there this morning to apologize, but that's when I found he'd disappeared ... been taken."

"Ah, but that was just a silly quarrel. He wanted to dance with you – he just didn't want to be asked out of pity."

Violet lifted her eyebrows in surprise. "How do you know what we were arguing about, or what Nicolas thought?" she asked.

"Your voices were somewhat loud and you were near my window," explained Madam Verger.

Violet remembered seeing the shutters open and close. She'd probably been trying to block out the noise.

"I'm sorry to have disturbed you—" she began, but Madam Verger raised a hand to stop her.

"I heard two young people who feel very passionately indeed. The only things standing in the way of you being together are your understanding and Nicolas's pride. If you were to find him, I have no doubt these little problems would melt away. True Love finds a way."

True Love? Violet hoped she was right. Up until the dance, everything had been so perfect between the two of them. It had just been one quarrel. Harsh words spoken in the heat of the moment. Maybe there was still a chance for them if only she could find him.

"You must go to the Far North," whispered Madam Verger, answering Violet's thoughts. She was still gripping the snow globe and she shook it again so the snowflakes swirled in their tiny world. "You must travel there and free Nicolas."

Violet shook her head slowly, speechless.

"I wish that, back in my youth, I had known what I know now. I wish I'd been able to help those poor people that disappeared. But I was just a child. This time, it can be different. You can find him; you can tell him how you feel; and you can bring him home."

"But how? How will I even know where to find him?"

The old woman clasped a bony hand around Violet's lower arm. It felt cool but comforting.

"You must get to the Ice Fortress. Once you are there, together, then your love will be powerful enough to melt through any chains, any walls. But you must avoid meeting the unicorn at any cost. Your power will only work when you have found Nicolas. If you see the unicorn before that, don't stop to think. Don't think you can fight him. Just get away, as quickly as you can."

"And I must do all this on my own? It seems impossible."

"Ah, but I will advise you before you go. I can tell you everything you need to know."

"But how do *you* know what to do?" Violet asked, thinking there must be more to this old woman than first appeared. "If you've lived in Millbrook all your life looking after the orchard, how do you know how to defeat the unicorn?"

Madam Verger smiled mysteriously. "Although I lived in Millbrook as a child, I moved away for many years. I've lived a long life, met many people, and received special gifts. One day, I will tell you everything, but for now those stories must wait. Right now, it is about you and Nicolas, and you must listen carefully to what you need to do."

Violet stared at Madam Verger in disbelief.

"How, Madam Verger? How could I possibly travel to the Far North on my own? I have never been outside Millbrook by myself. Indeed, I only started walking unaccompanied into the village a few weeks ago."

"Don't dwell upon what is standing in your way. If you really love Nicolas then you won't let anything stop you. You will do this on your own, and I will give you all the information you need. Here, take this. I have something else to show you."

Madam Verger passed her the snow globe, but Violet somehow failed to grasp it. It slipped from her hand and fell on the sharp corner of the table. The globe shattered, tiny splinters of glass scattering on to the table and floor. Clear fluid dripped from the table and seeped into the rug beneath.

"I am so, so, sorry," cried Violet, rushing to pick some of the larger pieces of glass out from the rug.

"It doesn't matter," said Madam Verger, coldly. Then, as Violet continued, she shouted, "Leave it!"

Violet stopped abruptly, pink spots appearing on her cheeks. She sat back on the chair, straight-backed, and Madam Verger joined her and gripped her forearm.

"The snow globe doesn't matter. It is a thing. An object. All that matters is Nicolas. Will you do this, Violet? Will you take it upon yourself to save your True Love and bring him back to Millbrook?"

Violet thought of Nicolas's words to her on the day she dropped her baskets:

If you really want to change, then you need to go out into the world and have some adventures. Stand on your own two feet. Make some mistakes. Find out what you're capable of.

Nicolas believed in her and now he needed her help. She had to be strong and not let worry stand in her way. Violet looked at Madam Verger, whose eyes were piercing and intent. She nodded. "I'll do it."

Madam Verger smiled, the broken snow globe forgotten. "A wise decision."

Violet still had absolutely no idea *how* she was going to do it, but she supposed she was about to find out.

CHAPTER FIVE

PERSUASION

As good as her word, Madam Verger told Violet everything she needed to know. All that was left was for Violet to persuade her parents to let her go, which was why she was standing in the wood-panelled hallway at home, straining to overhear a private conversation.

Most of Violet's parents' more interesting discussions took place in her father's study. After sixteen years of living at Millbrook Manor, Violet knew the exact point in the hallway that was best for eavesdropping. She was standing there now, close enough to hear what was being said within, but far enough that she could pretend to be passing by if the door suddenly opened.

Her mother was in there, relaying the news that Violet had suddenly decided to travel unaccompanied to a strange, frozen land. Her father's response was calm and unruffled.

"There is no need to make such a fuss about it all, Darling."

"Our daughter – our only child – gets a preposterous notion into her head about chasing a unicorn to the Far North because of some . . . village boy, and you tell me I am making a fuss?"

Her mother's voice rose to such a volume, Violet hardly needed to be listening at the door; she would have heard her from the other end of the house.

"Calm down, Helene," came her father's voice. *"I am telling you we have options, that is all. Yes, we can forbid her journey. We can lock her away in her room and endure the tears and tantrums. Or we can give her our blessing and assist her in planning for the journey."*

"Assist her? Have you lost your mind?"

Out in the hallway, Violet was as surprised as her mother; she never expected her father to agree to this.

"Think about it, Helene. Our daughter is not known for her hardy constitution or resilience. She's been known to turn back

from a walk in the manor grounds because of a pebble in her shoe. How do you suppose she will fare on a journey to the Far North?"

"I think she would find it impossible! Which is exactly why—"

"—Which is exactly why we let her go. We provide a safe coach and a chaperone to transport her wherever she chooses. In weather like this, in unfamiliar surroundings, she's unlikely to last more than a couple of hours before she's begging to come home."

"Well!" Violet whispered to herself, creeping away before they caught her eavesdropping. So that was what her parents thought of her. Not known for her hardy constitution or resilience! Charming. Well, it didn't matter what they thought. Violet had decided she was going to find Nicolas, and she wasn't going to change her mind. If they were going to help her along the way, then all the better for it.

THE JOURNEY

Her mother helped her pack in the end. They found an old leather knapsack of her father's, which was not a beautiful item, but was roomy enough to hold everything she needed. Her mother helped her choose appropriate items with a strained smile, selecting them from a pile the maids had already folded.

"You won't need anything beautiful," said her mother. "Plain and practical is the order of the day when you are travelling."

Violet knew her mother well enough to see she was trying to put her off. Well, she could try, and Violet would play along, but she wasn't going to change her mind about the trip.

"Oh, I absolutely agree. I wouldn't want to crease and crumple any of my fine things on the journey," she replied sweetly. "What made you change your mind about me going, Mother? You were adamant I should stay."

"What? Oh, it was your father's doing. He seems to think an adventure would do you good." Mother couldn't meet her gaze. She was not a good liar.

Her father appeared in the doorway. "Spiers the coachman will take you over the mountains as far as the carriage will go, and from there he will lead you on foot. You will need proper clothes and equipment for the journey. A sensible, thick cloak, not that flimsy velvet garment of yours."

"Yes, I'll wear a thick cloak, and this scarf and mittens I was making for Madam Tait. I'll knit her another set on my return."

"Just as well – those are more hole than mitten," said Mother, wrinkling her nose.

"We will ask Cook to bottle some of her soup. That will only last a couple of days, of course – you'll need to find your own food after that..." she continued, glancing at Violet to gauge her reaction. It crossed Violet's mind that her parents thought she might back out now, before she'd even left the manor. The thought made her cross. Did they really think she was capable of so little? Well, she would show them, when she returned to Millbrook with Nicolas.

She left after breakfast the following day.

Snow still lay on the ground and the servants bundled thick blankets and dry clothes into the coach, along with boxes and food packages.

The coachman, Spiers, was a quiet type, tall and slim, with eyes that darted around as if he would rather be anywhere else.

"May I take your luggage, Mistress Violet?" he asked, but she shook her head. She was travelling as lightly as possible on this journey.

"I will have my bag with me in the carriage, thank you."

Still, he took her bag and placed it inside the carriage, then stood beside the horse with his arms at his side.

"Thank you for taking me, Spiers," said Violet. He raised his cap and nodded awkwardly. She couldn't tell whether he was pleased to have been given this mission, which was surely an escape from the usual day-to-day routine, or if he saw it as a chore. He had no doubt been instructed to take very good care of her and to bring her home as soon as her resolve crumbled. Which it wouldn't.

Her father helped her into the carriage and kissed her lightly on the cheek.

"Stay safe," he said, with a smile.

"And warm," added her mother, with a tight but short embrace. She seemed more worried than her father. Perhaps she wasn't quite as confident as Father that Violet would return within hours.

They moved away from the coach, ready to wave her off. Violet thought they could have put on a better performance. If they really believed she was travelling all that distance away, then they would never give such a brief and cheery farewell.

Still, Violet played along and waved and smiled. The door of the coach slammed shut, Spiers checked it was secure, and there were a few seconds of quiet as he climbed to his seat. Violet shuffled in her own seat. It was comfortable enough, if chilly. The interior of the coach smelled strongly of beeswax, covering a lingering smell of damp.

Then they were away. Her father waved and her mother fluttered a lace handkerchief. Violet waved back and said a silent farewell to the home where she'd slept every night since her birth. The coach trundled slowly through the manor gates and down the hill.

They passed the snow-covered orchard and Madam Verger's cottage. Unusually, the old woman was standing outside, leaning on a long staff, her dress and hair both almost as white as the surrounding snow and sky. She raised her hand and Violet waved from the coach window in response, thanking her silently for the advice and encouragement.

Madam Verger had told her everything she needed to know and Violet felt prepared for what lay ahead.

As they made their way to the open road, Violet gazed out of the window at the thatched rooftops. She thought she could identify Nicolas's roof, although in reality they all looked the same. Then Millbrook was behind them and they were on the main road west, gaining speed all the time. At first, she leaned forward in her seat, transfixed by the passing landscape. Every new sight made her smile: the snow-topped trees, the patchily frozen lakes, a hare leaving a trail of tiny footprints in the snow. She wondered why she'd never felt the urge to travel before, when it was so much fun.

But after she'd sat that way for some minutes, the swaying movement of the coach combined with the twisting of her midriff made her feel most unwell. She leaned back and tried to find a comfortable position, a blanket wrapped around her. The seat looked padded and plush but was surprisingly hard, and an icy draught blew through the rattling windows. She wondered how the coachman was faring, exposed to the elements outside, and drew the blanket more tightly around herself. She thought about the next part of her journey, and about Madam Verger's instructions.

First, she had to lose Spiers the coachman.

"You will stop at Wending," Madam Verger had said.

"But what if we don't?"

"It is the obvious place. It is the better part of a day's journey from here, and the last town before you cross over the mountains. No doubt you will rest in the inn. When you have reached Wending, you must get away, any way you can. Remember, this journey can only be undertaken by you, on your own."

"But what if we don't stop at Wending?" repeated Violet.

"I am sure you will stop at Wending, but if you do not, then you will have to use your initiative to find your way there. I cannot predict every eventuality."

Madam Verger had reached into her glass cabinet and passed Violet a curved blowing horn. It was smaller than similar items she'd seen, no bigger than her hand, and Violet couldn't imagine what animal the horn might have come from. It had a polished surface, a leather carrying strap and a brass mouthpiece at the thin end, which Violet lifted to her lips.

"No!" Madam Verger had grasped the horn and pulled it from Violet's hand before she could make a sound. *"Do not blow this until you need it."*

"When will that be?"

And Madam Verger had told her. She'd given her clear instructions on how to get to the Far North and on what to do when she got there. Violet hoped she could remember them all.

While she was travelling in the coach, it didn't seem real. The cold coach windows steamed up with her breath and she didn't bother to wipe them. Without the view outside, she could be anywhere at all. After a while, she grew used to the lurching motion and began to find the movement soothing. Her eyes closed and she drifted off to sleep.

THE COACHING INN

Panic gripped Violet the moment she opened her eyes.

The coach had stopped. The lack of motion must have woken

her. How long had she been asleep? The sun was still high in the sky, so she couldn't have slept for that long. She would guess it was early afternoon. Where were they? Had they reached Wending yet? Violet hoped they hadn't passed the village; she would have no idea what to do next.

The coach window was foggy, and she rubbed it with her sleeve so she could see out. They'd pulled into a cobbled courtyard. Spiers was leading the horse to a stall.

She opened the coach door and stumbled outside, the jolt of fresh air waking her up properly. They appeared to be around the back of a coaching inn, a tall building with many windows, but there were no clues to its whereabouts.

Spiers looked relieved to see her standing there. Maybe he'd been worrying about how to wake her. He tipped his cap. "How was the journey, Miss Violet?"

"Most comfortable, thank you, Spiers – it went in a flash."

Spiers left the horse in the stall and walked back to the coach to meet her. He looked freezing, with a red nose, red fingers and tiny icicles in his beard. Violet felt a pang of guilt that she'd brought him all this way and half-frozen him, knowing what she was about to do.

"Where are we now?" she asked, casually.

"We're at a mountain town. Or village, I s'pose. Wending, it's called. Our last port of call before we head out there." He gestured vaguely over the mountains.

"Wending." Violet whispered the word. Madam Verger had been right about where they'd stop. This was the place.

"That's right. I know it's still early, but there'll be no better place to stop. I'll enquire as to rooms for the night," said the coachman, pausing as he watched Violet stare out into the mountains. "Unless . . . you'd rather we head back to Millbrook?"

"Of course not," snapped Violet. Her parents had obviously instructed him to ask her that at every step of the way, and to return the minute she relented. They probably thought this would be the moment, after hours sitting on a hard coach seat, then facing the reality of this bleak mountain town. But they were wrong. That is what the old Violet would have done, but not the new Violet. She was determined to do whatever it took.

Spiers carried Violet's bag around to the front of the building, and she followed, taking a good look at her surroundings.

The village of Wending was situated around a steep winding road, and the inn was right at the top, before the road began to travel through the mountains. Violet could see why it was an obvious stopping point for anyone travelling in that direction. The inn itself was white with dark beams, a little like her own home, but rougher around the edges. A wooden sign, depicting a howling wolf, hung above the door. It swayed in the breeze, creaking, and Violet had to squint to read the name: *The Full Moon.*

Inside the inn, she sat on a hard bench in the entry hall while Spiers went to find the innkeeper. Nobody would have given Violet a second glance as she sat there primly, hands folded in her lap. They would think she was on her way to visit relatives for Wintertide. They would never guess she was embarking on an adventure to save her True Love all by herself. Nor would they guess that at that very moment, she was making a mental note of where each door led, and working out the best way to escape undetected from the inn.

AN OLD, BROKEN QUILL

It was still early for supper, but Violet told Spiers she was tired and hungry from the journey, and requested a meal to be served as soon as possible in her room. The main hall would be full of coachmen and locals, and was no place for a lady.

When Violet's meal was brought to her room she found she *was* hungry, and ate gratefully. The hearty stew, with thick, crusty bread, would sustain her for some time. She washed at the washstand and dressed as warmly as she could, layering her clothes on top of one another. She packed up a leftover hunk of bread from her meal and stashed it in her bag on top of the other food and supplies. Then she felt ready for the next step in her adventure.

An old, broken quill and a nearly dried inkpot on the dresser worked well enough for her to scratch out a note in a torn-out page from her notebook.

Spiers, my heartfelt thanks for the part you played in transferring me safely to Wending. I appreciate that conditions were particularly cold and you made no complaint. Please return to Millbrook and inform my parents that I will continue this journey alone. They should place no blame for this on you, as I acted entirely independently. I am well-equipped and I know exactly where I'm going. Cordially, Mistress Reddmene.

She folded the note, jotted *Spiers* on the outside, and left it on the dresser. She doubted Spiers himself would be able to read it, but no doubt he could track someone down to help him.

When she heard singing and laughter from downstairs, she

felt sure the other customers were sinking jugs of ale in the main hall. She left her room and headed down an empty staircase, past the kitchen, and out the back way. For a moment, she hesitated as a chill blast of air almost took her breath away, but she wrapped her cloak tightly around herself, steeled herself against the cold, and started climbing up the road towards the mountain.

THE BLOWING HORN

"Head for the lower mountain slopes. Don't attempt to climb to the peak. Just far enough that you are no longer in the village – that you know you are in the mountains – and then blow the horn."

That was what Madam Verger had told her and it had sounded so simple at the time. She understood if she blew the horn, then help would arrive: someone would come and help her on her journey to the Far North. But now she wished she'd asked more questions: should she stay on the main road where the coach had driven, or turn off and make her own way up?

After walking a little way, she saw a steep footpath heading up into the mountains. It was not as wide as the road – no horse or vehicle could use it – but it was well-trodden despite the covering of snow. Perhaps it was used by farmers.

Violet's instincts told her to take the path. She took long strides, the muscles in her legs working hard to propel her. She remembered climbing the hill behind Millbrook with Nicolas, how he'd turned to help her up. There was no one to help her now. Her knapsack was heavy and she felt hot from the exertion. She had been worried about getting cold, but now she began to wonder if she'd worn too many clothes. She removed her mittens and placed them in her pockets.

The path dwindled to nothing and Violet decided to turn off again, into a dense copse of trees. At least their dark foliage would provide some cover if Spiers tried to follow her. She was glad it was still light, and she could see patches of bright blue sky between the trees. After walking for a couple of minutes, Violet found herself in a clearing, where the snow lay thick and white. She took a few steps into the whiteness and looked around.

Just far enough that you are no longer in the village, Madam Verger had said. The mountain loomed above her and the snowy ground on which she stood sloped down to the village of Wending. The village now looked tiny, although Violet didn't think she'd been walking for very long. Surely she'd come far enough. It was time to blow the horn and call for her guide.

Breathing deeply from the exertion of her walk, she reached

for the horn. She'd put it around her neck so it would be easily accessible, but for one moment, she thought she'd lost it. She unwrapped the scarf from her neck and scrabbled with her hand to find the leather strap, and there it was. Violet checked around her. She was all alone, of course, and she hoped the sound it made would not alert the townspeople of Wending. At least the people at the inn were making too much noise to hear anything else.

The horn smelled strange: dusty and metallic. She tried not to think about how old it was or how many people might have used it over the years. She wiped the brass mouthpiece on her dress, then placed it between her lips and blew gently.

No sound emerged, so she tried again, taking a deep breath of cold mountain air and puffing out her cheeks. She blew hard into the mouthpiece. This time it worked.

The noise that emerged was deep and hollow, as Violet had expected, but, after she stopped blowing, it took on a life of its own, changing to an *oooh* sound more like a call or a howl. The sound travelled away from Violet, fading away into the mountains, and returned to her stronger, like an echo.

Then there was nothing.

Violet let the horn drop back and stood, waiting for someone to appear, although she still didn't know who.

The warmth from the start of her walk had left her. The longer she stood still, the more the cold crept through the layers of her clothes, pinching at her toes, her nose and her earlobes. She was no longer worried she had worn too many clothes.

Violet shivered, put her hands in her pockets, and buried her face into the scarf at her neck, her breath warming the tip of her nose and her lips. She glanced around, unsure whether help would be coming from further up the mountainside or from down below. Madam Verger hadn't told her who her guide would be, only that the horn would summon them. Violet wished now she'd asked for more information, but Madam Verger was the sort of person who said what she wanted to say and no more.

The wind rustled the leaves on the nearby trees and a pile of snow fell heavily on the ground. Far away was a hammering sound. A woodpecker, perhaps. Violet would have preferred total silence to these unexpected and unsettling sounds.

What if nobody came? Violet would have to return to the inn, destroy the note, and pretend nothing had ever happened. The idea was quite appealing. In the morning she could tell Spiers she'd changed her mind about the journey and wanted to return to Millbrook. He'd be happy. Her parents would be happy. But she would know she'd failed to even try to rescue Nicolas.

As she tried to imagine how that would feel, the sky suddenly darkened, which was strange because nightfall was still a little way off. Maybe a cloud had obscured the sun for a moment. Violet looked up. Her breath caught.

It wasn't a cloud.

FLAPPING IN THE SKY

A winged creature was flapping in the sky above her. It was large, at least twice as big as her: a dragon or a giant bird. Violet screamed and ran to take cover in the trees.

She hardly dared look, but she could hear the beating of giant wings overhead. The creature was coming nearer, she was sure of it. Why had she screamed? It would have flown by without noticing her if only she'd kept quiet. She darted in between two tree trunks and bobbed down behind some bushes. She hoped she was well-hidden and the space between the trees was too small for the creature to squeeze into.

There was a soft thump worryingly near as whatever-it-was came in to land on the mountainside. Violet braved a quick glance around the bushes. It was sniffing about in the clearing. It was as big as she'd thought and had its back to her, which was grey and furry with a bushy tail. Its wings were now folded in and she couldn't see them properly. Not a dragon then, or any sort of bird. What was furry and had wings? All she could think of was a bat, but it was much, much bigger than any bat she'd ever seen.

It turned its head towards her hiding place and Violet darted away, but not before she caught a glimpse of a dog-like face, with sharp, pricked-up ears. A wolf! The villainous creature known for stealing sheep and chickens. No doubt young girls too, if they were foolish enough to venture on to a remote mountainside all alone. This wolf was bigger than any she'd heard of. And it had wings!

The Flying Wolves of Wending. She thought someone had once told her about them. Her parents, or more likely, Madam Verger. Would it carry her off to its mountainside nest before devouring her? Did flying wolves have nests? Fear made her unable to think straight.

If only Madam Verger's friend would appear. She needed someone familiar with fearsome wild animals; someone with a weapon.

The creature snuffled along the ground as if it were looking for a favourite treat. She backed even further into the trees until the roughness of the bark was scratching her back, even through the thick layers she was wearing. But there was no escape, and soon its snout was close to her foot. She drew her leg back. The wolf's amber eyes stared up at her.

Up close, it still looked huge, but not quite as frightening as she'd first thought. It had long, snow-sprinkled fur, grey around its head and ears but white on its face and throat. The wolf wasn't snarling, or growling, or looking like it might pounce. It sat back on its haunches and studied her. It actually looked quite jittery. She might be able to scare it away.

With shaking hands, she picked up a branch from under the tree and held it out at arm's length. She didn't expect it would do much harm, but it would put some distance between them. She had nothing else, apart from a small penknife somewhere in the bottom of her bag.

The wolf sniffed at the branch with its black nose, took it in its mouth and pulled gently. She let go with a yelp and the creature started to gnaw at it experimentally. Violet wrapped her arms around herself, desperately trying to think what else she could use. Her right hand reached once more for the horn hanging around her neck. Maybe it would finally alert her helper or scare the animal away.

Hands still shaking, she licked her lips, and brought the brass endpiece up to her mouth as she had before. This time, she blew as hard as she could, aiming the other end at the wolf's face, as if she was trying to blow it off the mountainside and away from her.

The sound that emerged was louder than even Violet had expected: that same deep booming sound that changed to a howl. She dropped the horn and it banged on her upper chest.

But the wolf didn't flinch or turn away. It abandoned the branch, pointed its nose to the sky and howled.

Violet gasped. Its call was an exact copy of the noise that had emerged from the horn. The wolf looked back at Violet, amber eyes unblinking, breath steady and calm.

Violet met its gaze. Did this mean what she thought it meant?

The wolf hadn't come to attack her. There was no need to call for Madam Verger's mystery helper.

The wolf *was* her mystery helper.

CHAPTER SIX

TO THE NORTH

Violet was sure she was right. She held out her still-shaking hand to the animal so it could detect her scent. It sniffed at it as it had done with the branch, then licked the back of her hand in a clearly friendly gesture. Relief flooded through her that she wasn't going to be the wolf's next meal.

So the wolf was her guide. But how could it help her? She tried to remember exactly what Madam Verger had told her. *Blow the horn at Wending and your guide to the Far North will arrive.* Something like that.

She inspected the creature, looking for a collar or a message-carrying device.

"Can you talk?" she asked in a whisper, and then felt silly when the wolf blinked silently back at her. Of course it couldn't talk. Still, she felt certain it understood.

"Have you brought me something? A map?" Violet's own voice sounded strange to her out here in the mountains. The creature continued to gaze steadily at her, then turned and walked back to the clearing where it had landed. It looked back at her, twice.

"You want me to follow, don't you?" asked Violet, not expecting a response.

She squeezed through the tree trunks and followed the wolf, admiring the magnificent pointed brush of its tail. It stopped near where she'd blown the horn, and stood watching her, the wind rippling the fur between its ears and around its neck.

"What now?" whispered Violet.

It crouched down before her and she had the horrible realization the wolf wasn't her guide to the north; it was her transport. She had been expecting another carriage, or at least a horse, not a strange wild animal.

"Oh no, no, I don't think I can do that." Violet backed away, but the wolf stayed exactly where it was, glancing back over its shoulder as if urging her to climb aboard. Violet began to realize that if she wanted to get to the Far North, she didn't have any choice.

She glanced up at the mountain range and the puffy clouds drifting by. How far up could this creature go? As high as the tallest mountain peak? Her legs trembled. Birds were meant to fly. Bats, dragons, even wolves, but surely not people. Perhaps she could convince the wolf of this.

"Would you mind dreadfully running to the Far North rather than flying? I don't mind if it takes a little longer that way." The wolf turned to face her and she saw the breath from its black nostrils curling into the air. She knew, without a doubt, it understood every word, although it didn't seem to think much of her suggestion.

"I'm sorry to make you wait after you were so gracious to respond to my call, but the truth is, I don't quite know what I'm doing. . ."

Her voice trailed away and she stepped a little closer. How was she going to ride this wolf?

At home, when she went riding, her pony was, of course, fitted with a saddle and bridle. She always rode side-saddle and had at least two stablehands helping her into position. She wasn't what you'd call a natural horsewoman, and rarely went above a trot. Still, she had promised herself she would save Nicolas, and could hardly give up at the first challenge.

She put on her mittens, ready for a cold journey, turned her back to the animal and used both hands to lift herself into her usual side-saddle position. Straight away it was clear it wouldn't work. Without the saddle and reins, she slid right off the wolf's back. There was nothing for it: she would have to climb astride the animal. Her woollen dress was too tight to allow much movement, so she bundled it up above her knees, instantly feeling the cold on her lower legs. Her billowing undergarments were split like trousers and came to just above her ankle. They were much less restrictive than the dress and she was able to climb on to the wolf with a leg resting on each side of its body. There, she felt more secure.

As soon as she was comfortable, bag resting on her back and leaning forward with her arms wrapped around the wolf's neck, it unfolded its wings. They were white and feathered, like those of a swan, with smaller feathers close to its body and longer feathers at the tips. Violet couldn't help but marvel at the beauty and size of them. Even not fully extended, they brushed the ground on either side. Still, she'd much rather it didn't use them.

The wolf began to run down the mountainside, going from

standing to high speed at an alarming rate. Its gait was uneven and Violet kept tipping over to the right. Her stomach lurched and her vision swam.

"No, stop! I've changed my mind!" she called.

The wolf didn't change course. It continued running, its strides lengthening, then flapped its wings and launched itself off the mountainside.

Violet screamed.

So much for staying on the ground.

The wolf rose rapidly until Violet's ears popped with the change of pressure. It felt as if she'd left her stomach down below. She took one quick glimpse at the mountains disappearing beneath her, before she squeezed her eyes tightly shut. She vowed not to open them until she was safely back on the ground.

Violet wanted to gaze around, to see what the scenery looked like from the back of the flying wolf, but she couldn't bring herself to open her eyes. They flew for a long time. She couldn't say how long, but hours, not minutes. Only once did she pluck up the courage to flutter her eyelids open. All she saw was white, which could have been the sky around them, the snow below, or even the wolf's wings – Violet didn't know. She didn't want to know. The giddy feeling came right back and she clamped her eyes shut, shuffling her body as close as possible to the wolf's, and burying her face in its fur to feel the comforting warmth from its body. All she had to do was stay like that, to cling on, and hope the journey would soon be over.

NOTHING BUT SNOW

The journey did end, eventually.

Violet knew they were descending because they slowed down, the flapping sound stopped, and her ears popped again. The wolf tilted backwards and she clung on tighter than ever before.

Just as Violet felt herself sliding along the wolf's back, there was a great thump, which reverberated through her body. They'd landed.

"Oh!" she said. She stayed where she was, eyes closed, mittened hands gripping the wolf's fur as best she could, hardly daring to move. What would she find when she opened them? She'd trusted the creature, but a small part of her wondered if she might find herself in the middle of a hungry wolf pack.

When she did open her eyes, all she saw was the bluey whiteness of snow, contrasted against the darkening sky.

Nothing but snow. This must be the Far North. The *Far North*! She could barely believe she'd arrived in one piece. That she'd arrived at all.

She reluctantly loosened her grip, dismounted and unhitched her dress. "Thank you," she said to the wolf, remembering her manners. She laughed, a little hysterically. Minding her manners with a wolf? What would Mother say about that?

The wolf didn't seem to notice and wandered a little way from her, leaving deep paw prints in the snow. It had a strange, uneven walk, which explained why they had kept tilting to the right on take-off.

Now Violet was away from its soft, warm body, she began to shiver. It was much colder here than in Wending, and night appeared to be coming. The orange sun was low – barely visible on the horizon – and the dark blue sky was banded with orange. Although she drew her cloak around her and pulled the hood low over her head, the wind blew through the weave of the fabric itself. How had she ever thought Millbrook was cold? How she longed to return to the warmth of Millbrook's snow, where uncovered body parts didn't feel as though they were about to freeze and drop off.

There was nothing here. No houses or paths. No signs of

life. Just snow, sky and forest. Without hills and houses, the sky appeared bigger than she'd ever seen before: unobscured even by clouds. Violet felt small and exposed.

The wolf, whose coat had looked almost white back in Wending, now appeared to be a darker grey against the backdrop of snow. It sat back in the snow, lifted its front left leg to its mouth and began licking the lower part. The paw hung limply and drew Violet's attention. This explained its unbalanced walk. "You're hurt, aren't you?"

The wolf stopped licking for a moment and fixed its eyes on Violet. Yes, it was hurt.

"May I take a look?" Violet approached cautiously and took the wolf's left paw. It had five toes surrounded by bristly hairs. On the lower part of its leg, where a human's ankle would be, was a slim yet stiff leather band, fastened with a stud. Violet gently brushed the snow away and the wolf flinched. The band was too tight. The fur beneath it had rubbed away and the wolf's skin was red and swollen.

"Who put this on your leg?" asked Violet. It seemed a strange and cruel thing to do to such a beautiful animal.

The wolf blinked.

"I'm going to remove it." The wolf replaced its paw in the

snow while Violet rummaged in her bag for her penknife, then held it up again when she was ready. Violet was surprised that it seemed willing to let her touch its leg, despite the pain it must be in.

Violet noticed there were letters engraved in the leather band.

"C-A-N-D-R-A," read Violet. "Candra. Is that your name?"

The wolf blinked again, giving nothing away.

As gently and carefully as she could with her mittened hands, Violet slid the blade of the penknife under the leather strip, and trying not to hurt the animal, sawed at the leather. Luckily, the knife was sharp and it didn't take long, but as she broke through, the wolf yelped in pain.

Violet stepped back, and the broken strip sunk into the snow.

The wolf watched her replace the knife in her bag, then it dipped its head towards her once. A thank you, perhaps.

There was a pause, then the animal pointed its black nose up towards the sky and howled.

The wolf's open mouth moved slightly as the howl changed in pitch. It grew in volume, then died away and the wolf lowered its head once more. It waited, and Violet waited too, although she didn't know what they were waiting for. An answering call? Or a whole pack of flying wolves. It could be anything.

Violet's heart pounded. She wished she were anywhere but here, in this strange place where she didn't belong and didn't understand.

The wolf looked left and right, as if searching for something.

"If I wanted to go back to Wending, would you take me?" she asked. Madam Verger had told her she could use the horn twice: once to take her to the Far North and once to bring her home. If she changed her mind now, the wolf could take her straight back, she was sure.

The animal cocked its head to one side and looked at her with wise amber eyes. But then it walked away from her again. It might have been wishful thinking, but Violet thought maybe it wasn't limping quite as much as before. It stopped, and unfurled its wings. Out here in the snow, there was enough space to unfold them to their full width, stretching them up and out like a tired child. They were bigger than Violet had appreciated.

Wait. Was the wolf going to fly away and leave her?

"No!" She ran in its direction, leaving her own, bigger footsteps next to its trail, knowing she could never catch it. She couldn't fly, or even run swiftly like a wolf, and her boots sank uselessly into the snow.

"Don't go!" Violet's voice came out cracked and squeaky.

Earlier, she'd been worried the wolf might want her for its dinner, but now it felt like her only friend in the world and she was desperate for it to stay.

The wolf lowered its head and began to run lightly, kicking up clouds of powdery snow. It made the most of the open space, panting from the exertion and taking great long strides. It was going; it really was going and leaving her. With a few effortless flaps of its wings, the wolf rose into the sky.

"Don't leave! Take me with you!" Violet called again. The wolf grew smaller and smaller, until it could have been mistaken for a bird. The beating sound of the wings grew fainter, until she could hear nothing at all.

The dark blue sky was left empty: devoid of clouds or birds or flying wolves. The undulating ground was untouched. She was alone.

ALONE

Violet adjusted her bag on her back, and turned in a slow circle, fully taking in her situation. Nothing in front of her, nothing behind her. Just a gentle snowy slope up to her left with the suggestion of some trees at the top. How could the wolf have deposited her here all alone as night was falling? She'd thought it was going to take her to the Frozen Unicorn's Ice Fortress, or take her *somewhere;* not to this empty place. Violet wanted to scream or cry, but it would do no good out here, with no one to hear. Besides, Nicolas was somewhere in this frozen wilderness. He needed her to keep going and to find him, otherwise they would both be lost.

When in doubt, head north.

That's what Madam Verger had told her, but which way was north? It all looked exactly the same, without any distinguishing landmarks. Thankfully, Madam Verger had given her a pocket compass to help her find her way. She pushed her hand into the bag and found the distinctive rounded shape of the compass. It was made of brass with an engraved lid: *Always North.*

With fumbling, mittened hands, she managed to flip open the lid. It revealed a star-shaped diagram with letters for each direction: North, South, East and West. A black needle spun around in circles, seemingly at random. Wasn't it supposed to tell her which way was which? What an irritating thing. She shook it but it didn't seem to help. It must be broken – probably everything would break in these freezing temperatures. As she closed the lid in frustration, the shiny metal slipped from her grasp and plopped into the snow. She tried to retrieve it, but the wet wool of her mitten wouldn't let her grasp it. She tugged off the mitten and plunged her bare hand into the deep, wet snow. With numb, pink fingers, she picked up the compass and dropped it back in her bag. She began to put her mittens back on but dropped one in the snow, so it too was wet and couldn't be worn. She thrust the wet mitten in her pocket, the other one back on her hand, and both hands under her arms for warmth, cursing herself. Why had she gone to all that trouble for a compass that didn't even work?

Now her hands were cold.

Her toes were cold.

And she was so tired. Nicolas was out there somewhere, but where? She pictured the Ice Fortress like the ruined watchtower in Millbrook: small and remote. She scanned the horizon but could see nothing like that. She wanted so badly to see him, but had no idea in which direction to head.

The only feature in this bleak landscape was the copse of trees at the top of the hill. She might as well walk towards it. Better to aim for *something* rather than *nothing*.

Violet tramped up the hill, her feet sinking mid-calf into the snow. As she drew nearer the top, she saw the trees were at the edge of a sizable forest. The trees were gigantic and pointed, and although they were covered in snow, enough of their green foliage showed through to make them appear dark against the sky. The sun was nearly down and it shone through the trees, casting long shadows across the snow.

Compared to the open, snowy plains, the forest felt inviting. The tree trunks made her think of the woods she and Nicolas had explored together, and she felt strangely comforted. As she approached the trees, a gust of wind swept a pile of powdery snow from a branch, which swirled in the air and hit her in the face. She gasped. She searched in her pocket for the wet mitten to wipe the snow away, but it had gone: she must have missed her pocket. She wiped her face with her dry mitten and continued.

She'd barely set foot in the forest when she heard a sound behind her. It could have been the wind, but it had a steadier rhythm: like someone breathing. She had a funny feeling, that made her shiver in the same way the cold had done, but this time the hairs on the back of her neck stood up.

She checked over her shoulder and saw nothing. Still, she couldn't shake the feeling that someone (or something) was with her, out here in the wilderness. And that feeling was much, much worse than the fear of being alone.

Violet paused. Ahead of her, a shadow fell on the white canvas of the snow: a long face and a pointed horn. The Unicorn.

NOT ALONE

Madam Verger's words played in her mind.

If you see the unicorn, don't stop to think. Don't think you can fight it. Just get away, as quickly as you can.

So Violet ran, with no idea where she was running to. In these dark woods, the ground was solid underfoot where it had been sheltered from the snow, and Violet could move quickly. She ran between trees, squeezing through gaps she hoped would be too small for a unicorn. She jumped over stones and lumps, and ducked under branches obstructing her path.

As she ran, a plan began to form in her mind; she would climb a tree. Surely a unicorn, even one with magical powers, couldn't follow her up a tree? She saw a strange pile of stones: a large stone with two smaller ones placed on top like a little tower. Behind it was a tree with low-hanging branches, perfect for climbing, even for someone with as little experience as her. She glanced back over her shoulder as she ran, to see how far behind her the unicorn was.

Nobody was there, which meant she had time. She kept looking behind her – just trees and snow. She turned her head back in the direction she was running, just in time to see the low-hanging tree branch at head height.

With some force, she ran right into it.

And everything went black.

$\mathcal{C}$HAPTER SEVEN

A WARM GLOW

When Violet awoke, the first thing she noticed was she was warm. Warm, and more comfortable than she'd ever been, despite a dull ache in her head. She was lying on something soft and could smell freshly baked bread, and the sweet scent of ginger and cinnamon. It was quiet, apart from the comfortable crackling of a distant fire.

She opened her eyes and stretched out her arms. She was in a bed, surrounded by more blankets and cushions than she'd ever seen in her life.

The last thing she remembered was feeling alone and afraid in the wintry wilderness. She'd been running away from the Frozen Unicorn and she'd hit her head.

Although she would normally be worried about how she'd got here, she just felt relief she'd survived. She was no longer surrounded by snow or being chased by the unicorn. She sat up and pulled one of the blankets around her shoulders. It was soft and cream-coloured. She rubbed it on her cheek and smiled. The bed was in a tiny space, hardly big enough to be called a room, and formed from carved wood. A circular opening led through to another room. Violet crawled to the foot of the bed, then poked her head through and looked out.

The next room was bigger than the one she'd been sleeping in, but still only about the size of the living area in Nicolas's cottage. There was a small round window set with tiny, colourful panes of glass, through which beamed irregular shapes of light. It had the strength of new morning light – she must have slept through the night. Most of the warm glow in the room, however, came from lanterns swinging from the beams overhead. A fire blazed in the hearth, which was set into the far wall and garlanded with silver pine cones. Every inch of floor was covered in rag rugs. Inviting chairs and floor cushions lined the walls. There didn't appear to be anyone at home.

Keeping the blanket wrapped around her, Violet stepped into the main room. She noticed her wet boots had been replaced with warm woollen socks. Underfoot, the rugs were so soft she had the feeling of walking on a cloud. She crept around the room, fascinated by everything she saw.

To her left were shelves of curiosities: books, bottles, teapots and pincushions. To her right were rows of deep, dark wooden drawers with gaps at the top. Each was labelled with a small brass tag. Violet examined a few. *Hilary, Bartholomew* and *Raphael*. Names, but of what, she wasn't sure. She peeped into the gap at the top of one drawer but could only see straw.

Above the hearth, some vegetables – potatoes or similar – were roasting on a spit, the fire spitting below. The baking smell she'd detected on waking came from the bread oven in the corner.

Who lived in a place like this? Whoever it was, Violet felt sure they could pose no threat.

Next to the hearth was a thick curtain. Violet pulled it to the side to reveal some twisting wooden stairs. A voice made her jump.

"So, you're awake. Awake and well. Good morning."

THE COSY COLLECTOR

The voice was low and muffled and came from the top of the stairs. Violet peered up, to see a small figure, around her own shoulder height, padding down the stairs towards her.

She was swaddled in layers of knitted clothes. A floppy purple velvet hat fell over her brow. Multiple scarves were wound around her neck and shoulders, covering her lower face. All Violet could see was a lock of dark hair and two large, appealing brown eyes with long lashes.

"I'm Elgu Ember, Collector and Gatherer. Elgu Ember," she said, thrusting out her mittened hand as she walked down the last few stairs. When she'd neared the bottom, Violet shook the offered hand but could only feel soft wool. The hand within must have been contained in numerous woollen layers.

"I'm Violet."

"Good, good. Viol-*et*," repeated Elgu, with an unusual emphasis on the last syllable. She jumped from the bottom step and shuffled straight over to the fireplace where she began removing the large orange potatoes from the spit. At first, Violet was a little concerned that Elgu's scarves were dangling so close to the fire, but she managed without any problems.

She split the potatoes and added a pat of yellow butter to each.

"Lots of butter," she muttered, then she unstoppered some bottles from the shelf above and added tiny spoonfuls from each. "Parsley, garlic and snufflepepper. Snufflepepper, garlic and parsley."

Violet didn't like to interrupt the activity, but she had many questions for this strange little person. "Thank you for your hospitality, Madam Ember. How did I come to be here?"

"Madam Ember! Madam! I've never been called that before. Elgu, please. Come, come," said Elgu, nodding at the chairs as she carried the hot potatoes through on a round wooden tray. "Eat, eat. Questions later, eat first."

Violet sank into one of the chairs and Elgu immediately placed the tray down on a low round table in front of her. She sprang over and tucked two cushions behind Violet's back, then whipped a patchwork quilt over her knees and tucked it in at the edges. With the blanket still around her shoulders, it was a little like being in a cocoon.

Only when she'd assured herself Violet was quite comfortable, did Elgu pass her one of the potatoes in an enamel bowl. Steam rose from the food and Violet blinked. "The steam seems to be *orange*," she blurted out in surprise, and then felt rude for commenting on her host's food. Her mother would have been quite perturbed by such an outburst. Elgu didn't seem to mind.

"Yes, yes. It has a warm glow," she said, a hint of pride in her voice. "A nice warm glow. Try, try."

Violet dug her wooden spoon into the warm mashed-up potato and brought it up to her mouth. Before she could take a bite, Elgu raised a hand to stop her. "Blow!"

Violet blinked in surprise and blew gently on the food, although she wasn't sure her mother would approve of that, either. The orange steam spiralled away from her in a satisfying curl, and Violet took a mouthful of potato. It was delicious. Buttery, herby and warm. Violet hadn't realized how hungry she was, but now she ate quickly, blowing between each mouthful.

She did wonder how her host was going to manage to eat, given half her face was obscured. But before tucking into her own food, Elgu unwound her scarves one at a time and placed them over the back of the chair beside her. Violet tried not to stare, although she was fascinated to get a good look at her host. Elgu had weathered brown skin and a long, protruding nose which was pink at the end. Her hair sprung out around her head like a beautiful, glossy mane and she looked almost, but not quite, human. Madam Verger had said trolls, elves and other fairy folk could be found in the Far North.

Violet wondered if the Collector was one of those, but she didn't know how to phrase the question without sounding impertinent, so she didn't ask. Instead, she said, "This potato is delicious."

Elgu smiled widely. "Thank you, thank you. I only ever eat food that gives me a warm glow inside. A nice warm glow."

Violet nodded at this as she didn't want to break up the meal with a long conversation. She went on taking spoonfuls until it was all finished. To complete the meal, Elgu brought out dishes of warm cloudberry pie, steaming with the same orange steam, and served with dollops of thick cream.

When Violet had finished, her insides did indeed feel glowing, and she could barely imagine it was cold outside. Elgu collected the dishes and scurried away and Violet brought her feet up into the chair, curling under the warmth of the blanket.

"Thank you for bringing me into your home," she said.

Elgu returned and sat back in the chair opposite Violet. Elgu wrapped her scarves back around her face and neck and pulled her hat down low. She reached into a patchwork bag next to her, pulled out some knitting in bright blue wool, and began to work away, needles clicking frantically.

"No problem, no problem. And tell me, how did you come to be in these parts? Candra brought you, did she?"

"Candra. . ." The writing on the leather band came back to her. Violet had been right – it was the wolf's name. She nodded, amazed at how Elgu didn't once look down at the knitting. "Yes. I called her . . . and she came." She felt proud she'd done that, by herself. Elgu wouldn't know it was unusual behaviour for her.

"But Candra didn't let me know you were here. I'm surprised. Very surprised. She sometimes brings visitors here, but normally she howls, to alert me to her presence. They howl, wolves."

Violet pictured Candra last night, throwing back her head and howling. The way she'd looked around afterwards, as if expecting someone to appear.

"I think Candra did call you!" said Violet. "I thought she was howling to another wolf, but there was no response."

"Hmm, I wonder. . . It might have been when I was trying on these." Elgu brought out a pair of knitted earmuffs. "They are very snug and warm. Snug, you see, but I couldn't hear an avalanche through them, let alone a wolf howl. Not an avalanche."

The needles clicked again.

So Candra had been howling to let Elgu know she was there. It was comforting to know her wolf friend hadn't abandoned her in the middle of nowhere; she'd brought her here, where it was safe and warm.

She wondered how Elgu had found her if she hadn't heard the howl. But another sudden thought overtook the first: if Candra had brought other people to Elgu's door, had she brought Nicolas?

She stared at the garment Elgu was knitting. It was growing at an astonishing rate. Elgu kept clicking as she met her gaze. "Do you have a question, Viol-*et*?"

"Yes. I wonder ... did Candra ... have you seen a boy ... or a young man really ... taller than me, with hair that falls into his eyes..."

"A human?"

"Oh, yes, a human."

"No, no, Viol-*et*. You are my first human visitor. My first human, though I had heard tale of your species and always believed you were real. Very real."

"Thank you," said Violet, unsure how else to react. Her heart sunk a little with the knowledge Elgu had seen no sign of Nicolas.

Elgu's knitting became a long, even shape – a scarf, perhaps. She added in a few pink and white stripes.

"It's a good thing you knocked before you collapsed at my door. Another good thing I'd removed my earmuffs and heard the knock. Otherwise you'd have been covered by the snowdrifts and I might not have found you until the spring. Not 'til the spring."

Violet was puzzled. A good thing she knocked? But she couldn't remember knocking, or even finding a house. "It's strange . . . the last thing I remember was running. I saw something that frightened me. Or I thought I did, and in my hurry to get away, I hit my head."

"What did you see? Wild harpies? Snow demons? Frost ogres?"

Violet blinked. She hadn't heard of any of those things. They sounded awful. "Why, no. You probably think me foolish to be frightened of the creature I saw, for they are usually so harmless. It's just I've been warned to stay away."

Elgu's large eyes were fixed on hers. "What did you see out there, Viol-*et*? Who did you see?"

Violet felt embarrassed to tell Elgu her fears when she was probably used to much more frightening creatures. She looked down at the colourful squares of the blanket. "I'm not entirely sure. I was so cold and tired. But I thought I saw a . . . unicorn."

Violet glanced up.

Much of the colour had drained from Elgu's face and she nodded slowly at Violet's words. "The Frozen Unicorn is *here*? The unicorn?"

The way she said it made Violet think it was unlikely. She began to doubt herself. *Had* she seen the unicorn? In her mind, she could picture exactly what it had looked like standing on the hill in Millbrook. A mighty beast with a white coat and dark mane, horn piercing the snowy sky. And she could visualize the same animal chasing her through the snowy landscape. She had known it was there and she had to run for her life, but had she actually seen it? Her head throbbed and she rubbed it. She'd seen a shadow – the shape of the unicorn's horn – but when she turned around there'd been nothing. Was it possible she'd been spooked by the shadow of some branches?

"I think I saw it, but I can't be sure. I was scared and I ran, hardly looking back."

Elgu reached over and patted Violet on the knee, then settled back with her knitting.

"If it was the unicorn, then you did right to run. Whoever brought you to my door saved you from grave danger. Grave danger, Viol-*et.*"

Violet thought of Nicolas, far away from home. "What sort of danger?"

"The Frozen Unicorn has no respect for anyone but himself. No one." Elgu sighed and her needles stopped clicking as she placed her work on her knees. "The Far North was a peaceful place, remote, but unspoiled. Peaceful. At first, when the Frozen Unicorn arrived, he brought a special kind of magic and beauty with him. He built a majestic building. Majestic."

"The Ice Fortress?"

"Yes. But it was all for him. No room for anyone else. No one. Few lived up there, in the Far, Far North, but he turned them out of their simple homes with no thought to their wellbeing. All of that space for him alone."

"What about his prisoners?" Violet was thinking not just of Nicolas, but of all those people long ago, taken from their homes in Millbrook.

Elgu wrinkled her brow. "I don't know of any prisoners. If he holds anyone there, then they are kept well-hidden. I have many visitors here. They tell me things, you see. That's why, if the unicorn had come this far, I think I would know. I would know. That shadow you saw yesterday – I wonder if it was your rescuer, not your pursuer," continued Elgu, stashing her knitting back in the bag. "Perhaps the wolf came back to find you and brought you here when you hurt yourself."

"You're right, I was probably mistaken," said Violet, although she still had a clear vision of the shadow she'd seen, and it was horse-shaped, with a pointed horn. Maybe she'd managed to stagger to Elgu's herself and couldn't remember it. Or maybe the wolf had come back and scared the unicorn away. Although if the unicorn was as powerful as all that, this seemed unlikely. Something didn't quite add up.

The bump on her head continued to throb and she rubbed it. Violet wanted to ask more about the unicorn, but not now. Right now, she was safe. She snuggled further under the blankets, bringing them right up under her chin.

But Elgu jumped up.

"Now you have eaten and you are warm inside, let me show you my collections."

ELGU'S COLLECTIONS

Violet reluctantly left the comfort of her chair by the fire and Elgu took Violet on a tour of her tiny home as if it were a great castle. It probably contained as much as a castle. Everywhere Violet turned, there was something new to see: pincushions, candlesticks, keys and cushions. But Violet thought collections were supposed to contain objects of one type: butterflies pinned behind glass, rows of jugs on a shelf. She couldn't see any similar items here; it appeared to be a random hotchpotch of stuff.

"What is it exactly you collect?"

Elgu blinked her large brown eyes at Violet. "Anything cosy. Anything that might generate a warm, comforting and relaxing atmosphere. Do you feel cosy now?"

Violet smiled. "Yes, I rather think I do."

Elgu pointed out various items proudly: a long, slim-handled candle snuffer; an engraved wooden bowl full of walnuts and a nutcracker; a snow globe that made Violet think of Madam Verger.

Violet picked up each item and examined it carefully. But she was most keen to find out what was in the rows of drawers she'd found on waking. "Can you tell me what's in the drawers? I saw the name tags and I was intrigued."

"Ah, come and see," said the Collector. She led Violet to the drawers and opened the first one, the same one Violet had peeked at earlier. In the middle of the drawer, nestled in the straw, was a plump brown dormouse, with its pink paws drawn up to its chin and its tail curled around its body. "This is Bartholomew."

"Oh, how adorable!" whispered Violet. "Don't let me disturb him."

"Oh, there'll be no waking Bart until the spring. Or any of the others. There's Hilary here, and Raphael. They're all dead to the world for the winter months. They know they can stay here, cosy and warm with me."

She opened the other drawers to show Violet, who saw that Hilary was a tortoise and Raphael was a raccoon or something similar.

"I won't open Vernon's door," she said, indicating a large cupboard at the end from which deep snores were emanating. "He hasn't been asleep for very long and would be grumpy if we woke him."

Violet agreed hastily. She was a little curious about what sort of creature Vernon was, but if he was big and grumpy, she was quite happy not knowing.

They passed the dwindling fire and Elgu stopped to try and poke some life back into the smoking logs.

"Hmm," she said, and stood away from the fire with her hands on her hips. She twisted one of the silver pine cones from the garland above the mantlepiece.

"Stand back, stand back!" she instructed, and Violet obeyed.

With a flamboyant movement like that of a sorcerer conjuring a dove from her sleeve, Elgu threw the pine cone, which sped with some force into the dying fire. For a second or two, nothing happened, and then the pine cone burst open with a loud bang, exploding in a blaze of silver light. Silver sparkles flew out with trails behind them, like tiny shooting stars. Then, the silver light was gone but the fire was renewed and blazed steadily as it had first thing that morning.

Violet blinked and smiled. "That's better," she said, holding her hands up to appreciate the warmth from the blaze.

"Yes, yes," agreed Elgu. "It won't do for the temperature to drop too low."

Violet smiled again. This Cosy Collector was a funny mass of contradictions.

Elgu looked at her quizzically. "What is it, Viol-*et*?"

"It's just ... I was wondering, since you like warm places so much ... why do you live in a cold place like this?"

"I should have thought it was obvious. I don't like *warm* places; I like *cosy* places. Cosy. No one's ever cosy in the summer, are they?"

Violet supposed that was true. "But when do you gather all these things, if you never leave this house?"

"During the summer months. They are the time for collecting and gathering. For combing the riverbanks and searching the hedgerows."

"Summer? I didn't think you ever had summer in the Far North."

Under her scarves, the Collector laughed long and hard.

"Forgive me!" she said. "I don't mean to laugh, but you're not in the Far North, my dear. You are far from the Far North. You have a long, long way to go. No, this is the Near North, where we enjoy pleasant summers and reasonably mild springs."

The Near North? Violet had never even heard of the Near North. She had been sure her guide – Candra – was supposed to take her to the Far North. Wasn't that what Madam Verger had said? Although now she thought about it, perhaps she'd just spoken about the *first part of your journey.* Violet wished she could remember. She hadn't written down Madam Verger's instructions, in an effort to keep the detailed plans hidden from her parents. Anyway, it was too late now. Not only was she nowhere near the Ice Fortress but she wasn't even in the right land.

Her face must have fallen, because Elgu looked at her with concern. "What is the matter, Viol-*et*?"

"I have travelled such a long way already, and I thought my journey was nearly at an end. But now I've found out it's only beginning."

"Journeys are for enjoying, not for rushing and getting over with. I don't recommend you go out again in this treacherous ice and snow. Risking frostbite and nosenip and chilly toes? Stay here, where it's cosy. You can hibernate like them. Hibernate."

"Oh, no, I can't. I mean, that's very generous of you, but I don't hibernate."

"You wouldn't have to go in a drawer. You could have the big-person bed. It's soft."

"I know. It's the softest bed imaginable." Violet sighed, thinking of Nicolas. Wherever he was, he didn't have a soft bed. "I can't lose any time. I must continue on my journey to the Far North."

"Your journey. Upon what journey could a young woman like you possibly be embarking? What journey?"

"Someone is lost out here. I must find him."

Elgu blinked her big eyes. "And you think the Frozen Unicorn might have something to do with his disappearance?"

"Yes." The Collector peered at her then, as if she could see what Violet was thinking.

Violet blushed.

"Ah. I see from your reaction this person means a lot to you. A lot. Could this person possibly be your True Love?"

Violet nodded and the Collector nodded back. "Looking for a lost love. A lost *True* Love. I understand now your journey must continue. For you are searching for the warmest glow of all."

The Collector paused for a moment and wound her scarves back around her neck and head.

"In that case, you will need the proper attire for the Far North. Proper attire."

"I wore my warmest clothes," said Violet, not wanting to appear foolish. She had known it would be cold here and thought she'd prepared accordingly.

The Collector laughed a muffled laugh under her scarves.

"Of course you did, my dear Viol-*et*, but clothes that are warm in your land will do nothing to protect you in mine, let alone in the Far North. Nothing."

Violet wondered what the Collector could possibly find her that would keep her warm in the freezing terrain outside. She was a little concerned she might end up looking like the Collector herself.

But the Cosy Collector reached for one of the many boxes on her shelf and tipped out a pile of tape measures, which she proceeded to unravel. Tiny, all of them. "This one's for newts, and here's one for bats. I need a longer one... I've never clothed a human before..."

Eventually, she found what she was looking for.

"Stand over here – arms straight out like wings."

Violet obeyed and the Collector dragged over a small stool, which she stood on to bring herself nearly to Violet's height. She began to take measurements: the circumference of Violet's head, her wingspan, even the length of her nose from tip to mid-eyebrow. She scribbled the details on to a tiny notepad, muttering as she went along.

Then the little person sat back in her favourite chair and pulled out a long pair of knitting needles.

"You're going to make me some clothes?" asked Violet incredulously. "But won't that take rather a long time?"

Elgu blinked her big eyes, knitting needles already clicking furiously with new wool. "You will need to stay for one more night. One more. But by the morning, you will be equipped for the Far, Far North."

Violet agreed. She didn't want to waste any more time than necessary, but wearing the right clothes would save her time in the end. One more night in the cosiest bed she'd ever slept in, and then her journey to find Nicolas could truly begin.

THE PROPER ATTIRE

In the morning, Violet was awoken by the smell of baking once again. The bump on her head was considerably reduced and she felt well-rested. She wished she could stay in Elgu's welcoming little home, that she could hibernate, like Hilary and Raphael. What a way this would be to spend the winter. But Nicolas was waiting for her in a far from cosy place. She must put any thoughts of her own comfort aside.

After a breakfast of warm oats and stewed pears, which provided Elgu's usual warm glow, the Collector led Violet up the little spiral staircase. A full bath was waiting for her at the back of the room, and some clothes hung from a fox-shaped brass hook, covered in a protective sheet.

"Your cosy clothes are ready."

Violet fixed a smile on her face, ready to feign joy at a mismatched pile of hand-knitted scarves, but then Elgu whisked away the sheet.

Violet's fake smile was replaced by one of real wonder. A full winter outfit in shades of white and cream was waiting for her. These were nothing like Elgu's own clothes. Violet turned to thank Elgu, but she raised a mittened hand.

"Bath, then dress. Bath first," she urged, and retreated downstairs.

Clouds of sweet-smelling steam rose from the wooden bathtub. It looked decidedly appealing and smelled like a cake. The tub was round, deep-sided and lined with white fabric. Rose petals floated on the surface of the water so that it looked, as well as smelled, beautiful.

Violet peeled off her clothes, stuffed them into her bag, leaving the blowing horn on top, and climbed into the bath. The water was a perfect temperature. Of course it was. Violet was beginning to realize Elgu had a knack for these things. She could have stayed there for half the morning, but she wanted to make the most of the daylight hours. She scrubbed her skin well, then ducked her head under the water and used the jug of fresh water to rinse it clean. Along with the grime of the journey, she washed away the insecurity she'd felt on the flying wolf and the loneliness of arriving here in this snowy land. Most of all, she washed away the fear of the unicorn. She emerged from the bath feeling stronger and more confident than ever before. After drying herself off with a length of linen and combing her hair, she began to put on the new clothes Elgu had made.

The undershirt was fashioned from some soft, cream fabric and the body-hugging leggings felt unusual to Violet, who'd only ever worn long skirts. She stretched out one leg at a time, enjoying the freedom of movement. They all fitted perfectly. She looped the strap of the blowing horn around her neck. She would need it for the journey home.

To wear over the top was the softest, warmest garment Violet had ever come across. It appeared to be woven from an array of feathers in white, grey and brown. When Violet put it on, it fell to her knees. It had loose sleeves and a long, tubular neck and hood in one. The main part of the body was soft and downy, whereas the hem, cuffs and hood were adorned with longer, sleeker feathers. She thought of Candra's wings, soft yet strong.

Violet pulled the feathered tube up over her face and tucked the opening under her chin and over her brow. Her face was cocooned all round, and white feathers circled her dark hair. There were diagonal openings to deep pockets by her hips, and even a drawstring she could tighten so just her eyes were visible, Elgu-style. For now, Violet left the tube bunched around her neck and the drawstring loose.

These clothes were far more elegant than she'd been expecting and, although she'd been willing to sacrifice style for warmth, she was glad she didn't have to.

Smiling, she walked down the stairs through to where Elgu was still knitting, needles clicking away. Violet lifted her arms high and turned in a circle so Elgu could see how well it all fitted.

Elgu smiled a satisfied smile at the sight.

Violet stroked the downy feathers along her front. "What is this garment? It's incredible!"

Elgu looked rather proud. "A snoncho. Snoncho, Viol-*et*. Made from the finest cygnet feathers, oiled individually for protection from the elements. Should keep you warm in the cold and cool in the heat."

Cygnets. Of course. She should have recognized the colours. But that gave her quite a different view of the garment – she was rather fond of swans and their fluffy babies. "Were the birds—?"

"—No! Not harmed at all. Each feather was naturally moulted and collected by hand. I'm a gatherer, not a hunter."

Violet examined them more closely, the way they fell in neat rows, feather tips all aligned. It was a work of art. "You wove them all together? Last night?"

"Why, yes. Last night was spent weaving, knitting and stitching by the light of the fire. A cosy evening indeed. Cosy."

"When did you sleep?"

"I didn't, I didn't, but no matter. I can sleep all day; all winter if I choose. Right now, we need clothes. Clothes. Here, I have more essentials for you."

Elgu pushed another pile towards Violet, containing gloves, long stockings and felt boots. The Cosy Collector's touch was more evident here, where she had included bright colours and patterns. The boots were cream, but with a woven band at the top in a red-and-blue geometric pattern. She had also added furry pom-poms that served no apparent purpose other than decoration.

Violet slid them on and, again, they were a perfect fit and so snug.

"Made from dried alpaca wool. No seams, you see. The cold won't find any place to creep in."

Her outfit was complete, and Violet smiled again, although this time it was with mixed emotions. How easy it would be to stay here with Elgu where it was warm and safe, rather than facing the dangers waiting for her.

Elgu seemed to sense her hesitation. "You look most fine, Viol-*et*. And I think you will want to be looking fine when you find your lost love. Most fine. Before you go, there are some other things you will need to keep you warm and cosy."

She presented Violet with a pewter flask containing hot broth, and a bundle of bread rolls and cake. In addition, there were two unusual items made of bones with leather thongs attached.

"What are these?" asked Violet.

"Ice skates, for skating on ice," said Elgu.

"Oh, how wonderful," cried Violet, "I've wanted to skate since I was a little girl, but it was never cold enough. Then when the cold winter did finally come, I had other things on my mind. . ."

"Ah yes, but now is your chance perhaps. But ice-skating is not a simple activity, oh no. You must push your feet like so. Push, push." Elgu acted out the ice-skating motion and Violet smiled, stashing the skates in her bag.

Next, Elgu handed her a cloth bag full of firecones. "Whenever you need an immediate and steady blaze, throw one of these down and it will provide you with all the warmth and comfort you need."

"I can't take all these," she said, but the Collector didn't seem to mind.

"Take them, take them," she urged. "I know where to find more."

Violet thanked her, then stayed for one more hot drink, until her hair had dried by the fire. Then it was time to go.

As she prepared to say farewell, Violet felt suddenly overcome with gratitude. "You have done so much for me: brought me in from the cold, fed me, clothed me... How can I ever thank you?"

"I don't need thanks. The cosy feeling of helping another is enough!" She paused. "Although there might be something..." From her pocket, Elgu brought out Violet's remaining mitten: the one she was wearing when she arrived. It looked somewhat old and bedraggled compared to her new wardrobe. Elgu looked at Violet with large hopeful eyes.

Violet laughed. "You give me all this, and you want my old mitten in exchange?"

Elgu nodded and stroked it gently. "You seem to have just the one, and it's different to anything I can collect from around here. And already worn. Soft enough for the purpose."

"Of course you can have it, Elgu, but what do you want it for?"

Elgu smiled and opened one of the wooden drawers, marked with the name *Mistle*. She took out a sleeping creature which looked like a child – a girl –but was no bigger than Violet's thumb, with delicate folded wings.

"She's a River Fairy," explained Elgu. "I found her here, in Ember Forest, days ago, after a storm. She must have blown here. Her arm is broken but she will heal."

A fairy. Violet had been sceptical when she'd heard Nicolas's tale about fairies in the woods, yet here, without doubt, was a real-life fairy. "She's so tiny!" whispered Violet.

"Yes, tiny, tiny. And delicate. She keeps rolling around in there," whispered Elgu. She tucked the fairy into the mitten and popped her back in the drawer.

"I will let her rest, yes, and return her to her own kind when it is warm outside."

Violet felt a strange comfort knowing, even when she was back out in the bleak, cold winter, her glove would be safe with Elgu until spring.

With Mistle safely tucked away, it was time for Violet to be on her way.

"I wonder if you could give me some directions? I was told to travel north and I was given this, but it doesn't seem to work." Violet showed the Collector the compass.

Elgu peered at the inscription. "*Always North*. Yes, yes." She flipped open the lid and held it flat in the palm of her gloved hand, not upright as Violet had done. It spun a little and came to rest, one side of the arrow.

"Not broken, see? This gold tip on the arrow points north. *Always North*, see? You point, you walk, you point again."

"Thank you, Elgu," said Violet, a little embarrassed she hadn't even known how to work her own compass.

Elgu handed it back to her. "Put it in your pocket now. Go back to the plain where Candra left you, then use the compass to head north, through River Forest. Once you reach Forest River, follow it north. Then put compass away. Follow the river. When the sky turns bright in the afternoons, then you've reached the Far North. Keep on. Follow the river. River will lead you all the way to the Ice Fortress.

"And how long will that journey take me?"

It could have been Violet's imagination, but Elgu didn't seem to want to answer the question. She lowered her lashes briefly and then opened them again.

"How long? How long? Don't think about how long, perhaps, but about what you can gain from the journey."

"That sounds like good advice," she said, although deep-down she knew Elgu didn't want to tell her quite how far she still had to travel. Violet didn't mention, either, that she could never enjoy the journey, when Nicolas was surely getting colder and weaker with each day.

She bit her lip, but Elgu took Violet's hands in her own and met her gaze. "Farewell, Viol-*et*. May you reach the Frozen North safely. May you find your True Love, and may you carry a warm glow wherever you go."

CHAPTER EIGHT

ONWARDS

As Elgu opened the door, Violet braced herself for freezing winds and swirling snowstorms. She was pleasantly surprised to find sunshine, a cerulean sky and sparkling snow. She blinked a few times into the brightness, trying to pinpoint where she was in relation to the plain where Candra had left her. Elgu's house was at the edge of the forest. Most of the snow-covered trees looked identical, but Violet did recognize some low-hanging branches and a tower of stones. She now realized the tower marked Elgu's pathway, which meant when she'd blacked out, she'd been almost at Elgu's house. Was it possible she'd staggered to Elgu's front door without remembering? Had Candra returned and dragged her there? And was the unicorn shadow just a figment of her tired imagination?

It had been only two evenings before, but it felt like a long time ago. Two nights was too long to spend in one place when Nicolas was in danger. She had no more time to waste. She smiled at Elgu, waved, and turned to walk deeper into the forest, but Elgu called out.

"North! North, Viol-*et*. Not through the forest but the other way – out of the woods and down the hill."

"Thank you!" called Violet, pulling out her compass and checking. Yes, north was in the opposite direction. She changed course. So her instincts that first evening to head to the forest had been completely wrong. It was fortunate she'd ended up at Elgu's house, otherwise who knew how many miles she would have walked in the wrong direction.

She walked away, turning back and waving at Elgu again as she went. She left the forest and tramped down the snowy hill. It was disheartening to think she'd made no progress at all since Candra had brought her to the North. By now, Spiers would have returned to Millbrook with an empty coach and explained to

Violet's parents that she was missing. She hoped Mother wasn't too angry with him.

Still, she tried to focus on the positives. She had food and firecones, knew how to work her compass, and had the right clothes for the weather. It was so much easier to walk in her new boots, which were made for the snow and fitted her feet perfectly. She didn't sink as far as she had in her old boots, and the cold had yet to penetrate their woolly warmth.

She reached the plain where she'd first arrived and checked her compass for north. As she trekked through the snow, she was able to appreciate her surroundings in a way she hadn't before. The all-white landscape was now a variety of colours. In places where the sunlight hit the snow, it was a bright yellowy-white. The shadows were a contrasting bluey-white. Violet needed a brand-new set of words to describe these colours, and she amused herself by making them up as she went: *whellow* and *bluwhite*.

In the silence, her ears and eyes were open to any change: anything new. She noticed every gust of wind and every bird that flew overhead. Strange there were birds out here, in this frozen landscape.

After a time, she saw a new forest in the distance that must be River Forest. As she trudged up the hill towards it, a herd of reindeer emerged, walking in a long line, the leader's hooves making a deep groove in the snow. The others, heads down, followed in the trampled trench. They paid little heed to her and she felt more than ever like an unimportant speck in this vast land.

In amongst all the new sights and sounds, Violet didn't hear any water, although she kept listening for it. Elgu had said she must follow the river – Forest River – north. Although she knew she might not reach it for a while, she rather thought she might see it, or hear it, from a distance. She hoped that didn't mean she was still a long way off.

Every so often, she checked her compass and readjusted her path, proud of herself for finding the way.

She was relieved when she reached the edge of the forest, thankful for a break from the shining brightness and the deep snow underfoot. She chose to have a break in there, sitting on a fallen tree trunk to give her feet a rest. Her poor feet that were used to short strolls around the manor grounds were finding this journey quite a shock.

She took out one of Elgu's firecones and dropped it on the forest floor, where it cracked open like an egg. Some small, unsatisfactory flames burned at its centre. It was disappointing. Elgu had thrown hers in a special way. Violet would have to remember to do the same.

Still, she was close enough to feel a little of its warmth. That, combined with a few sips of the spicy, warming broth Elgu had packed, restored her energy. She resumed the journey with her insides full of the promised warm glow, trying not to concentrate on her aching feet.

After walking a little further among the trees, she passed through the forest and found herself next to a wide, winding river, lined on either side by snow-covered trees and stretching to the horizon and beyond.

Forest River. At last.

And Violet saw straight away why she hadn't heard flowing water as she approached. It was obvious when she thought about it: the river was frozen.

FOREST RIVER

Of course the river was frozen in this cold climate. The millpond had frozen even in Millbrook, and it was much warmer there. Violet checked her compass again. She was standing at a bend in the river.

One way led west, and the other slightly north-east, so it was clear which she should follow. The only question was how.

There were steep banks of snow on either side. She could walk on the banks, following the river round. She would know then she was going the correct way, but she would be walking on an uneven, angled slope. She could see that there were also places where the trees got in the way, which would make progress slow. She could go back into the forest and try to keep the river in sight, but it would be easy to lose track of it.

The quickest way would be to travel on the frozen river itself. And, Violet remembered, she had the perfect method by which to do so. Ice skates.

She would never dare to skate on the river in Millbrook, unless her father had declared it safe. There had been a boy who'd tried – perhaps inspired by Madam Verger's tales – and he'd broken through the ice. He'd survived but only because he'd been fished out and warmed up rapidly.

Still, here in the Far North, or the Near North, or whatever place she'd reached, she could be certain the water was frozen solid. At least, she hoped.

She teetered down the bank to where she could sit on a flat rock, untied her bag and brought out Elgu's ice skates, which were near the top. She fixed one to the sole of each boot, criss-crossing the straps over her feet and tying them tightly.

The bones were straight and inflexible, and felt like no shoe she'd worn before. She managed to get herself down to the river, scrabbling with her hands backwards. Once she was there, she stood on its frozen surface, wobbly but upright. She took a deep breath and readied herself, then managed a couple of tiny steps, knees high and feet flat.

It worked! Violet smiled. After all these years, she was finally going to realize her ice-skating dream. She would skate gracefully all the way to the Ice Fortress, a rosy glow in her cheeks, wearing her beautiful feathery outfit. She would rescue Nicolas and they'd skate back to Elgu's together.

What a shame there was nobody there to see her now.

Feeling confident, she pushed with her right foot, but it slid forward at dramatic speed and her left foot didn't have time to follow.

"Aaaargh!" she cried, landing with her left leg folded beneath her and her right leg stretched out in front. She scrabbled to push herself to an upright position, hands slipping on ice.

It didn't hurt that much, just a slight ache in her left leg where she'd twisted it. Still, she felt tears pricking at her eyes, more from the shock than anything else. Elgu had warned her skating wasn't easy. She should have listened. What was it she said? *"Push, push."*

Violet took a deep breath and tried again.

"Push, push," she muttered to herself, attempting to scissor her feet forward in the manner Elgu had suggested. But she hadn't reckoned on the bones being able to move sideways, as well as backwards and forwards. Slowly, her feet slid outwards. Trying to bring her feet and knees in, Violet fell forwards, landing on all fours.

Why had she ever dreamed of an audience to watch her skate? Now, hands and feet on the ice, behind in the air, she was grateful there was no one to see her humiliation. But as she struggled to a standing position once again, she thought she heard something. A high, twittering sound, very much like laughter.

LAUGHTER

"Who's there?" called Violet, looking around. The sound had been nearby, but there was no one on the river, no one on the riverbank and, by the looks of things, no one hiding in the trees.

She was imagining things. It was the birds. Her own embarrassment had translated their singing as laughter.

Perhaps she'd been too cautious. Plenty of people ice-skated. How difficult could it be? She tried again, with a new resolve to speed up the push, push motion.

Both her legs flew out rapidly from beneath her and she sat down hard and suddenly on the ice.

Once again, as she was picking herself up, Violet heard laughter. Loud laughter. This time, there was no mistaking it – peals and peals of high giggling, coming, from the sound of things, from more than more person. And it was close by, yet Violet couldn't see anyone. Were they invisible?

"Who is that? Show yourselves!"

Gradually, emerging from the ice like steam, came a white cloud. The cloud dispersed into smaller fragments, and Violet saw each one was a tiny, winged person, around the size of her palm. There were thirty or forty of them altogether, delicate and white like snowflakes, with leafy, shimmering clothes. They flew at random, twisting and turning as they performed their own little dances. At certain angles they were transparent, and Violet kept losing sight of them.

Violet watched for a while, open-mouthed, before she realized what they must be. They resembled the fairy sleeping in her mitten at the Collector's house. More sparkling and full-of-life, but otherwise the same.

"River Fairies?" Violet whispered, and they laughed again and nodded.

"I saw one of your kind, in Ember Forest. She is safe and well with a kind Collector named Elgu. Her name is Mistle."

At that, the fairies threw their hands up in glee, grins on their tiny faces. They blew her kisses and danced together, linking arms and swinging one another in circles. They chattered in tinkling voices and swarmed towards Violet. For a moment, she was alarmed and batted them gently away, but it made no difference. They kept coming at her, and attached themselves to her legs, clinging to her leggings from knee to ankle, although Violet couldn't feel their weight. Approximately half the group aimed for one leg and half the group aimed for the other. One sat on the top of each of her boots, reclining against the tied leather straps. They were still laughing and didn't seem to mean any harm. A single fairy flew back down to the surface of the ice and performed a little pirouette. He turned his back to her, then skated off a little way, gliding skilfully in a curvy line. He didn't appear to be wearing any skates himself, but his tiny feet looked like blades themselves. He stopped, turned and bowed, as if expecting applause. Violet couldn't help but smile; the little fairy creature looked so pleased and proud.

She felt pulling on the leggings of her left leg and looked down. The fairies on that side were heaving with all their might on the fabric. Instinctively, she moved that leg forward, her foot gliding along the ice. When the fairies on her right leg did the same, and her foot moved again, she realized what was going on.

"You're teaching me to skate!" she cried, and they all laughed again. The fairy leading the way flew into the air and back down. Then he turned and skated off once again. All Violet had to do was follow.

SKATING

Considering how impossible Violet had found ice-skating to begin with, she got the hang of it very quickly.

After a few minutes, the fairies let go of her legs and she continued skating unassisted. They all joined the guide up ahead and skated side by side, legs moving in perfect unison. Their wings moved steadily like butterflies', and their long hair flowed out behind them. Violet was never going to look as graceful as them, but it didn't matter: she was as good as she needed to be. At first, she felt hot, despite the cold air, because of all the effort needed. But gradually, she found a rhythm of pushing and gliding that allowed her to travel a long distance with less exertion. She leaned forward, smiling, whizzing past the sparkling trees. The long, winding river stretched out ahead of her, leading to her destination. The river was white in places, midnight blue in others, hinting at its depth. Violet wondered if it was frozen right to the bottom or if there were little pockets where animals rested, ready to emerge in the spring. Elgu had told her how she'd come to the riverbank to forage in the warmer months. It probably looked quite beautiful then, with green grass and trees. Right now, it was impossible to imagine this land without its thick blanket of snow.

Her skates made a scraping sound, and cut white lines into the thick ice, unlike the fairies, who made no dent at all. She liked the fact she, Violet Reddmene, was leaving her mark somewhere in this vast landscape. It made her feel less small.

They skated for a long time. Perhaps all afternoon, although it was difficult to tell. Violet's feet hurt from the unfamiliar motion and she was fairly certain blisters were forming by her heels and ankle bones. But she tried to push aside any thoughts of discomfort. However much her feet hurt, she wasn't suffering half as much as Nicolas, alone in his icy cell. He needed her and she would find him.

It couldn't yet be sundown, but the sky had begun to change. Since Violet had arrived, it had been nondescript, like a blank page. But it was beginning to come to life with broad strokes of colour, as if someone was sweeping paint across it. It was like no sky she'd ever seen, with distinct horizontal stripes. There were familiar sky colours: blues, oranges and pinks. Also, more unusual shades: violet, red and even green.

Violet remembered what Elgu had said about the sky turning bright in the afternoons. This must have been what she meant.

"Are we in the Far North now?" Violet called to the fairies.

They nodded and fell about clutching their sides as if she'd said something hilariously funny. Violet had come to realize that this was their usual response to her. She didn't mind it, actually, as she couldn't think of many other times when people laughed at the things she said.

At least she knew they were getting closer. Closer to the Ice Fortress. Closer to Nicolas.

DANCING IN THE SMOKE

It was difficult to know how long they'd been skating, or how many miles she'd travelled. Eventually Violet's shins began to ache as well as her feet. The sun was dropping in the striped sky, and Violet sensed twilight was approaching. She would like to get another couple of hours of skating in before nightfall. As for where she would spend the night, she didn't yet know. Perhaps she'd keep skating all night long. But for now, she needed something to eat and drink and to rest her weary legs.

"Can we stop now, for a break? My legs are tired."

That was, of course, funny. The fairies' legs were tiny compared to Violet's, but they showed no signs of tiring, even with all the jumps and turns they managed. Their wings and skate-like feet gave them an enviable advantage.

Still, the fairies led her to a spot where she could easily climb from the frozen river on to the bank. As soon as she stopped skating, she was cold – very cold. She drew the drawstring of her snoncho tight (to the fairies' amusement), removed her gloves for a moment, and managed to untie the straps of her skates. She stashed the skates in her bag. Without them, walking felt peculiar, as if her feet wanted to glide through the snow.

Violet headed into the forest. She half-expected the fairies to flit away and leave, but they came with her, buzzing around her head like a friendly swarm of bees.

A short way in, she found a large clearing with a fallen tree at its centre. She stopped there, shivering. It was the perfect space for another fire. After the last disappointing attempt, she thought she'd try a new technique.

She tried to remember how Elgu had thrown the firecone into the fireplace. It was with some vigour, and a certain flourish.

"Stand back, everyone," she cried. The fairies obligingly flew into a perfect circle around the clearing, as if they were playing a children's party game.

This time, Violet laughed. The fairies made everything more fun.

Palm facing up, Violet jerked her wrist and flicked the firecone as forcefully as she could down on the forest floor. It instantly smashed into fragments, and bright flames shot out as they'd done at Elgu's house. Tiny silver stars were visible within the blaze and the fairies shrieked and pointed with glee.

"So that's how it's done," Violet said proudly, moving closer to the fire and feeling it defrost her bones. She held her hands up in front of the blaze, letting the warmth seep in through her gloves. The fairies circled it at shoulder height, gazing down at the flames as if they'd never seen a fire before. Perhaps they hadn't.

One little fairy shot forward so he was directly over the middle of the fire, a few feet up. Surrounded by smoke, he spun in a pirouette, as they'd been doing on the ice. The others watched, entranced, and then ventured forward themselves to play in the spiralling plumes of grey smoke.

Violet was a little bit worried about them; they looked so small and fragile, like snowflakes. Would the fire hurt them? Melt them, even? But it had no effect on them at all.

Silvery smoke twisted up and they flew around it, and through it, joining and releasing hands in a beautiful, synchronized ballet. Even without music, it was the loveliest dance Violet had ever seen. At the Wintertide dance, her family and the villagers had thought they'd been light on their feet. Compared to these fairies, they'd been like a gaggle of geese. She sighed. Would she be home in time for Wintertide? And would Nicolas be with her? Thinking about it made tears prick at her eyes, and she tried to put those thoughts out of her mind.

She would have joined in with the fairies' dancing, but the blisters on her feet hurt too much. She wanted to rest them while she could, so she sat on the peeling bark of the tree trunk and enjoyed the fun from a comfortable place.

She opened her flask and offered some broth to the fairies, who shook their heads, giggled and continued dancing. She had no idea what fairies ate but, guessing from their reaction, it wasn't soup. She was glad, because she needed it herself. She was hungry and worn out from all the skating. The soup had somehow stayed hot and tasted deliciously hearty. She drank it all up, feeling the warm glow radiate from within.

Violet closed her eyes for a moment, enjoying the fire, the food in her stomach and the laughter of the fairies. She felt a little bad for enjoying any moments of happiness when Nicolas was locked away, but she would be no use to him if she was too tired to move. Soon, she would be on her way, and would get in another couple of hours skating before darkness fell. In the meantime, she wanted to give herself a chance to rest fully.

Violet sat there with her eyes closed for only a few moments before she heard the flutter of wings in the forest some distance behind her. A bird fleeing, she supposed. Someone was there, watching from the cover of the trees, she was sure of it. She opened her eyes. The fairies were still dancing, lost in their own fun.

Violet turned slowly. She was right. She was being watched.

It was the unicorn.

She gasped and the fairies stopped dancing, their little faces creased with worry.

He was standing in amongst the trees outside the clearing, some distance away. His white coat was visible through the trees and the front part of his mane flopped over his forehead. She met his gaze, and saw his eyes were a dark, liquid brown. She felt the eyes were asking her a question – begging her not to run. Violet had the same strong feeling as she had in Millbrook; she wanted to approach the creature.

He flicked his mane, and the sudden movement brought her back to her senses. Of course the unicorn could convince her he was good – he was magic, wasn't he? But she was too sensible to fall for his tricks. Perhaps the fairies could help her. They were magic too, weren't they? Some of them had noticed her looking out into the trees and were following her gaze. Violet bobbed down so she was closer to their height and whispered, "Help me! I need to get away from that unicorn. He means me harm."

They all turned to look at the unicorn, frowns on their tiny faces.

"Please, will you help me find a place where I can be safe?" asked Violet

She didn't need to ask twice. They whirled up, little wings whirring at top speed as they circled the fire. Then they blew, directing their pursed lips towards the flames. The fire was extinguished. From the dying embers, a cloud of tiny sparkling stars shot out, a little like those created by the firecones. There were more of them, though, and they shot out high and wide, forming a wall between them and the unicorn. She could no longer see him.

As Violet stashed her belongings in her bag, the fairies beckoned for her to follow them deeper into the forest. She did, darting between the trees, running for her life.

CHAPTER NINE

TENTS IN THE SNOW

This was the second time Violet had run through the forest to escape the unicorn. This time she didn't look back: she wasn't going to risk hitting her head on a branch again.

How had the unicorn tracked her down? Every time she thought she'd shaken him off, there he was following her. How was she ever going to sneak into the Ice Fortress undetected? It would be impossible.

At least she had the little fairies to keep her safe for the time being. Violet's feet smarted with pain as they weaved through the trees away from the river, until she was sure she would never be able to find her way back. Every step took her further away from Nicolas, but right now she felt she had no choice.

They emerged onto a snowy plain, rather like the one Violet had crossed on leaving Elgu's house. Out of the cover of the trees, the striped sky loomed large. The fairies stopped and pointed as Violet fought to regain her breath after the run.

Breaking up the acres of snow were about a dozen tents, made from a hotchpotch of different materials cobbled together. Pipes and tubes stuck out at odd angles from the tents, and smoke was rising from the centre of each. The most noticeable thing about them was that each tent had a colour of its own, with all the materials dyed to match. The colours all reflected hues from the sky above. One was a bright yellow, another red, and there were various shades of blue and green. Some distance away was even a violet tent. The effect was inviting, as if Violet had opened the lid of a treasure box and discovered glowing jewels inside.

Nobody was about, although wooden sledges lay outside many of the tents. In the centre of the camp was a large contraption with a pipe emerging from it: some sort of stove, perhaps.

The fairies pointed to the tents and pulled at Violet's arms, urging her to hurry up, but she wasn't quite sure what to do. She felt shy at the prospect of approaching a stranger's home, even if the fairies told her to.

She peered back into the forest. There was no sign of the unicorn. They must have shaken him off. Knowing she had to hide before he found them, she tentatively followed the fairies towards the entrance of the closest jade green tent.

"Thank you for everything you've done for me," Violet said to the small creatures. "For teaching me to skate and for bringing me here—"

The fairies didn't wait to hear the rest of Violet's sentence; they pushed her once more towards the entrance and flew off, waving and giggling. She was on her own again.

Violet approached the tent, wondering who would camp in this deep snow. They must be freezing inside. Up close, Violet realized the tents couldn't possibly contain humans – they were a little too small.

A flap covered the entrance to the tent and there was no door to knock on. Violet didn't like to stick her head inside uninvited, so she called out, "Hello?"

INVENTOR CREATORS

A child, who looked a little like a smaller version of Elgu, appeared at the tent flap, his large brown eyes close to Violet's. There was a double flap, like a sort of porch, so Violet could see nothing of the inside of the tent.

"Yes, yes?" he asked.

"I... The fairies told me I might find a safe haven here?"

The boy-Elgu blinked.

An older voice from somewhere within the tent – his mother, perhaps – called, "From who or what do you seek refuge?"

"What or who?" came another voice.

"I have been running –" Violet inexplicably felt tears welling up in her eyes. "– from the Frozen Unicorn."

There was a pause, and Violet wondered what would happen if the fairies were wrong. What if they wouldn't offer her protection? Then there was a rustling from behind the inner tent flap. The owner of the first voice emerged. She also looked similar to Elgu, but with a shorter nose and smaller eyes. She pulled the little boy unceremoniously back inside, pushed past Violet and looked out of the tent and all around.

"Is he here, the unicorn?"

Violet shook her head. "I ran, and I think I lost him."

"Hmm," she replied, doubtfully. "Come in now, inside."

She pulled at the outer flap and began to secure it with ties. Violet crawled inside, on her hands and knees. It was the only way she could manage, being a couple of heads taller than the occupants of the tent.

Once past the inner flap, the tent opened up into such a large space, Violet was able to stand up, although her head-height was limited. The floor was wooden and there were rugs laid down and cushions scattered around, all in the same jade green as the exterior of the tent. In the centre was a stove, and clothes hung from poles by the ceiling. The pipes she'd spotted sticking out of the tent continued inside, travelling in different directions. A pail stood under one of the pipes, and every so often, a lump of snow slid into it, making a disconcerting thump. It was much warmer than she had imagined; she wouldn't have known she was in a tent at all.

A family, or maybe two families, were going about their lives. Someone by the stove was melting the snow from the pail in a cooking pot. Another nursed a tiny infant. Their eyes all followed Violet as she entered their space and, once again, she felt guilty for disturbing their peace. She stood near to the centre of the tent, where there was the greatest head-height. She wasn't sure what to do, so she smiled awkwardly. A little one, who looked no more than about three, stared at her suspiciously, then started to cry quietly, and took refuge on his father's lap.

"I'm sorry," said the father, patting the child's back, "he hasn't seen many like you before."

"Oh, that's quite all right," said Violet, "I understand."

She continued to stand, feeling quite out of place and not sure if she was entirely welcome.

"Who brought you here?" asked the one next to her, stirring the pot.

"River Fairies," said Violet. "They taught me to skate."

"Hmm, River Fairies don't help just anyone," said the father.

"Not everyone," agreed the snow cook. "You must have impressed them. Made them laugh." She looked at Violet doubtfully, as if being humorous was an unlikely skill for her to possess. Violet decided not to illuminate them with tales of her repeated falls on the skates, especially now she was becoming something of an ice-skating expert.

Silence fell in the tent and Violet searched for something to say.

"It's cosy in here," she said nervously. "Are you cosy collectors?"

They all stared and she hoped she hadn't offended them.

"No, you're thinking of Collector Gatherer Trolls," said the pot-stirrer. So Elgu was a troll, just as Violet had suspected. She'd always thought trolls were big and green. Northern trolls must be different. She was glad she now knew.

"We're Inventor Creator Trolls. Collectors are normally found in the south," added the father.

The thought of Elgu living in the south made Violet smile, as it had seemed so far north to her. They continued with their explanation. The trolls took turns in speaking, so in order to follow the conversation, Violet found herself looking around the tent in a dizzying manner.

"Collector Gatherers are solitary trolls."

"But we Inventor Creator trolls like to work together."

"Many minds make many ideas."

Violet lost track of who said what, but she tried to follow the conversation as the troll who'd let her in bustled past her, having secured the tent flap. She stood, arms folded across her chest, eyeing Violet with what looked like suspicion. "Enough about us. Tell us about yourself – you are running from the Frozen Unicorn?"

Violet nodded and the little one cried harder at the mention of the unicorn, his wails reaching a high pitch. His father patted his back in a comforting manner, and the others all ignored him until his cries died away.

An older troll, who was bundled up in shawls and scarves almost to the extent Elgu had been, beckoned to Violet and patted the cushion next to her. She had a small pot of snow, which she was fashioning into pebble-sized lumps with her hands. She then placed these ice pebbles in another pot. The whole process was very rapid, and the ice pebbles piled up. Violet joined her with some relief, enjoying taking the weight off her poor, blistered feet.

"The Frozen Unicorn is here now? You've seen him?" the troll asked as she poured the boiling-water-that-was-once-snow from the pot into a line of wooden cups. She passed one to Violet first, who took it gratefully. Red berries floated in the cup, and the water was gradually turning pink.

"Yes, I've seen him twice in your land."

"Where?"

Violet took a sip of the steaming drink. The taste was a little sharp, but delicious.

"Once in the Near North and once over there, in the forest by the river." Violet didn't confuse things by saying that the first time, she'd only seen a shadow.

"He's here? But why would he come to these parts?" The troll at the stove sat down next to the father and his child. They too began to fashion ice pebbles with their hands. The look of fear and disbelief on her face reminded Violet of the way Elgu had reacted.

"We are settled here now. The unicorn can't make us move again," said the troll who'd let her into the tent.

"He made you move before?" asked Violet.

They all nodded at once.

"We'll tell you all about it, but first, introductions," said the troll who'd let her in. "I am Hefta, and this is my husband Hooan, our little boy Tipto and baby Mitty. My sister-in-law is Alline, and my mother-in-law we all just call 'Grandmother'."

Violet tried to commit all the names to memory.

"I'm Violet."

Once they were all settled on the floor cushions, sipping their drinks and fashioning ice pebbles, Hefta told Violet their story. Hooan and Alline interjected regularly.

"We liked living in the Far, Far North."

"We had permanent homes."

"Beautiful homes."

"We had fishing systems."

"And salt-extraction machines."

"It sounds idyllic," said Violet. She had stopped trying to follow exactly who said what. It didn't matter, as they were all telling the same story.

Hefta looked at her seriously. "It was. It really was."

"But the unicorn destroyed it all!" That came from little Tipto, who had overcome his initial fear of Violet and was now brave enough to speak.

His father nodded. "We were not used to visitors in the Far, Far North, until the unicorn came."

"We were the only ones living up there. The only ones who liked it."

"Then he fell from the sky and we knew he was magic."

Violet hadn't expected to hear that. She was so surprised, some of her drink went down the wrong way. She coughed, and Grandmother thumped her on the back. "He came from the sky?" Violet asked, when she'd recovered.

"Yes," said Hefta. "At first, we welcomed him. Then he wanted us to work for him, to build his great fortress."

"But we said no."

"We don't mind hard work."

"Oh, no."

"No, no."

"But we work for ourselves. We think for ourselves, to have our own ideas, to share and create together for each other."

"Not build what an icy unicorn tells us to."

Violet nodded. "I can understand that," she said.

Alline shuffled over with the teapot and topped up Violet's berry drink, which was getting low. "But he got angry. He pointed his horn all around and worked his magic."

"He covered our homes in thick ice. Most of our possessions were lost."

"He said he would do the same to us."

"Freeze us where we stood."

"We had to flee."

"We came here, near to the river but hidden by the forest. We worked hard to make new homes."

"They're beautiful," said Violet, meaning it.

Hefta looked pleased. "Beautiful, yes, but not as lovely as our old homes."

"We plan to make something more permanent, but we worry he will chase us away again."

"If he is here, further south, then maybe he wants more. More land, more power."

There was a pause as they all sipped their berry drinks. Ice clinked steadily into pails from all sides.

"Did he do the same to you?" asked little Tipto, his eyes wide. He reminded Violet of Nicolas's younger siblings.

She began to tell her story. "In my village, Millbrook, we don't often see much snow, but many years ago, he brought a cruel winter to my homeland." The tears were threatening to rise again. "He even took *people*."

Tipto gasped.

Violet looked at the berries in her cup, swollen now with the water they'd absorbed.

"This all happened a very long time ago. Before I was born. But it sounds as if what happened here was more recent?"

"Some years ago now. Before Tipto and Mitty, but not long enough to forget," said Hefta and the others nodded their heads in agreement.

"Feels like yesterday to us," added Alline.

"That's most strange," said Violet. "Perhaps he had another Ice Fortress, somewhere else, before he came here. Do you know where he lived before he came here?"

"No," said Hooan.

"All we know is it was in that direction." Heffta pointed up.

"Of course, you mentioned he came from the sky," said Violet. "It sounds like something invented. . ."

"We didn't invent it."

"Even though we're Inventor Trolls."

"We invent things, not truths."

Violet was worried she might have offended her hosts. "Oh, I know – I didn't think you were making it up. All I meant was it sounds like something out of a storybook." She sighed. "When I heard those stories, as a child, I didn't know whether to believe them or not. But I know now it was all true. The unicorn returned, three days ago, and took someone very dear to me. I have come here looking for that person – for Nicolas – but the unicorn seems to know I'm here, and he's been chasing me."

The trolls gazed at her, eyes wide. She could see they understood her hurt and, at their sympathy, the tears that had been threatening began to fall freely down her cheeks.

"I must rescue him. He is held in an Ice Fortress and he's all alone. I'm the only one who can help him—"

Grandmother placed her hand reassuringly on Violet's knee. Alline looked particularly concerned.

"You cannot mean you plan to *go* to the Ice Fortress? All on your own?"

The others all shook their heads as if the idea was utter madness.

"The Ice Fortress is a big place," said Hefta.

"It is hard to reach," added Hooan.

"And the Frozen Unicorn is so powerful. He was too powerful for all of us," said Alline.

Violet hung her head. It was beginning to feel like an impossible task. But she had come all this way – how could she possibly turn back?

"It is the only way I know to rescue my friend. I have no choice. And someone back home told me I possess a power of my own."

"What power is that, Human?" asked Hefta

Violet flushed. "The power of True Love."

The trolls all nodded, their faces serious.

"True Love is powerful indeed," said Grandmother, her voice low.

Violet wiped her tears from her cheeks with her sleeve and tried to change the subject. "Anyway ... as you can tell from my story ... I'm sure it's not your homes he's after this time. It's me he wants, and I will leave as soon as possible. I don't want to bring more trouble to your community."

Grandmother patted her arm. "You must stay the night here with us, in safety."

"Thank you." Tears welled up in Violet's eyes. This was such a kind, hospitable family and the Frozen Unicorn had brought them nothing but hurt and misery. She felt suddenly angry. "I don't understand how the unicorn could cause all this pain. Where is his compassion? Where is his heart?"

Hooan sighed a long sigh. "That's just it: he *has* no heart. No heart, no soul. That's why you can see right through him; everything inside him is frozen."

"The Frozen Unicorn is not a *real* unicorn at all."

"They say he was once a man – a sorcerer – who took the form of a unicorn to cast powerful spells, but ended up frozen like that."

They continued to talk, giving their opinions on quite how heartless he was, but Violet stopped hearing their words. It was all noise in the background. She could only hear Hooan's words, over and over in her mind. *You can see right through him.*

Violet thought back to the two occasions when she'd seen the unicorn. Once on the hill at Millbrook, and once out here in the forest. Although she hadn't looked for long on either occasion, she could recall the sight most clearly in her mind's eye. He'd been anything but see-through. He'd been solid and powerful, muscular and smooth. Perhaps the trolls didn't really mean he looked like ice; it was a turn of phrase.

She interrupted their chattering to check with Hefta. "I'm sorry – what did you say about the unicorn? That he is frozen, like ice? He actually *looks* like ice?"

"Yes, like the thick ice on the river. White in places but frozen inside and out. No warmth at all. It's where he gets his name."

Violet gaped. "But, the unicorn I saw . . . he had a white coat . . . and a dark mane and tail. . . His coat looked warm, not frozen."

The trolls all exchanged glances and Hefta patted Violet's arm sympathetically. "That doesn't sound like the Frozen Unicorn."

"Not him," agreed Hooan.

And, in case Violet hadn't quite understood, Alline added, "That sounds like a different unicorn altogether."

A DIFFERENT UNICORN

A different unicorn? Of course. It all made sense: there were two unicorns all along. Violet tried to remember if Madam Verger had ever actually described the Frozen Unicorn. She didn't think she had.

If there were two unicorns, then it explained a lot. It explained why Elgu and these trolls had been surprised how far south the

Frozen Unicorn had ventured. He hadn't. It was a different unicorn.

She thought about the expression on the unicorn's face in the forest earlier. He hadn't looked predatory or evil. He had looked like he wanted to ask her something, or tell her something. Could he be a friend, not a foe? There was still some piece of the puzzle missing: why was he following her at all? He had been following her: she was sure of that.

Violet realized she hadn't spoken for a long time, and all eyes were on her.

"I fear I have misled you," she said, finally. "The unicorn I've been running from cannot be the Frozen Unicorn. He must be a different creature, as you say."

She felt foolish and thought they'd be cross with her for bringing fear to their tent, but instead they were all smiles and full of relief.

"We are just glad the Frozen Unicorn hasn't come to ruin our lives again. He needs to stay up there, locked in his own Ice Fortress, and leave ordinary folk alone."

Grandmother spoke in a raspy voice barely above a whisper. "Most *real* unicorns are pure of heart. The one you saw was no doubt trying to approach you. To help you."

Trying to help her. She wondered if this might be true. Someone had left her at Elgu's door, hadn't they? She had no recollection of how she'd ended up there, and all she'd seen had been the shadow of the unicorn. What if that hadn't been the Frozen Unicorn at all, but the Other Unicorn? And for whatever reason, he'd helped her?

The enormity of it all began to hit Violet. If there were two unicorns, and the one following Violet was helping her, then the *actual* Frozen Unicorn didn't know she was here. It was possible she was safer, more hidden, than she'd realized. She might still be able to sneak into the Ice Fortress and rescue Nicolas without meeting the Frozen Unicorn at all. The impossible rescue attempt was beginning to look like a possibility.

"She smiles!" said Tipto, pointing to her mouth, and Violet smiled even wider.

The trolls all laughed, but suddenly, they seemed distracted. There was a sound outside the tent, like a horn or a bugle, and they were listening, alert.

"What is it?" asked Violet, thinking immediately that the unicorn had arrived at the camp. She had to remind herself this was unlikely. She'd not yet set eyes on the Frozen Unicorn. Only the Other Unicorn.

No, the sudden change in atmosphere was caused by something else entirely, and the answer came again from little Tipto.

He grinned.

"The sky is pink tonight!"

PINK SKY

Violet had no idea what the relevance of a pink sky might be, but the trolls were in a hurry. They picked up their pails of ice pebbles and layered on scarves and hats, although they kept their feet bare. She had noticed they all went barefoot in the tent, but had assumed it would be different out in the snow. If Violet tried it, her toes would no doubt freeze off in minutes! Violet guessed troll feet must be a lot hardier than human feet.

Violet reluctantly moved from her warm, comfortable position. "Can I do anything?"

Hefta pointed to the bucket of ice pebbles Tipto had been preparing. "Take those."

Violet did as she was instructed and limped after the trolls into the snow, every part of her newly warmed body objecting to getting cold again.

Outside, Violet looked up at the striped sky, which was changing. Most bands of colour had narrowed. A bright, peachy pink dominated, in a wide band at the top. Trolls rushed out from every tent. Violet felt conspicuous as she was the only non-troll and much taller than all of them. A few looked in her direction but no one paid her too much attention once they saw she was with Hefta. They were all concentrating on their individual tasks. Hefta ushered her to the back of a queue of trolls who were all carrying pails of ice pebbles like hers. As the queue moved forward, Violet shuffled along with the others, trying to figure out what was going on. The band of pink in the sky steadily grew, until all the other colours were just suggestions by the horizon.

In the centre of the camp was the stove-like contraption that Violet had noticed on her arrival. It was set over a blazing fire, with a long pipe, pointing straight up, attached to the top. Another pipe, with a funnel attached, jutted out in the direction of the queue.

A troll in a hat striped like the sky was stoking the fire and issuing instructions to those in the queue. On her command, each troll poured their bucket of pebbles into the funnel, then raced off for a refill.

When it was Violet's turn at the front of the queue, the troll in the striped hat widened her large eyes, perhaps noting Violet's difference, but saying nothing. The troll held her hand up, stopping

Violet for a moment. She checked the sky – for birds, perhaps. Then she nodded once. "Pour."

Violet obediently poured her pail of pebbles into the funnel, enjoying the satisfying clattering sound. When she was finished, she moved away just as the trolls ahead of her had done. A loud popping sound made her jump and clutch her hand to her chest. "Oh!"

One or two of the trolls laughed and pointed to the long pipe on top of the stove. More popping sounds followed as ice pebbles shot from the pipe, one after the other, straight up into the sky, forced out by the pressure within the stove.

As the pebbles continued to fire out, Violet shielded her eyes with her hand and tried to track their path, but they were so tiny she lost sight of them in seconds.

Alline hurried up to her and filled Violet's pail with more clear pebbles.

"Where do they end up?" Violet asked her.

"In the sky. They absorb its colours before they fall back to earth."

Just then, the troll at the stove shouted something Violet didn't quite hear. All the trolls dropped to the ground where they were standing and covered their heads with their hands.

Violet was a couple of seconds behind them, but Alline pulled at her arm and urged her to do the same. As soon as she was curled up, she heard soft thuds all around her, like heavy rain. The sound of ice pebbles hitting the snow.

"Ouch!" One hit Violet on the back of the arm. She guessed she would have a bruise there later. A sore arm to go with her blistered feet and bumped head.

When the thudding stopped, the stripy-hatted troll called out something like, "All clear!" and everyone jumped to their feet again, gathering the pebbles that had fallen. They glistened pink like fallen blossom in the snow.

Violet picked one up and saw the colour was even all the way through. It wasn't quite as cold as she expected. "Won't they melt?"

"No, they are troll-made." Alline was concentrating on picking up as many pebbles as she could, tilting the pail and throwing them in. Violet didn't really understand her answer, but didn't want to interrupt her. She bent down to help, putting one or two pebbles in her pail, but Alline shook her head and sent her to the back of the queue again with her clear pebbles. "We all have different jobs to do," she explained.

In the queue, Violet watched the trolls at work. Some of the tiny trolls ran off into the trees. She tapped the shoulder of the troll in front of her. "Where are the little ones going?"

"They go searching in the forest to find any pebbles that have fallen there."

"Many will be lost, but we find what we can," added the troll in front of him.

They continued like that, funnelling in clear pebbles and gathering pink ones. The sky darkened to a deeper pink, and then almost black, contrasting against the smattering of stars. At that point, the groups of trolls called their children in from the forest, gathered up their pails of pink pebbles and returned to their tents.

Hooan showed his, nearly full to the brim, and Violet grinned in amazement, but Hooan shook his head sadly. "It's not been a good night."

The others gathered around him.

"It's not the same here."

"At home, the sky is bigger."

"More sky, more colour."

And Violet thought how beautiful their real home must be if they were disappointed by an evening like this one.

The trolls all returned to their tent, and Violet traipsed after Hefta, Hooan and the others.

They poured their pink pebbles into a small pail that stood next to a much larger bucket of green pebbles.

Once they'd settled again, back in their original positions, Violet felt able to ask more questions.

"Why are all your pebbles in here green, but the new ones are pink?"

"Each tent has a different colour."

"Our tent is sea green."

"We gather sea-green pebbles."

"But pink nights are scarce."

"Not so many pink nights."

"We all work together then."

"And what do you do with them?" asked Violet. "The ice pebbles, I mean."

"Ice pebbles have many uses."

"Clear ones we use for fixing, sealing and re-icing."

"Coloured ones we use for homes and beautiful creations."

"We melt them down for dying cloth – see?" Alline held out her skirt.

Violet had noticed that the trolls' clothes, as well as the soft furnishings, were the colours of the sky here in the Far North.

Grandmother leaned forward.

"Pink pebbles are for healing. Your feet hurt, I think," she said.

Violet wasn't sure how the old troll knew. Perhaps she'd been limping a little. But Grandmother was right: they did really hurt and now she was resting them, they were throbbing.

"I can help," she offered and Violet gratefully accepted.

She gently removed Violet's boots, examining them as she did so. "Are these troll-made?" she asked and seemed pleased when Violet said they were.

"Troll-made!" she announced, holding them up, and Hefta, Hooan and Alline all nodded and smiled. "The best."

"The best," they all agreed.

Grandmother was even more intrigued by Violet's feet. She ran a long fingernail along the sole of each, which made Violet laugh aloud. She held those up too. "See the human's feet! They are so soft!"

They all scurried forward to get a good look.

Violet had large blisters at the back of each ankle and on many toes. Grandmother tended to them gently, soaking wads of cotton in a cool, pink liquid (made from the ice pebbles), and strapping the wads to the sore patches.

The pain ebbed away and tiredness took over. Since leaving Elgu's house that morning, Violet must have travelled miles. It felt like the longest day she'd ever lived, and now she could barely keep her eyes open.

INSTRUCTIONS

Violet tried to hide her yawns behind her hand, but the trolls noticed, and announced they would get her bed ready. Near the door flap was a circular iron handle, which Hefta turned and set some creaking and squeaking in motion. A blanket draped over a sort of washing line inched its way across the tent, forming a separate area: a tent-within-a-tent. Violet hoped she wasn't taking anyone else's sleeping area, but they insisted and she accepted. The space, although not quite as comfortable as the bed at Elgu's house, was warm and private. Listening to the low muttering of the trolls and the lumps of snow thudding into the pail, Violet fell asleep.

She didn't wake until she heard Alline putting the morning snow into the pan to melt.

Violet was served another cup of hot berry drink and a breakfast of warm grains. She ate sitting with the family in the same way as she'd done the night before.

They had welcomed her into their home so unquestioningly, she wished there was something she could give them in thanks. After breakfast, she looked in her backpack for any suitable token. Not the food or the firecones of course – she needed those. She rummaged further. Her clothes from Millbrook would be of limited use in this climate, and there were no hibernating mice here as far as she knew. Her hands felt the familiar shape of the compass. She suspected the trolls, with their technical minds, would enjoy such a gadget. She didn't really need it any more. As long as she was following the river, she couldn't get lost.

Violet approached Hefta, who was scrubbing the breakfast dishes in sea green liquid, and handed the compass to her. Hefta took it and examined it, turning it this way and that and finally opening the cover. She creased her eyebrows together.

"The needle always points north," explained Violet, as Elgu had told her. "So you can find your way."

Hefta immediately called the others over and they stood around the compass, all making sure they got a good look. Little Tipto ran a fingertip over the inscription. "What does it say, Mama?"

"*Always North.* This pointer points north always."

The trolls all gasped happily.

"North, where our homes lie."

"North, where our hearts lie."

"Thank you. We shall treasure it always."

*

The trolls insisted on walking Violet back to the river. Although they were certain Violet's unicorn was not the Frozen Unicorn, they still wanted to protect her.

Grandmother stayed behind with the little ones and the three adults walked with her.

With Hefta on her left, Hooan on her right, and Alline ahead, spears held firm, she *did* feel protected. It was a shame they couldn't come with her all the way to the Ice Fortress, but their fear of the Frozen Unicorn was too great.

They walked through the woods, following the same route she'd taken the night before. It was only after they'd been walking a little way that she noticed her feet felt better after Grandmother's care the night before. If there were any blisters left, then she couldn't feel them.

She shared that with the trolls. "My feet are no longer sore. I shall be able to cover many miles. Do you think I'll make it to the Ice Fortress today?"

"Oh yes, yes. No problem on skates," said Hefta. "All you have to do is stay on the river,"

"Stay on the river," repeated Hooan.

"Don't leave the river," agreed Alline, somewhat redundantly.

"I'll make sure I don't leave it."

"When you have passed four big bends, you will be in the Far, Far North, and you will see the Ice Fortress in the distance."

"A blot on the landscape."

"A monstrosity."

Violet nodded.

"Once you have the fortress in view, you will pass a place winter hasn't reached. Whatever you do, and however lovely it looks, don't set foot inside," ordered Hefta.

"Stay on the river," said Hooan.

Violet's mind was spinning again from trying to keep up with the trolls' advice. She thought she had the message now (stay on the river) and nodded. "Don't worry, I won't be distracted by anything on the riverbank. I will skate on by."

"But," said Hefta, gripping Violet's arm, "once you've passed the place winter hasn't reached, be careful. The ice might start to creak and crack—"

"—It will crack and creak—" interrupted Alline earnestly.

"—and when it starts to creak, you must seal the crack." Hooan handed Violet a small drawstring bag and urged her to open it.

Ice pebbles. Clear ones, which they had explained were for fixing, sealing and re-icing.

"Thank you," said Violet, taking the bag and tucking it into the top of her knapsack. "You've all been so kind—"

"—Remember, once you've sealed the crack, stay *off* the river." Hefta interrupted Violet's fond farewell, concerned Violet would remember these instructions.

Violet nodded again. It was straightforward, she thought. She had to stay on the river until she passed the mysterious "place winter didn't reach", then get off the river the moment it began to creak and crack.

They had reached the river already. It wasn't far from their encampment.

"Thank you," she said again, expecting them to wave goodbye, but they insisted they see her on to the ice. They climbed down the slope to the riverbank with her, and watched as she fumbled for her skates and began attaching them to her boots. They even helped tie them on, Hefta attending to her right foot and Alline to her left.

"You should bring the blades forward, nearer your toes," muttered Hefta, adjusting the skate.

"No blisters," agreed Alline, doing the same.

The skates did feel better, and Violet wished she'd put them on like that before.

"Thank you again, kind Inventor Creator Trolls, for everything you've done," said Violet, and they nodded solemnly. She hitched her bag on to her back and tottered off the bank and down to the icy surface of the river. The trolls raised their right hands in unison and waved her off.

Violet felt a little self-conscious setting off with three pairs of troll-eyes watching her. She worried she might wobble, but a full day of skating had made her something of an expert and she headed off smoothly, waving as she went. Her smile and warm glow (as Elgu might have put it) lasted for an hour or so. Her feet certainly felt better than they had in a long time.

But then, loneliness set in.

Skating without her fairy guides felt strange. She was so used to following the rhythm of their feet and sharing in their delight at every little thing. She kept wondering if they might appear, and watched for little fairy clouds, but the only clouds were those her breath made as she exhaled. Perhaps River Fairies didn't come as far as the Far, Far North. Perhaps even they were frightened of the Frozen Unicorn.

Snow was falling. Great big, soft snowflakes that settled on her snoncho and her boots. It was a wonder to Violet there was any more snow left in the sky.

She remembered to look out for bends in the river. Four big

bends, the trolls had said, before she would see the Ice Fortress. But, although she skated round one sharp bend right near the start of her journey, after an hour or so, she hadn't encountered any more. She was relieved when the river finally took a sharp turn to the left, then shortly afterwards, another turn to the right.

That was three bends in the river. After the next one, she'd see it. But it took for ever to come. The river had straightened out once more and she was just skating, skating. One foot in front of the other, legs and feet getting sore again. She needed to stop for a break, but she wasn't going to; not until she'd had at least a glimpse of the Ice Fortress. Until she knew it was real.

And then, up ahead, the river headed left again. She approached it tentatively, not knowing quite what to expect when she turned the corner.

There it was. The trolls had been right. As she skated around the fourth bend, the shape of the Ice Fortress loomed large on the horizon.

THE MONSTROSITY

After the trolls' description, the Ice Fortress had grown in Violet's imagination from a small watchtower to a large building, with ramparts and towers. Something like the great stone castles she'd seen in her schoolbooks. Something like Essendor castle, but made of ice. The reality was different.

It was dark and distant, beyond the snow, but Violet could tell it was big – taller than the trees – and imposing. If she hadn't been expecting it, then she might at first have mistaken it for some sort of natural formation: a hill or a mountain. She was too far away to see any detail, but its top was jagged and uneven. There were two ghostly shapes near the top, which Violet supposed were windows, but from this distance could be mistaken for eyes. And lower down, a dark shadow of a mouth. *A monstrosity,* Hooan had called it, and it did look like a sort of monster, ready to pounce and swallow her up.

An Ice Monster.

And she was skating right into its jaws.

CHAPTER TEN

SPRING GARDEN

The sight of the Ice Fortress unnerved Violet. She hadn't been quite prepared for how she'd feel when she saw it. Nicolas was in there somewhere, though who knew exactly where.

I'm not far away now, Nicolas. Soon we'll be together again. Hold on!

She was so deep in thought, and so exhausted from skating all morning, the sight she saw next took her by surprise. She stopped pushing with her feet and came to a slow, gliding stop.

Up past the banks of the river, the forest gave way to a clearing, in which stood a garden. A proper spring garden, here in the snow, with lush green grass and bright, quivering flowers. Violet gazed at it in wonder, unable to look away.

She had, of course, been warned. *A place winter hasn't reached*, the trolls had called it, but she hadn't expected this sudden jolt of beauty and colour.

For days, almost everything she'd set eyes on had been white. White sky, white snow, white river. The snow was so bright – relentless. Now, her eyes drank in new colour like a thirsty person in a dry desert. The flowers! There were so many of them: tall foxgloves and bulbous tulips. Vivid lilac and narcissi. All clustered together behind a low wooden fence.

The trolls had told her to skate on by, and she was sure they had their reasons, but they did seem a little overprotective. Violet knew there was no way she could skate past such an amazing sight. She had to have a proper look; she would just make sure it was from a safe distance.

Now she was stationary, she began to feel the cold Far North wind with which she was becoming so familiar. She was tired and needed a break. If she were to stay on the river at all times, as the trolls suggested, then how could she stop and eat the provisions they'd so kindly packed?

Luckily, there was a wide, snowy bank by this part of the river. It would provide enough space for her to light a firecone, eat the provisions, gaze at the flowers and move on. It wasn't quite staying on the river, but it was close enough.

Violet climbed off the ice on to the bank and removed the skates from her boots, flexing her toes and swivelling her ankles to relieve her tired feet.

She unbuckled her bag and took out one of the last two firecones. But, as she was about to throw it to the ground, the wind changed direction so it blew from the garden. With it came a perfumed, heady scent of flowers.

It was the strangest thing: the essence of flowers carried on an icy wind. The aroma brought with it a wave of memories. The manor gardens in the sunshine, with hyacinths bobbing in a warm breeze and the bees clustered noisily around the rosemary. Oates the gardener raising his cap as he toiled away in the flower beds. Even the local honey at the breakfast table, with its floral flavour. It felt as though home was calling her, and she thought of her parents, of Madam Verger, and of course, of Nicolas. If she couldn't be with them, she wanted to be where she could breathe in that smell and all those special memories.

She tucked the firecone back into the pocket of her snoncho, forgetting about the fire, her tired legs and her hunger. She left her bag on the bank in the snow and, entranced, she climbed up towards the garden. From the fence, she had an even better view. The flowery smell was stronger there. A white cottage, covered in wisteria and partly hidden by trees, stood at the far end of a stepping-stone path. There was no sign of anyone at home. A solitary bee buzzed around her and disappeared up the frozen river. How strange it was to see a bee out in the snow, but then no stranger than seeing this full bed of flowers in bloom.

At the centre of the fence was a closed gate. Violet paused there, running her hand along the smooth, well-kept wood. It would be foolish to go against the troll's advice and approach the house, but surely it wouldn't hurt to have a quick look at the garden. She unlatched the gate and stepped inside.

It was like walking into a late spring day. There was not a single flake of snow to be seen, and even the air felt warmer. Violet knew there must be some magic behind it, but she didn't care; she wanted to enjoy the moment, and take a short break from all the snow. She pushed back her hood, although she didn't feel too hot. Elgu had explained that her clothes would work in any weather.

She'd never seen such an abundant and unusual combination of flowers in one place. It brought the old song into her mind. The one she and Nicolas had discussed in the woods on the day of their kiss. She spotted all the flowers from the lyrics and many more. There were red wallflowers, poppies and roses. She spied orange marigolds. Yellow ones too, along with cowslips and daffodils. She began to sing it to herself, surprised she could remember the words so well.

The loveliest of roses will always be the red;
Marigold brings orange cheer to every flower bed.
Yellow cowslip sparkles in the early morning dew;
In lush green grass, forget-me-not – a pretty,
welcome blue.

Violet stopped for a moment. Forget-me-nots were dotted in amongst the cowslips, but she could see no wild indigo or violets, the next flowers in the song. She wasn't quite sure what indigo even looked like, but she supposed the deep blue of the hyacinths would be about the right colour. There were lots of pretty pinky-purple flowers too, even if they weren't quite violets. She continued with the last lines.

Indigo, the wild and false, standing straight and
tall;
But don't forget the violet, the sweetest of them all.

Her gaze was suddenly drawn to a small, familiar flower, nestled at the edge of the flower bed. There *were* violets! It was like spotting an old friend.

She rushed over and fell to her knees on the grass. She could smell the flowers' sweet, familiar fragrance. Without thinking about it, she plucked one and held it gently between her thumb and forefinger, spinning it by its stalk. Two heart-shaped leaves sprang from the stem under a single flower: five perfect petals of purply-blue, streaked with white towards the golden centre. How she loved violets. Nicolas had promised to bring her the first sweet violet of the year, and now that might never happen. Tears slid down her cheeks. She was so lost in her thoughts that a sudden voice from behind startled her.

"Oh, hello, my dear. I didn't realize I had a visitor."

Violet turned to see a troll wearing a white apron.

"A troll!" she blurted, and then, as she realized how rude that sounded, she added, "I'm terribly sorry, you startled me."

But the troll didn't look cross. She smiled, her crooked teeth on display, cheeks round and rosy. Her black hair was drawn into a bun, and she was carrying a wooden spoon, as if she'd been disturbed in the middle of baking.

"So, I take it you've met trolls before?"

Violet sprang up, still guiltily holding the violet. She wrapped her fingers loosely around it, hoping she hadn't been caught picking flowers. "Yes, I met a Collector Gatherer in the south and some Inventor Creators not far from here."

Violet slipped the flower inside her feathered pocket and wiped her tears away with the back of her hand.

This troll continued to grin. "I am Vyvlle, a Planter Nurturer. I suppose my brothers and sisters told you all about me?"

Violet wasn't sure what to say. The others had told her nothing about her, other than to stay away from this place. "I . . . er. . ." she began.

"What is a human girl like you doing all the way up here?"

"I am heading to the Ice Fortress."

Vyvlle's smile fell away. "The Ice Fortress? That's a dangerous place. You should think twice before you go there all alone. And you must be frozen from your journey! Come inside, warm yourself."

"Thank you for the offer, but I was just stopping for a moment to admire your garden." The warnings she'd received seemed a little over the top now Violet had met the kindly troll who owned the place. Still, she thought she'd better be on her way. "It really is a beautiful place. And so unexpected out here in the snow. It's almost as if it's late spring . . . or summer here, and yet I know that cannot be."

"Why do you say that? Spring is just a feeling, like any other, wouldn't you say?"

"I'm not sure. . ." Violet was fairly certain springtime was a season, and not a feeling, but she didn't like to disagree. There was something about this place that confused her, made her unable to think straight.

"Anyway, I'm glad you like the flowers, my dear." Lines around the troll's eyes crinkled as she smiled broadly, although she offered no further explanation as to how the garden came to be. "And you're fond of sweet violets, I see?"

"Yes, they're my favourites. I'm named after them. They were in bloom when I was born."

"Violet. Such a pretty name, but I think Marigold suits a bright and sunny young woman like yourself, don't you? Let's call you Marigold. We'll forget about those other flowers."

"I'm sorry?" said Violet, sure she must have misheard. The troll pointed her wooden spoon at the violets. They began to shrink, petals folding in on themselves until they shrivelled away, then wormed back down into the earth. All that was left was a patch of bare brown soil, giving no sign the violets had ever existed.

"Oh," said Violet, staring at the ground. "But where did they. . ." Vyvlle was still smiling kindly, but something was very wrong. Violet's heart began to race, and she had a sudden urge to be out of the garden and skating on the river. She should have listened to the other trolls and left this place well alone. She began walking towards the gate, but Vyvlle bustled along behind her, moving remarkably swiftly despite her short legs. She intercepted Violet and leaned against the gate so the only exit from the garden was blocked.

Then she reached up and tapped the spoon gently on Violet's shoulder. It didn't hurt, but it felt warm and tingly, spreading from one shoulder to the other and down both arms.

"No more tears now, Marigold," said the troll. "Follow me."

She felt a little unsure as she followed her along the pathway of irregularly shaped stones. The name Marigold didn't sound quite right, but she could think of no other name that suited her better. And she didn't know what Vyvlle meant by "no more tears". Had she been crying? She didn't feel sad. She didn't feel anything.

Just warm and safe. She had a feeling she had been trying to get somewhere, but she didn't know where.

Marigold smiled. It didn't matter any more. None of it mattered. She was right where she wanted to be.

PAINTING, PASTRY AND POETRY

Inside the house, Marigold was happy. There was so much to do. They brought in bunches of flowers from the garden, and arranged them in jugs along the window sill, where some full vases already stood. Rows and rows of flowers.

"They look so vibrant," said Marigold. "It makes me want to paint their likeness."

Vyvlle chuckled. "It is delightful to have a young person about the place at long last, with all your enthusiasm. If you want to paint, then that is what you shall do! I have some paints and brushes here somewhere." The troll turned her back to Marigold and clattered about in a cupboard. She brought out a set of six paint pots, a palette, brushes and a canvas, which she placed on the table. The paints were untouched and their bright colours rivalled the flowers themselves.

Vyvlle selected two of the pots: a red and yellow ochre. She pushed them forward. "If you mix these two together, then you will have the perfect colour to paint your special flowers."

Marigold took a dab of each on her brush and swirled them together on the palette. She felt slightly surprised when a deep orange emerged. She'd been expecting purple. How silly of her. She creased her eyebrows together, squinting at all the jugs of flowers on the ledge. "You'll think me foolish, but I can't remember which ones are my special flowers."

"Why, the marigolds, of course!" Vyvlle moved the jug of orange blooms closer and Marigold smiled and began to paint.

Marigold was unsure about her painting skills, but the troll complimented the picture and promised to put it on the wall when it was dry.

Next, they moved on to cooking, which Marigold enjoyed, although she was clueless about everything. She had no idea which spoon was which, or how to make even the simplest thing. They were baking a mushroom pie for their lunch, which was completely beyond her capabilities.

"Where did you grow up, to be unable to make pastry?" asked the troll, with her usual smile. "In a palace, perhaps? A pampered princess?"

Marigold didn't know, although she had a feeling there had been an orchard. And a millpond.

"Well, you'd be the first miller's daughter I've heard of who couldn't pop a lid on a pie. Here, let me show you."

And Vyvlle did show her. It turned out Marigold's cool hands made excellent pastry. She enjoyed criss-crossing strips over the top to make a lattice. She enjoyed the smell of the pie in the oven and eating it together.

Afterwards, they sat feeling full and content. Vyvlle selected a book from the shelf, and pushed it across the table.

"Read to me, my dear."

And Marigold read. It was a book of old poems and songs. She read one about ships on the ocean, and one about a black, beady-eyed bird. The troll closed her large eyes and nodded along to the rhythm of the words.

On the next page were some verses about flowers. Marigold enjoyed the first line:

The loveliest of roses will always be the red—

It sounded delightful, but Vyvlle didn't seem to agree. She reached forward and snapped the book shut.

"I'm tired of reading," she said, as she put the book back on the shelf.

Marigold didn't mind. She was happy to do anything. She folded her hands in her lap and sat politely, the last line she read playing in a loop in her mind.

"I do enjoy having company," said Vyvlle. "I have been lonely here for so long with not a soul to talk to. There used to be visitors: animals, fairies, pixies, even the occasional boy or girl, until he trapped me here and drove all the others away."

"Who trapped you?"

"The Frozen Unicorn."

That didn't sound quite right to Marigold. Unicorns were supposed to be kind and pure, she was sure of it. She didn't know quite how she knew it: possibly from a book like the one they'd just been reading. She had a fleeting memory of another cottage, a woman and some stories. But then Vyvlle continued speaking and the memory disappeared.

"He wanted me gone, and I refused. This garden took me years to build. Years of planting, nurturing and special spells. Where we are sitting was once an ordinary part of the forest. And they wanted me to leave it all behind."

"They?" Marigold had thought they were talking about a single unicorn.

"The unicorn and his interpreter. He can't speak for himself, so she speaks for him. A sorceress."

"She was the one who cast the spell. I can't go further than my gate. I have all of this – my special garden – for ever, but no one to share it with. That was my burden. Until you came along, of course. Do you see?"

Marigold nodded, although she didn't really see; it was all quite confusing. "Can *I* go further than the gate?"

For a moment, the troll's smile faded. "Well, of course you *can* go further than the gate, Marigold, but would you *want* to? It's all snow and ice out there. So cold. You wouldn't last a moment, would you?"

Marigold shook her head.

"You stay here with me where it's safe and warm, and we'll do as much painting, pastry and poetry as you want. You'd like that, wouldn't you?"

"Oh yes," said Marigold. She thought for a moment, looking at the jugs of flowers. "I do love the garden too."

"Well, you can go out in the garden whenever you like. In fact, that lily of the valley in the vase is looking a little droopy. Why don't you go and pick some more?"

PICKING FLOWERS

Marigold skipped down the garden, Vyvlle watching and waving from the window. Near to the house were some low rose bushes, in pink and red, and the first line of poetry from the book came back to her:

The loveliest of roses will always be the red;

The words came to her in a tune, and she was surprised to find she remembered more lines. Nearly a whole song, in fact. She sang her way down the stepping-stone path, naming a flower each time she brought her foot down on a stone.

Marigold brings orange cheer to every flower bed.
Yellow cowslip sparkles in the early morning dew;
In lush green grass, forget-me-not – a pretty,
    welcome blue.
Indigo, the wild and false, standing straight and tall;
But don't forget the—

She couldn't remember the last flower.

But don't forget the something, *the sweetest of*
them all.

What was missing? She tried singing other words in the space –
don't forget the primrose, or *don't forget the pansy* – but none of
them sounded quite right. How funny the one flower that the song
told her not to forget, was the one she couldn't remember!

She turned and waved to Vyvlle, and then went to the flower
beds to gather the lily of the valley. How she loved the pretty white
flowers and their perfume.

It was a strange thing, but however many flowers she picked,
there were always more. The flower beds were spilling over with
blooms. Yet there were a few bare spaces at the front that bothered
her. Balancing the freshly picked bunch of lily of the valley in the
crook of her arm, she investigated the soil with her fingertips. She
drove them deeper and deeper, searching for something, although
she didn't know what. All she was left with was dirty fingernails;
the beds were definitely bare. She would speak to Vyvlle and see
if she could plant some seeds. Something that would spread and
cover the bare earth.

Her thumb hurt. A tiny trickle of blood ran down it. She must
have nicked it on a sharp stone. It wasn't deep at all, a scratch really,

and nothing to worry Vyvlle about. If she had a handkerchief, she could wrap it around her thumb for a moment until the scab formed. She pushed both hands in her wonderfully deep pockets, searching for a handkerchief. She found nothing but a silver pine cone and a single, purple flower.

THE FORGOTTEN FLOWER

She tucked the pine cone back in her pocket, but held the flower in the palm of her hand, the cut on her thumb forgotten. A lovely flower, with five blue-purple petals. Not a bloom she recognized, and not one she could spot in the flower beds. Whatever was it doing in her pocket?

Then she smelled it. Its sweet, heady scent drifted up her nostrils, bringing with it a rush of memories. Laughter in the woods, perfume sprayed on her wrists. A purple gown. A dance.

"Why, it's a violet!" she said aloud.

Vyvlle was still watching her from the cottage window, too far away to hear, or to see the flower in her hand.

"Don't forget the violet – the sweetest of them all."

She spoke the words aloud. In the bare patches of earth, the soil began to shake and move as stubby green shoots pushed their way out of the ground before her eyes. Something was growing. Violets. With the shoots, came the realization she shouldn't be in the garden or the cottage at all; there was somewhere else she should be.

The shoots divided into heart-shaped leaves, the loose soil falling from them as they unfurled and grew towards the light. She knew her name wasn't Marigold at all. It was Violet. The troll in the cottage had enchanted her somehow and made her forget. She had to get away.

As the buds sprang open into sweet violet flowers, Violet noticed Vyvlle was no longer watching at the window. The cottage door opened. Violet dropped the armfuls of lily of the valley on the grass and ran towards the gate.

AT THE GATE

The gate was less than a minute's run, but somehow, Vyvlle was right behind her. Violet could hear her calling out, "Marigold! Marigold, come back!"

The troll snatched at her sleeve and caught it, wrenching Violet's arm back at an unnatural angle. Violet kept running and managed to grab hold of the gate with her free hand. There was a sickening rip as Elgu's neat stitches were pulled apart. Violet somehow managed to open the gate and make it through, leaving her snoncho sleeve in the troll's hands.

They stood on either side of the gate facing each other. Violet held on to the wooden post, red in the face and taking deep breaths to recover from her sprint. The troll held the long feathery sleeve in her arm, where it dangled limply like a swan's neck. Tears were in her eyes and she looked a pathetic sight.

"Don't leave me, Marigold," she said, making another swipe for Violet.

Violet whisked her hand away and stepped back, surprised at the feeling of snow once again crunching underfoot. As long as she was this side of the fence – the winter side – there was nothing Vyvlle could do to her.

"My name's not Marigold," she said. "It's Violet. And I cannot stay here. I am looking for someone, and I'm not going to stop until I find him."

"It's not safe out there," whispered the troll. "The unicorn's magic is more powerful than mine. You'll be no match for him."

"I have to take that risk."

"But it's so cold. Look at you, you're shivering already."

It was true, Violet was shivering, no longer hot from running. This wasn't the sort of weather in which to stand around for long.

"Come back inside. Have some cake and a warm drink to help keep you warm on your journey. I'll sew this back on for you."

It was a tempting offer, but Violet knew she couldn't trust this troll.

"I must go," she said, and began walking back towards the riverbank, leaving the warmth and brightness of the spring garden behind her. She dropped the violet but didn't stop to pick it up.

Vyvlle's voice followed her down to the riverbank, full of pleas and promises, but Violet tried to block it out. She had to get away, to continue her journey. Her bag was right where she'd abandoned it by the riverbank, stiff and frozen, covered in a thin layer of snow, like dusted sugar. Thankfully there hadn't been another heavy snowfall, or she would have had to dig it out.

She put on her skates, heaved the bag on to her back and set off north again, towards the Ice Fortress, with shouts of, "Marigold! Marigold! Come back!" fading away behind her.

CHAPTER ELEVEN

BACK ON THE RIVER

Violet skated away from the troll and her bright flower garden, tears rolling down her cheeks. She felt shaken by the experience, but also frustrated with herself. Why hadn't she listened to the Inventor Creators? *Stay on the river,* they'd told her. An easy instruction to follow, yet she'd been distracted by pretty flowers.

How much time had she wasted at Vyvlle's house? Not to mention hitting her head and ending up at Elgu's. Yes, she now had sensible cold weather clothes, but if she weren't so foolish, then she could have rescued Nicolas by now. As it was, it had been three days since Nicolas vanished and he could well have frozen to death in his icy prison. Madam Verger had told her no one would last long in the Ice Fortress. A few days, or a week, she'd said. Violet pictured him huddled on an icy floor without a blanket, and the tears flowed harder.

"No, no, no!" If she thought like that, then she would get herself in too much of a panic to do anything. She gulped back the tears and tried to think more positive thoughts. Nicolas could have been treated well. Maybe the Frozen Unicorn even had Nicolas working for him, as the trolls had refused to do. Nicolas was young and fit: used to physical labour. Maybe he was working on the Ice Fortress right now. Violet had to assume that he was well and she would reach him in time. All she could do was get to him as quickly as possible. So she put her head down and skated.

Vyvlle had been right about one thing: it was cold. Colder than it had been so far on the journey. The chill seeped into her bones and made her feel stiff and uncomfortable. Violet wasn't sure how much this was down to the missing sleeve of her snoncho. She still had the long sleeve of her tunic underneath, of course, but the fabric was thin. Even with a spare scarf wrapped on top, she couldn't recreate the warmth provided by Elgu's garments. The cold seemed to travel via this one exposed arm to every other part of her body.

Even with the drawstring of her hood tightened as far as it would go, and even with the heat she was generating from the skating, Violet still felt frozen. What's more, her hand hurt from the nick in the spring garden and her feet and legs ached from all the skating. She could feel the bruise from the ice pebble. The bump on her head, which she'd barely noticed since Elgu's house, began to throb under her feathery hood.

Despite Vyvlle's trickery, she felt guilty for leaving her behind. Vyvlle had been treated badly by the Frozen Unicorn, after all, and now the troll had no one. Violet knew how that felt. It was strange; she was accustomed to being alone, and always thought she was content with her own company. Yet she would have given anything for some companionship right now. Some Collecting or Inventing Trolls, some River Fairies, even the Other Unicorn. Especially the Other Unicorn.

She kept thinking about the way the creature had gazed at her, as if it had a question ... or information. If he appeared again, around the next corner, she wouldn't skate away. She would approach him as she had always wanted to do.

But the unicorn didn't appear around the next corner, or the one after. Maybe she'd run away too many times and he'd given up on her. She kept skating. One foot in front of the other, eyes on the murky shape of the Ice Fortress, which loomed on the horizon like a hostile cloud. She thought only of her destination, and of Nicolas.

As she skated closer to the fortress, its details became clearer, the lumpy mass of white becoming solid and real. Less cloudy and more building-like. She looked for signs of life but saw nothing. She wondered if, somewhere inside, the Frozen Unicorn was looking out and could see a tiny figure skating up the river towards his stronghold.

For a long time, Violet concentrated her gaze above the trees and towards the horizon, hoping to gather new information about the place. But she discovered nothing more. Presently, Violet's attention shifted to what was happening beneath her feet.

CREAKING AND CRACKING

The frozen river had been Violet's route for so long now she'd begun to think of it as a walkway through the forest. But the ice that had been so solid, so reliable, so *frozen*, felt suddenly different. She had an unnerving feeling of it shifting beneath her. She stopped immediately. She heard a strange creaking sound and remembered Hefta's words.

Once you've passed the place winter hasn't reached, be careful. The ice might start to creak and crack.

She looked down. What had been white and frosty before was now darker, and unless she was imagining it, she could see through the ice to the water below.

With a worrying crack, like china breaking, a fine fissure shot out from under her left foot. It zigzagged in the direction of the riverbank, and Violet swallowed, thinking of that boy who went through the ice in Millbrook. He'd lived, but if the ice broke here, then there was no chance she would survive.

Her instinct was to skate to the bank as fast as she could, but what if she skated over an even thinner patch of ice? Heart beating fast, she stood as still as she could, trying to gather her thoughts.

When it starts to creak, you must seal the crack.

Of course! That was what Hooan had said when he gave her the ice pebbles. The last time she'd ignored the trolls' advice, she'd nearly ended up trapped in a spring garden. This time, she couldn't get it wrong.

The bag of ice pebbles was in her knapsack. She kept one eye on the frozen river as she undid the flap of her bag and fumbled for the smaller leather pouch inside. She found it by touch alone, its bumpy weight familiar, like a bag of marbles.

None of the pebbles had melted. Troll-made, they'd said.

As she brought out the pouch, another crack like the first shot out from beneath her left foot.

"Don't break, don't break," she muttered desperately to the river, as she undid the pouch.

The crack to her right began to widen alarmingly, until it was the width of her finger. She gasped and, without stopping to think, threw one of the pebbles at it, as she'd done with the firecones. It was an accurate hit, and it made a dark oval hole directly on the line of the widening crack.

"No! What have I done?" she cried. Throwing a pebble at a crack was only ever going to make it worse! She should have asked the trolls how to use them properly. Why did she never think of these things at the time? Now the gap to her left was widening too. And the creaking and cracking was getting louder. But, unbelievably, the ice pebble she'd thrown was working some kind of magic under the ice. Maybe she'd used it correctly, after all.

The ice was hardening. The widest of the cracks and the oval hole iced over and turned opaque white. The thinnest cracks disappeared altogether. The hardening continued under her feet and along the crack by her left boot. Then the sound stopped.

"I sealed the crack!"

Violet tested the area around her with her skate blade. It was solid. Her heart rate returned to normal as she skated across it and over to the bank. Sitting on the rotting trunk of a long-ago fallen tree, she untied her skates and thrust them to the bottom of her bag. She wouldn't be wearing them again until she was sure it was safe.

"It's so odd," Violet murmured. "The weather is getting colder the further north I travel, yet the river is melting."

She glanced at the snow that had fallen between the forest and the river. It was as thick as ever. It was a mystery to Violet, but then this whole land was a mystery.

Still, she was in no hurry to get back on the ice. She was exhausted and this would give her poor feet a break from the skates.

"I may as well take the time to eat, as well."

Although her food supplies had been dwindling, with just a couple of bread rolls left, the trolls had kindly packed her up a luncheon. A warming bun, they'd called it. As she unwrapped it, it didn't feel warm at all; it felt as cold as the other contents in her bag, and it looked almost exactly like a snowball. A little disappointing.

When she broke into it, though, a tempting herbal steam tickled her nostrils. The filling inside, a mash of chestnuts and herbs, was the warm part. Violet tore off pieces of the outer casing, and scooped up the flavoursome filling. It was doughy, delicious, and most definitely warming. With a full stomach, she felt more positive. She was nearly there. It wouldn't be long until she and Nicolas were together again. She tried not to dwell on the fact she had no more meals left.

Violet set off again on foot, trudging through the calf-deep snow. After skating for days, walking felt a strange way to get around. It was slow: so very slow. Rather than watching the trees flash past, she seemed to be expending more energy and getting nowhere. A new, fierce wind had whipped up, making each step a battle, and she was more sensitive to the cold, now that she was no longer generating heat from the skating.

Although she walked through the forested areas, she tried to keep the river in sight by following its curve. She was nervous to stray too far from it as, having given the compass to the trolls, she had no other way to navigate.

As she walked, she observed the changes in the river. Where the ice had been solid, it was now broken into sections with great fissures in between like the path in the spring garden. She was glad she'd stopped skating when she had. As she progressed further, she noticed the water was flowing freely. It was strange to see it moving along like a living thing; she'd been so used to its stillness.

The other surprising thing was the river's current flowed first one way, and then the other, pulsing like no river she'd seen before.

When she turned a corner, nearly at the edge of the forest, she saw the reason why. The reason why the temperature had dropped but the ice had melted. The reason why the water was moving backwards and forwards rather than in one direction.

It was still a long way off, but there was no doubt about it. Violet had nearly reached the ocean.

THE OCEAN

Violet stood, squinting into the distance. There it was, before her: the deep blue of the sea, forming a continuous band below the horizon. All this time, it had been hidden by the tops of the trees, but here, at the edge of the forest, it was revealed to her.

Violet had never seen the sea before. She'd never *expected* to see the sea, and the sight shocked her. It was as if she'd reached the end of the world. The wide sky was streaked with its usual stripes, although it was as yet unclear which colour would dominate. Below the sky was the rippling darkness of the ocean, dotted with icebergs. It was calm, yet she could hear it, like a faraway roar. She could even taste a faint hint of salt on her frozen lips.

It looked so big, so wild, so . . . impossible.

She wondered why Madam Verger, Elgu and the other trolls had all failed to tell her she was heading to the ocean. Perhaps they'd thought it was obvious. It hadn't been to Violet.

Now she thought about it, perhaps it *should* have been obvious. Even though she'd never seen an ocean, she knew that most rivers led to the sea eventually.

The Inventor Trolls had mentioned fishing and salt-extraction machines. Of course these things would be found by the sea. They had even said how big the sky was in their real home. Violet had never seen the sky look bigger and more beautiful than it did here.

The most surprising thing of all was that the Ice Fortress wasn't built on land as she'd expected. It was somehow floating in the middle of the ocean like an island.

She stared. She had a clearer view of the fortress than ever before. It was white and uneven and looked as though it had been carved from a great iceberg. Right at the top of the fortress was a lump of ice topped with a protruding icicle, which looked very like a unicorn's muzzle and horn.

This was the place she had been heading to ever since she'd

arrived in the North. This was where she would find Nicolas. Where was he? Held in a cell, at the monstrosity's core?

"Nicolas!"

She shouted it, knowing he wouldn't hear. Even if he was out there, her voice would be lost in the sound of the sea; it would never carry to him. She hoped somehow that her thoughts might reach him. Maybe he would know she was here.

She closed her eyes, wondering if she could sense him, but she felt nothing. What did that mean? Was their love not strong enough after all? Or was she too late to save him?

The only way to find answers to these questions was to go to the fortress and see for herself if he was alive or dead. But that was easier said than done. She was still so far away. Reaching the fortress had been her journey's goal, but although it was so clearly in sight, it might as well be on the moon. It was still a few miles away, and in the middle of the sea, with no clear way to reach it.

And night was beginning to fall.

THE LAST FIRECONE

Tonight was going to be a blue night. She could see the wide band of colour creeping to the top, which meant it would soon be dark. Violet was so tired that she couldn't think straight. Her bumps and bruises hurt, and her limbs were stiff with cold and fatigue. She could go no further until the morning, which meant she was going to have to find a place to spend the night.

This was the first time she would have to find shelter by herself. Up until this point, she had relied on the kindness of others, but now she felt alone. She *was* alone. She knew from the Inventor Trolls that no one but the Frozen Unicorn lived here any more. They'd said that they were the only ones to inhabit these parts before they were forced from their homes.

Violet was going to find no kind host to open their doors to her out here.

She had no one to rely on but herself.

Another blast of icy wind swooped and whistled over the flat expanse of coastline, reminding her that it was going to be cold.

There was no point heading nearer to the ocean. She couldn't see the beach from where she was, and had no idea if it was sand, stone or just more snow. Either way, the forest was likely to provide more shelter. Violet turned and headed back in the opposite direction to the fortress. It was the only sensible thing to do; she might find fuel there, wood for a shelter, or even something to eat.

The blue sky darkened to nearly black so that the night sky looked little different to the one in Millbrook. The stars were bright, and the brightest of all was the unicorn constellation – mocking her misfortune. She reminded herself of what the Inventor Trolls had told her: not all unicorns were bad. Not all unicorns took people from their family and friends. Just the Frozen Unicorn, and he wasn't even a proper unicorn at all, but an evil sorcerer adopting that shape. Most unicorns were good, including the Other Unicorn, that had followed her for a time. She hoped.

When she thought of it like that, she could convince herself the stars were on her side. The same stars twinkling above Millbrook looked down on her now. Maybe even watching over her.

She found a small clearing in the forest. It was big enough for her to make a fire and stretch out next to it, but small enough to provide shelter from the vicious wind. She turned in a slow circle, assessing the wind direction and the best place for a sheltered fire.

Most of the trees had slender trunks and high foliage with snowy white coats, but she headed towards one with branches that almost swept the ground. It had an indentation in the base of its trunk that looked perfect for sheltering. She could sleep with her head and shoulders within and her legs stretched out by the fire.

Next, she began a search for firewood. Any windfall was buried in layers of snow beneath the trees. One tree, however, was brown and dead-looking, and she managed to break off a couple of brittle branches, covering herself with powdery snow. She kept one branch for firewood and used another like a broom to sweep as much snow as possible out of the way. It wasn't as deep here as outside the woods, but there was still enough to cover the ground. The branch was quite effective and soon she'd swept a patch of ground clear.

With stiff, cold, fingers, she checked inside her knapsack to see what supplies were left, but she was running pitifully low. No broth, just one hard bread roll which was stale or frozen or, in all likelihood, both. A few ice pebbles in their bag. No compass, of course. Only one of Elgu's silver firecones remained. She would use it to start a blazing fire to keep her warm through the night. It would last until the morning, and then she wouldn't need any more fires: she would rescue Nicolas and they would be on their way home.

But somehow, as she took it from the bag, the firecone slipped from her hand. She made a grab for it, but it hit the ground and broke open, like a dropped egg with a cracked shell. The flame that emerged was small and greenish, just as it had been the morning she'd left Elgu's.

"No!" she cried and knelt on the ground next to it. Although she'd cleared most of the snow away, a few patches remained, and the cold and wetness seeped through the knees of her leggings. She held her hands around the flame, desperate for it to stay alight. She broke off a bit of the broom branch, and held it there, hoping it was dry enough to catch fire.

It caught, sizzled, and produced a lot of smoke, but not much else. Violet coughed in the smoke and snapped the other branch into smaller pieces. She managed to build a small fire with tiny flames, but however hard she tried, she couldn't seem to coax it into much more life. After a little while, she stopped, worried if she carried on poking at it, she would put out the few remaining flames, and her last hopes of warmth.

Why, oh why did she have to drop the firecone when she needed it so badly? She had a long, cold night stretching ahead of her and these smouldering flames weren't nearly enough.

Staring at the half-dead fire wasn't going to change a thing; she'd have to make the best of the situation. She laid the first branch at the base of the tree hollow, then broke off as many others as she could, layering them on the ground. On top, she placed a folded blanket from the bottom of her bag, which she'd packed in Millbrook but not yet used. There were two. She held one up to her cheek. It smelled of home: a cross between the starch the maids used and her mother's perfume. Yet it was almost laughably light for this climate. She shook her head at the Violet that had packed this bag. What had she thought the Far North would be like? She could no longer remember.

Violet tucked the blanket on top of the branches for added softness. She would use the other one as a cover. But it wouldn't be enough.

She thought of the trolls melting snow for their tea. She could do the same. She filled the flask with snow and put it in the fire. It quickly melted and she soon had hot water even if there were no berries to flavour it. She warmed the bread roll too, and heated a couple of rocks by the side of the fire to use like warming pans.

The boughs above provided a sort of natural shelter, and she leaned more broken boughs up against the tree trunk to protect against the elements and keep her hidden from view. She'd seen no wild beasts out here, but would still rather not be exposed.

Before she settled down for the night, she layered on any remaining clothing she could find in her bag. This included the long hand-knitted scarf and two pairs of woollen stockings, which she put on over her gloves. If it worked for Elgu, then it would work for her.

She crawled inside the makeshift shelter and squashed herself into the slight hollow of the tree, shuffling around so it didn't dig into her back. She ate half the bread roll, saving the other half for breakfast, and drank some warm water.

She would sleep sitting up and her near-empty bag would be her pillow. With the smouldering fire, makeshift shelter, layers of clothing and warming rocks, Violet didn't think she would freeze overnight.

She pulled the blanket up to her chin and waited for sleep to come and for the warm sun of the next morning.

THE LONG, COLD NIGHT

Despite her all-consuming tiredness, Violet couldn't sleep. Just as the cold seeped through every gap in the branches and seam of her clothing, dark thoughts seeped into her mind.

Sounds were amplified and strange. A distant howling was either the wind or wolves. Crackling was either coming from the embers or rats scurrying through the fire's remains. She flinched and tried to pull the thin blanket more tightly around her, but it was of little comfort.

She didn't belong out here.

Nicolas was depending on the wrong person. All her life, there had been someone there to pick her up: her parents, her maid, even Nicolas himself. She smiled at the memory of him helping her out of the puddle back in Millbrook.

Even out here, in this brand-new land, she had found assistance at every step of the way. First from Candra the wolf, then from Elgu Ember and the other trolls. Even, perhaps, from this Other Unicorn. She'd been lucky to meet the right people, but now there was no one left to help her.

Nicolas had said she had to stand on her own two feet, but what if she couldn't? Perhaps some people simply weren't made for tough adventures. There was no way she could get to the Ice Fortress in the middle of the sea. Not without being seen by the Frozen Unicorn. He would no doubt freeze her into a cube of ice the moment he saw her, just as he'd threatened the trolls.

It was impossible for her to rescue Nicolas.

She sighed, the sound disappearing into the dark night.

Perhaps she should have stayed in the spring garden and made mushroom pies for the rest of her days, without ever knowing what she was missing. Or perhaps she should never have left the manor. The thought of her own warm bed and home-cooked food was almost too much to bear. Her parents and staff fussing around her. She hadn't changed at all. She might have been pretending to be someone adventurous, someone different, but she was still the pampered girl from the manor. There was no point pretending any more.

Her hands reached for the leather thong around her neck: the strap of the blowing horn, which had remained in place for the entire journey. It was her ticket home. If she blew it now, would the sound reach Candra the flying wolf? Would that majestic creature arrive to take her home? She imagined her parents' emotional greeting. They would tuck her safely away and make sure she never ventured far again. They would send someone else for Nicolas. Perhaps.

She brought the mouthpiece to her lips.

But then she thought what that would really mean. Violet tried to imagine telling her parents she had defied their wishes and caused them heartache all for nothing. They probably still thought Nicolas had run away and her stories of evil unicorns were ridiculous notions. She tried to imagine telling the Evergreens she had come this close to rescuing their son, only to give up because she was cold and hungry. She couldn't do that.

If she called for help now, it might mean a warm bed for Violet, but what about Nicolas? He would be left here freezing and alone, just as she was now, but without hope; with no one to rescue him.

She couldn't leave him trapped in the fortress. She would rather die trying.

She dropped the blowing horn and let it hang back where it had before. She would use it when she had rescued Nicolas: not before.

She shivered and opened her eyes a little. The few weak flames had gone, leaving glowing embers and little heat. She didn't try to poke and prod it any more. She would leave it to fate to decide. If she could somehow survive this night, then perhaps she was strong enough to succeed. And if not, then maybe it was better for everyone.

Violet closed her eyes, ready to give in to whatever the night would bring.

A SIGN

Despite the freezing temperatures, she did fall asleep, although she couldn't have said how long for. A couple of minutes, an hour, it was impossible to tell. Even in her sleep, she was uncomfortable, arms held stiffly around her, tense against the cold. She slept lightly, dreams and visions disturbing her.

She dreamed she'd found Nicolas in the fortress, chained to the wall of his cell. He was right in front of her, so close she could touch him, but a sheet of thick ice separated them. His lips moved. He spoke, but she couldn't hear the words. She ran frantically this way and that, trying to find a way through, but the glass-like wall was unending. She beat her hands and fists on the ice, but it wouldn't break. She cried out:

"Nicolas! Nicolas!"

And then she felt a nudge on her shoulder. Gentle, but persistent.

The nudge wasn't in her dream at all. It was real and it was waking her, dragging her away from her sleep. She didn't want to go; she didn't want to leave Nicolas. She cried out again, "Nicolas! Nicolas!" but she realized she wasn't shouting; she was mumbling, muttering incoherent sounds.

It was a strange feeling. Every exhausted part of her body fought to remain asleep. Her mind, though, was cleverer. Her mind knew the nudge was important, and forced her to open her eyes and remember where she was. Her mind asked who it was doing the nudging, out in this wilderness. A friend?

Gradually, her body caught up and she rubbed her eyes, blinking in the near darkness. All trace of the fire had gone.

The nudge came again. A friendly nudge – not an attack from a stranger.

"Who is it? What do you want?" Her own voice sounded strange to her in the silence of the night: thick with sleep and confusion. There was no reply. She registered it wasn't a hand nudging her, but the muzzle of a horse, a white horse, poking through the branches of her shelter.

She pushed the branches away, eyes adjusting to the weak light, and looked past the horse, searching for its rider. But she saw only a beautiful white horn, glowing on its own as if a light burned within.

It was the unicorn!

Not the Frozen Unicorn. The *Other* Unicorn.

"You!" she cried, scrabbling to her knees, her first instinct to run away as she had every other time. But then she remembered this wasn't the unicorn who'd taken Nicolas, or who'd forced the trolls from their homes. This creature wasn't a Frozen Unicorn, made of ice. This was some other unicorn, who had been following her, perhaps helping her in its own way. She'd wanted to find the missing piece of the puzzle, hadn't she? Well, now was her chance. The only way to find answers from this creature was to ask him.

"Who are you?" she asked, sounding more like herself. "What do you want from me?" She gazed into the unicorn's eyes. They seemed as anxious as her own, which calmed her. If this unicorn had meant to hurt her, then he would have had plenty of opportunity while she was curled up here, asleep and vulnerable.

She stayed like that, on her knees, staring. She was shivering uncontrollably and must have been even colder than she'd realized.

Wispy white breath emerged from the creature's nostrils. His eyes were large, and a thick lock of dark mane fell across his forehead. He tossed it back, out of his eyes, and Violet felt a twinge of recognition.

The creature moved forward and rested his chin on her shoulder. There was no doubting this gesture was a unicorn's embrace. She felt the creature's warmth and the shivers eased. How could she have ever thought this warm creature could be the Frozen Unicorn? Any doubt had gone: he was a friend, not a foe. Of that much she was certain.

"Thank you," she said, and the unicorn made a low sound in his throat as if in response. Violet felt tears rising up, and she wasn't sure why. Perhaps from relief she was no longer alone.

"I'm Violet," she said into the unicorn's mane, which was softer than any horse's. He nodded: a small gesture but definitely a nod. Did he know who she was? If so, how? Her brain was still not fully awake.

"Who are you?" she repeated, not expecting an answer, but the creature took a step backwards and moved his mouth a little, as if he was about to reply.

But he didn't speak. He was holding something in his mouth. Something small, which he dropped deliberately in the snow by her knees. He bowed his head, then gazed back up at her as if he was trying to tell her something.

She peered down, unable to see what it was. A leaf? No, a flower. A small purple flower.

CHAPTER TWELVE

THE VIOLET

Violet peered at the flower, then picked it up. A sweet violet. Could it be the violet from the spring garden? The colour of the petals, the dot of yellow and the fine white lines were all the same. She'd dropped it when she was running away. Where else would the unicorn have found a wild violet in all this snow? They didn't usually appear until the spring.

An idea came to her. A confused idea, beginning to take shape in her mind. What had the Inventor Trolls told her about unicorns?

Unicorns were usually good.

Sometimes, unicorns weren't even unicorns, but people.

The Frozen Unicorn himself wasn't a real unicorn but a sorcerer, who'd taken that shape.

What if this Other Unicorn before her hadn't always been a unicorn? What if he was a person too, trapped in another body?

She peered at him.

"Nicolas once said he would bring me the first violet of spring; that nothing would stop him."

The unicorn nodded his head vigorously, as if he knew. Which was impossible. Nobody knew. There had been nobody there, that winter day in the woods, but the two of them.

Unless...

Violet paled. She hardly dared to ask the question, in case she was wrong.

Yet she was certain she knew the answer.

"You can't possibly be..." Her breath caught in her throat. "Are you ... Nicolas?"

NICOLAS

The unicorn nodded, then reared back on its hind legs and neighed at such volume Violet dropped the flower in surprise. She couldn't be in doubt of the response.

The unicorn *was* Nicolas!

She saw it now. The creature's eyes, although larger, shared his expression, as though they were telling her something he couldn't put into words. Even his dark mane was a giveaway: the way it fell forward and he kept shaking it back.

How could she have missed it? He hadn't disappeared. He had been there all along.

All those times when she saw him as she travelled north, she'd felt a connection with this unicorn, and a desire to speak to him rather than run away. It hadn't been a clever spell from an evil unicorn – it had been Nicolas. She should have listened to her own intuition.

"Nicolas," she whispered again, and he nodded.

It was true.

She rose up and flung her arms around him, breathing in his scent. That same combination of apple pie and woodsmoke, even as a unicorn out here in the Far North.

"I thought you were locked up in the Ice Fortress, but you're here. You were always here." She pulled away and looked into his eyes. "He didn't imprison you at all – he turned you into a unicorn!"

Somehow, this magical transformation didn't seem so difficult to believe. A moving, flowing body of water could transform into a solid walkway when the temperature dropped. Why then, should a person not transform into a unicorn given the right conditions? It was still him, and just as the river had begun to thaw, she knew Nicolas the person would come back to her again.

"Oh, Nicolas, how I've missed you."

A tear slid from his eye and she saw then his happiness and relief. How hard he must have been trying to reach her: to tell her his secret. And all she had done was run from him. She threw her arms around his neck again. It was all going to be all right. She'd found him at last. She wept warm tears into his soft mane. Then she stood back and gazed at him. Nicolas. Her True Love. Any worries she'd had all melted away.

Then tiredness hit her, and she saw his eyelids, too, were drooping. There was nothing more to say. It was night-time and they both needed sleep. They could talk more in the morning.

"We must sleep," she said. "Here, where it's more sheltered."

She began to rearrange the branches at the base of her tree, but he didn't seem to want them.

He dropped to the ground, legs folded beneath him, and the side of his long head resting on his lower front legs. His tail was close to the tree trunk on one side and his horn on the other, so the curve of the tree hollow and the curve of his body made a circle. A safe, warm circle in which she could finally relax, like one of Elgu's hibernating creatures in their drawers. She curled up facing the tree, the blanket over her and his warmth behind her. Her own chilled body gradually relaxed and returned to a more normal temperature. His breath was slow and steady, and she felt calmer as her breathing regulated to match his.

She was so tired, so confused, she couldn't think straight. All she knew was Nicolas was there and he wasn't angry with her. He couldn't have been, to come all the way out here. Everything was going to be all right.

She fell asleep in seconds, and this time, she didn't dream at all.

QUESTIONS

When she opened her eyes, the sun was high in the sky. She'd slept late. But Nicolas's warmth had gone and she was alone by the tree trunk. Had last night been just a vivid dream? There was no unicorn, no Nicolas. Her tired imagination had given her the story she'd wanted.

Then, as she sat up, she spotted him a little way away, tearing at the bark of one of the trees with his teeth. At the base of the tree was a small pile of seeds and berries. Her heart skipped. It hadn't been a dream! He'd woken before her and was looking for breakfast.

She looked down at what she was wearing. Socks on her hands and an Elgu-style scarf wound around her arm? Had she really greeted Nicolas like that last night? She removed the additional clothes and stuffed them into her bag, then loosened the drawstring of her hood and pushed it back around her shoulders.

"Good morning," she said. It was strange talking to him when he couldn't reply, but she didn't know what else to do. A moment of doubt crept in. Was it him? It had all been clear the night before, but now she felt rested and well, she wondered if she'd been mistaken.

He turned and bowed his head towards her. His breath made

white clouds in the air as he exhaled softly through his nose. Those eyes. That mane. It was him. She smiled.

She'd found him. He was alive and free, not locked away in a dungeon. But in the cold light of the morning, things didn't look quite as positive as they had the night before.

Nicolas was a unicorn. And she had no idea how they were going to turn him back.

She stood and straightened her clothes. The harsh wind had died down and it felt much warmer than the night had done. Maybe Nicolas would be able to help her answer some of her questions.

"Nicolas, I'm so glad to find you. All this time, I thought you were imprisoned, out there in the Ice Fortress. I kept thinking of you, all alone. I was worried you might die—"

He trotted towards her then, dipping his head, and she kissed him softly between his ears, on the familiar dark hair that made up his mane.

"I'm so sorry we argued on the night of the dance. I just wanted to dance with you, and when you turned me down, I felt sad and humiliated. Still, I shouldn't have spoken so harshly. I came to find you the next day, to apologize, but you'd gone."

He nuzzled into her. He didn't seem angry. Madam Verger had been right: it had all just been a silly argument.

"Of course, you hadn't really gone." Talking about the events aloud like this straightened them in her mind. Everything began to make sense.

"I know now it was you on the hill in Millbrook. I thought you were the Frozen Unicorn and I ran away."

He nodded and she frowned.

"All this time, I've been running from you, even when you helped me. How could I have missed it?" How she wished he could respond. "Madam Verger told me to keep away from the unicorn. Otherwise I feel sure I would have found you before."

Suddenly, Nicolas's body language changed. He looked up and stepped away, ears back, then stomped on the snowy ground, sending powdery snow flying around his legs. Violet understood how frustrated he must be. She'd encountered him right near the beginning of her journey, when she'd arrived in the Near North, but she'd run away. If only she'd realized sooner.

She lay her hand back on his neck, gently.

"I'm so sorry. Things would have been different if only I'd known it was you."

It was no wonder he was angry. She had been so glad to find him alive and not locked in a fortress, she hadn't considered how it must be for him. Nicolas *was* in a sort of prison, stuck in this changed shape, unable to converse with her or tell her how he felt.

"I must think what to do next..." she said. "Let me get something to eat."

She sat and pulled out the last half a bread roll from her bag. Nicolas brought over a cluster of red berries on a stalk, and she plucked them and ate them one by one, enjoying the tart, acidic juice. He'd also found some walnuts, which he helped break open under his hoof. She drank the dregs of the water from the flask, which was ice cold, but not yet frozen again.

With food inside her, however little, she was able to think straighter. She considered their options.

They could return to Millbrook. She could blow the horn as she had come so close to doing last night. Perhaps Candra would arrive to take her home, and Nicolas would travel on foot. But when they returned, what kind of life would they lead?

Most would think Violet had lost her mind, disappearing for days and then returning with a unicorn she claimed to be Nicolas. Madam Evergreen would perhaps recognize her son, but what about everyone else?

"Back in Millbrook, there's a chance we might find a person of magic – someone who could turn you back to your proper self..."

Nicolas looked at her with such despair in his eyes that Violet trailed off. She didn't really believe there was anyone back in Millbrook who had the right skills. It was a simple place – not the sort of place to find sorcerers. Perhaps in Essendor, but even that was a gamble. What if there was no one with the right powers of transformation?

The reality of it all began to dawn on Violet. "I was beginning to hope, now I've found you, we could go home. But we can't, can we?"

He shook his head sadly.

The only one who could be guaranteed to undo this spell was the one who'd cast it. The Frozen Unicorn.

She knew suddenly what they had to do and felt excited at the prospect of a new plan. Together, she and Nicolas could put things right.

"Nicolas, was it the Frozen Unicorn who made you like this – who cast the spell?"

Violet had been expecting confirmation – a quick nod of the head to show she had understood correctly – before sharing her plan. She was surprised then when Nicolas shook his head slowly. It was different to a human headshake, his heavy head low and swaying, but Violet was in no doubt it meant the same thing: no.

THE PLAN

No? There must be some misunderstanding. It had to have been the Frozen Unicorn who'd made Nicolas this way. If not, then what were they both doing here, in the Far North? For a moment, she felt light-headed. What if Madam Verger had got this terribly wrong and Violet had come to the wrong place?

"Who, then? Who changed you into a unicorn?"

He turned and pointed his muzzle across the ocean, towards the Ice Fortress. Relief flooded through her. They were, at least, in the correct location.

"But that's where the Frozen Unicorn lives."

Nicolas nodded. Yes. She felt more confused than ever.

"Someone else in the Ice Fortress put you under this spell?"

Nicolas nodded again and Violet sighed. How she wished he could speak back. This conversation was entirely one-sided, and she felt as though she were asking all the wrong questions.

"So, whoever it was that changed you is working with the Frozen Unicorn? They are there with him now?"

Nicolas nodded for the third time. That was enough for Violet. It didn't really matter who had cast the spell. Violet and Nicolas still had to get to the Ice Fortress and somehow convince, trick or force them into changing Nicolas back. There would be no hiding away any more.

"We need to go there, don't we? To the Ice Fortress?"

Nicolas nodded reluctantly.

Violet finished the food in silence and Nicolas walked a little way away, to give her space, or to run through things in his own mind.

Violet packed their little camp away with a new determination. She kicked snow over the place where she'd made her pitiful fire, and flung the branches into the undergrowth. They would soon be covered by a white layer of fresh snow.

She examined the empty clearing. There was no longer any sign they'd been there, except for the single violet she'd discarded on the snowy ground in surprise.

She bent and picked up the single flower. It still looked as fresh as when she'd picked it in the spring garden.

"You," she said, twirling it by its stem, "are very important."

For without the violet, she might never have discovered Nicolas's true identity.

"I'm glad I dropped you the first time, or Nicolas wouldn't have found you. But I should never have dropped you a second time. I never shall again. You are too precious."

Violet pressed the flower between the pages of her notebook to preserve it, and then picked up her bag.

"To the Ice Fortress, before we waste any more time."

CHAPTER THIRTEEN

THE JOURNEY CONTINUES

Violet was no longer alone, and she no longer had to trudge painfully slowly through the snow.

She'd finally discovered the best way to cross this frozen landscape: on the back of a unicorn!

At first, she'd felt a little wobbly without a saddle, but she reminded herself how she'd managed to stay on Candra's back. This was much easier. She soon got used to it and discovered what a glorious way to travel it was.

Nicolas didn't worry about staying close to the river. He

galloped through the forest on a twisting trail through the trees, leaving hoofprints in the snow. The world was monochrome: dark tree trunks sprouted from the white ground, snow-covered foliage white all around them.

The brightest white of all was Nicolas's unicorn horn. It contrasted with his black mane, which bounced as he moved. Every so often, he would hurtle down a steep slope or leap over a wide dip, and she would hold on tight, bag banging against her back, knowing he wouldn't let her fall. The distances he jumped grew increasingly wide, as if he was daring himself, or showing off to her.

He enjoyed this part of being a unicorn, she could tell, especially the jumps. Maybe it hadn't been such a prison for him after all. Once, he turned to look at her, and she smiled back to show him, yes, she liked it too. Powdery snow whipped into her face, from the trees or the clouds, she didn't know which.

For a time, the only sound was his hooves thundering on the snowy ground. But after a while, Violet heard the low roar of the ocean as she had the night before. She knew then they were getting nearer.

All too soon, they were at the edge of the forest, and the journey was over.

THE WATER'S EDGE

The trees stopped abruptly and gave way to a steep cliff edge. Nicolas slowed to a standstill, panting heavily from the gallop, and Violet dismounted. She took a couple of steps back and held on to a slender tree trunk as she peered out at the view. She felt a little giddy from the ride and from the change in perspective.

The cliff plunged down to the ocean, which was such a dark blue it was almost black. Numerous flat icebergs of all sizes were scattered in the sea, the pale orange sun glinting off them as they moved and shifted with the tide.

In amongst these icebergs was the Ice Fortress itself, which for the first time, Violet was able to see in detail.

It was enormous, at least three times as tall as the manor back home, and it floated on an iceberg with a border around it like the brim of a bonnet. It was opaque white and reminded Violet of the candles on the dinner table, where layers of white wax had dribbled down the sides then set and cooled. But this was one big lump of candle. Not quite a monstrosity, as the trolls had called it – such a structure must have taken great skill or magic to create – but crude somehow.

Violet could still see the darker, bluey patches that had formed a face when she'd viewed them from the river, but now she could see other shapes and details too. There was the unicorn at the top but also, lower down, what looked like a slender man with a hat and wand, looking straight out at her. Violet didn't know if these shapes were intentional, or if she was imagining them like pictures in the clouds. Either way, the multiple eyes made her feel watched and she found herself looking over her shoulder for the Frozen Unicorn.

"Do you feel like he's watching us?" she whispered, and Nicolas side-stepped a little closer. Maybe he felt it too. After a few moments of gazing out across the water, Nicolas left her side and began to walk along the cliff edge, to where the ground sloped downhill. Violet followed, hoping to find a way across to the fortress.

The slope may not have been the sheer drop of the cliff, but it was still steep and rocky. Nicolas turned to check she was coping, and she thought of how he'd helped her down the hillside back home.

She'd changed since then, and had tackled much worse than steep hillsides by herself.

"I think it's best I manage this on my own," she said, and he nodded and began stepping slowly down the slope. She followed afterwards. The snow was less deep than she was used to, and she could feel the rocky surface beneath. She watched where Nicolas put his hooves and copied, placing her feet on the flatter parts.

Within moments, they were standing on the beach, jagged grey stones protruding through the snow, the tide rolling gently in and out. Violet navigated her way across the stones to the water's edge, fascinated by the calm sea.

Nicolas came and stood behind her, chin resting over her right shoulder, and she stroked the long bridge of his nose.

"It's the sea, Nicolas. The real, actual sea!"

From up on the cliff edge, the water had looked dark, but up close it was as clear as the millpond back home – clearer even. She didn't have to drink it to know it was salty, though; she could taste it in the air. Chunks of ice had washed up on the sand, and Violet could see the large, smooth stones lying on the seabed. The way it moved, in and out, foaming white as it came towards them, was like nothing she'd ever seen before.

Nicolas left her side and trotted right up to the water as the tide went out, then ran away as it rushed back in. She laughed. Would he do the same if he was in his human form? She had no doubt he would.

On impulse, she picked up a smooth, flat stone.

"Watch this," she called to Nicolas and flicked it towards the water, imagining it skimming daintily over the gentle waves. It didn't, though: it plunged into the sea and sank, as it had every other time she'd tried.

She shrugged. "No need to worry – your stone-skimming record's not in danger yet."

He threw back his head and made a whinnying sound that could only be unicorn laughter. She wished he was standing next to her as the Nicolas she knew. It was a reminder of why they were there. Not to skim stones or play on the beach, but to get to the Ice Fortress and find a way to turn Nicolas back.

But she knew they were both thinking the same thing: how?

She'd rather hoped by the time they got this close, a solution would have presented itself. Sometimes, things looked better after a good night's sleep. But Violet could see nothing different from the night before. The fortress hadn't floated closer in the night. No secret tunnel had appeared.

They gazed out to sea, as if expecting inspiration to wash up with the tide.

LOOKING FOR ANSWERS

"There must be a way to reach it," said Violet, stating the obvious. After all, the Frozen Unicorn couldn't fly. Or could he? He had magic, and had somehow built his fortress out there in the middle of the sea.

The floating icebergs almost looked like stepping stones, yet were too far apart to leap across.

"Any ideas?" she asked Nicolas, knowing if he did have a solution, he wouldn't be able to share it with her.

He looked at her steadily, as if thinking, then dragged an old tree branch, washed ashore, into the water. Violet tried to guess what he was thinking.

"Maybe we could build a raft? Or a sort of bridge?"

Saying the words out loud to Nicolas helped her process her thoughts. She'd missed having someone to discuss her problems with. The bridge idea might work. The water was shallow near them. But one tree branch wasn't enough.

Violet continued to stare out to sea, hoping for a solution.

Strangely, the longer she looked, the more she saw.

There were other structures, like the Ice Fortress, but smaller, floating on their own icebergs around the larger one. They were more uniform in shape: like little domes with a point on top. Each mini-fortress had its own familiar colour: pink, orange, jade and violet. Sea green as well.

The trolls' homes. Violet would recognize those colours anywhere. She even knew which one had been Hefta and Hooan's. They had said their homes were beautiful and unique and she could see it was true. They were made from ice and every colour of the sky. She tried to imagine what they looked like inside. No doubt as cosy and homely as their makeshift homes by the forest. That was why the Frozen Unicorn had wanted their skills. He'd obviously tried to copy the look of their houses when he'd built his fortress, but even with all his power, he couldn't make something so beautiful. The fortress was lumpy and ugly in comparison.

Strangely, each house was encased in its own block of clear ice, visible but entirely inaccessible. That must have been down to the Frozen Unicorn too. They'd told her he'd covered them in ice.

"Heartless," she whispered. "How could he?"

Nicolas looked at her quizzically.

"Those smaller, colourful houses belonged to the Inventor Creator trolls. My new friends. The Frozen Unicorn cast them out of their homes."

He snorted angrily and she nodded. It made her angry too.

But thinking about the trolls gave her the germ of an idea.

"Trolls can't fly either," she muttered. Realizing she should offer some explanation to Nicolas, she said, "They must have had some way of getting from the shore out to sea. Boats perhaps, or some other way. . ."

She smiled.

Of course.

She'd been carrying the solution with her the whole time.

ICE PEBBLES

Ice pebbles. The Inventor Creator Trolls used them for everything. To drink, to dye clothes, even to build their homes, by the looks of things. Why not to build walkways across the sea, too?

She opened the bag and showed Nicolas. "The trolls gave me these. I used them to seal a crack in the river when it began to melt."

There were only a handful of pebbles left.

Nicolas tilted his head, interested. Violet shook the pebbles in their bag. Would they work as they had done on the river, or would their powers be lost in the wide expanse of sea? Did she have enough to create a path all the way to the Ice Fortress?

The only way to know was to give it a go.

She reached into the bag, took out a single pebble, and threw it a little way, halfway between the shore and the first iceberg. It landed in the water with a gentle plop and Violet waited.

After a few moments, a loud cracking sound filled the air as the water turned white and froze. The frozen section was wider than a garden path, but not quite as wide as the river had been. It stretched from the shoreline to the first iceberg.

Violet grinned at Nicolas, and he tested the new ice with his hoof, then walked tentatively on to the pathway. It was solid. He lifted his head and whinnied, ears pointing towards Violet.

"It worked!" she cried, and ran to join him, careful not to skid on the slippery ice. They crossed over to the first iceberg and assessed the situation. Between them and the fortress, a few icebergs floated in a staggered line. Violet checked the ice pebbles.

"Four left. That should be enough."

Nicolas whinnied approvingly as Violet threw the next pebble. It looked as though they were going to walk right across the middle of the ocean, up to the door of the Ice Fortress.

CHAPTER FOURTEEN

WALKING ON WATER

Crossing the ocean in this way was either Violet's best idea ever, or complete foolishness – she had no idea which. So much could go wrong. Out here they were so noticeable: the only figures in a desolate landscape. If the Frozen Unicorn was watching from his fortress, then they would be instantly visible. What would he do if he saw them here? Would he be angry? Would he come out and break their icy path? Violet would rather they surprised the Frozen Unicorn, than the other way around.

She threw the next pebble into the sea, waited for a new icy pathway to form, then walked across, with Nicolas trotting behind her.

They had crossed the shallows, and were walking further out to sea. Dark blue, almost black water swirled on either side of their ice path. Nicolas kept checking back over his shoulder. Violet wondered if they were thinking the same: was this icy trail permanent, or would it eventually melt? If it did melt, would they be stranded on an iceberg in the middle of the ocean?

She tried to force the negative thoughts from her mind. It was best she concentrated on getting from the shore to the fortress before worrying about what came next.

Walking on the ice without skates was challenging, and as they crossed to the third iceberg, her right foot slid out beneath her. Luckily, she was able to catch hold of Nicolas as she fell, which prevented her from flying into the icy waters. Violet felt shaky at the thought; she wouldn't last a moment in there. It was lucky he'd remained so close. From then on, as they progressed from iceberg to iceberg, she concentrated on where she put her feet.

When they reached the final iceberg, Violet stopped. There was a problem. The last iceberg was much further away from the fortress than it appeared from the shore, and she was down to her last pebble. So far, the ice pebbles had only frozen relatively small stretches of water and she doubted this single pebble would be enough.

Nicolas stood next to her, waiting for her to continue; she could hear him breathing steadily.

"The gap's bigger than I expected and there are no more pebbles," she confessed. She ran her hand around the bottom of the bag, hoping to find another, even a broken shard, but there was nothing.

Nicolas hung his head. Frustrated at the situation, probably. She rolled the last pebble in her gloved hand. Then she realized what she was doing and clenched it tightly. She didn't want to drop it as she had done with the firecone.

The Ice Fortress loomed before them, surrounded by a narrow iceberg path and separated by an impossible stretch of water. At this proximity, they could no longer see its shape at all: just a great white slab of ice, reaching up into the sky.

"I can't bring myself just to throw it," she explained. "It would be such a waste if it doesn't reach."

He nodded and tilted his head to one side as he thought.

Violet thought too. They stood as they had done on the seashore, moments before, waiting for answers. And, once again, inspiration struck.

"I've got it!" Violet held up the last remaining pebble. "I skim the pebble."

SKIMMING PEBBLES

Why hadn't Violet thought of it before? If the ice pebble froze the water every time it hit, then this was a way to make their icy walkway much, much longer.

Nicolas held his head to one side. She sensed scepticism.

"I know, I've never yet managed to skim a stone."

He cocked his head to the other side.

"Yes, I know I've tried on multiple occasions. I wish you could do this for us too, but ... well ... you can't. It has to be me."

He nuzzled the side of her arm.

"Thank you for the support," she said. She could understand why he wasn't entirely sure about the plan. She had failed to skim a stone every single time she'd tried. But it had never mattered before.

She gazed at the gentle waves. At least the sea was calm. She didn't even need to skim the stone particularly well. Three or four hops would be enough to close the gap.

She had to at least try – they had no other plan.

On examination, the ice pebble wasn't quite the sort of flat-bottomed stone Nicolas had advised her to select back in Millbrook, but she'd seen him successfully skim all sorts. This would have to do.

She held it in the curve of her forefinger and squatted like the Millbrook stone-skimming champion himself.

"Is this right?" she asked.

Nicolas nodded. She knew he would rather be doing this himself. But he couldn't. And she could. She'd managed to learn other things, hadn't she? Ice-skating and fire-starting. Why should stone-skimming be any different?

She took a deep breath.

Four hops. Or even three would do.

She aimed the stone at the water and swung her hand back a few times in the way Nicolas had taught her. She glanced at him. His eyes were squeezed shut.

She let out her breath and threw the stone, parallel to the water.

It left her hand, curving away from her forefinger, with just the right amount of spin, and headed towards the gentle waves.

She would never understand quite how it happened.

Perhaps ice pebbles were the right shape and weight.

Perhaps ice pebbles contained a little bit of magic.

Perhaps fortune was on her side.

But, this time, when the stone hit the surface of the water, it didn't sink below, but sprang up as if it had a life of its own. There was a first time for everything.

"It hopped!" she shrieked.

Nicolas opened his eyes and they watched together as the pebble bounced away from the waves. It hit the sea again, leaving an icy path in its wake.

Amazingly, the second hop was even higher than the first. For a moment, Violet thought she'd done it, but then the pebble disappeared into the water with a plop and didn't re-emerge. The icy path ended abruptly some distance away from the Ice Fortress.

Violet's excitement at her first successful stone skim faded rapidly.

"Two hops. We needed at least three."

He nuzzled her arm sympathetically.

"Oh, Nicolas! I thought I'd done it. I really did. Still, maybe it's close enough."

They walked along the icy walkway, hoping that it would reach further than it looked. It didn't.

Despite Violet's magical stone-skimming efforts, they were still not quite close enough.

PLAN B

From up close, Violet could see the gap to the fortress was as wide as the distance between the other icebergs.

A cold wind whipped up, and the waves around them grew bigger, crashing into the path on which they were standing, like a reminder of the sea's power.

"What shall we do now? I have no pebbles left. Do we have to return to shore?"

There was a short pause, then Nicolas turned and began walking back in the direction they'd come. There was her answer. It surprised Violet, as Nicolas wasn't the sort to give up. Maybe he had a plan and was going to retrieve the wood from the beach.

Nicolas walked as far as the previous iceberg but then turned again so he was facing in the direction of the fortress.

He lowered his head and narrowed his eyes. Violet had a funny feeling she knew what his plan was. He wasn't walking back to the beach. He was preparing for his run-up.

"Nicolas, you can't intend to jump to the fortress?"

The sparkle in his eyes told her that was exactly what he was planning.

Violet checked the gap once more.

"But that stretch is as wide as a small river! It's too far."

Nicolas craned his neck to get a better look, then whinnied in a reassuring way. Her heart sank. He really was planning to do this.

"But how am I going to get across?" As she asked the question, she knew what his answer was going to be.

He flicked his head towards his hindquarters.

"No. No, no, no. I'm not sitting on your back here. It's too slippery. Too dangerous. . ." Her gaze turned once more to the dark, swirling sea, and then back to Nicolas.

His eyes were wide. He fixed them on her. Violet knew that look from when they'd climbed the watchtower in Millbrook: *trust me.*

She sighed.

"Of course I trust you. But some things are out of your control. What if you slip when you're taking your run-up? What if you can't make the jump?"

At that, Nicolas snorted, breath puffing out white from his nostrils. His confidence made her laugh, and she began to feel a bit better about it. Besides, what choice did she have? She was all out of ideas.

THE JUMP

Sitting on his back, she felt safe and secure; Nicolas was more stable on the ice than she was. Maybe having four legs helped. Once she was settled, he turned and looked at her briefly. She leaned forward and put her hands either side of his neck, head close to his mane, breathing in his Nicolassy scent.

"I'm ready," she murmured, although she felt anything but.

He broke into a gallop and Violet gasped as his hooves chipped bits of ice from the path. If he slipped, they would both plunge into the icy water. But he didn't slip. He kept a straight path, looking as though he was going to gallop straight into the water itself. At the very last moment, as his front hooves reached the edge, he reared back and jumped.

Violet gasped as she slipped sideways, but grabbed his mane to prevent herself from being thrown off. The jump was bigger than any he'd made on their journey there, and the landing area was narrow, but he made it, just, and slid to a stop.

Violet unwrapped her hands from his mane and clung to him for a few more moments, their heart rates returning to normal. She didn't know whether to hit him or thank him. In the end, she laughed, as she slipped off his back on to the snowy iceberg. She leaned against the wall of the fortress and raised her eyebrows. "Well! That was close."

He looked at her, eyes sparkling with humour and pride, in a way that was such pure Nicolas, that she kissed him on the forehead.

He snorted gently and they both looked around at their new surroundings. They had reached the Ice Fortress and were closer to the Frozen Unicorn than ever before. This was really happening. But what next? Should they walk left, or right? Violet had no idea where the entrance was, where they would find the Frozen Unicorn, and if they were likely to be attacked on their way in.

Nicolas wasn't looking any more decisive than she was.

"Now what?" she asked.

CHAPTER FIFTEEN

DECISIONS

In the end, Violet made a decision and turned to her right.

"The base of the fortress is roughly circular, so one way is as good as the other," she said to Nicolas.

They walked in silence, following the wall around, looking for a way in. In some places, the surrounding ledge was wide enough to walk side by side; in others it narrowed so that Violet had to walk ahead while Nicolas followed. There were no doors or windows in this vast structure, just thick, lumpy ice, as if layers upon layers of icicles had been stuck together. Violet trailed her gloved hand along the surface. In some places it felt bumpy but smooth. In other places, she could see and feel the sharp ends of the icicles.

A couple of times, Violet stopped, thinking she saw the shape of a doorway, but it was an illusion, like those faces she'd seen from the shore. She wondered if the entrance was concealed somehow, but if it was, she had no idea how to find it.

They trudged on.

When they had walked around to the other side, and could no longer see the shore, or the path they'd taken, they found the entranceway. On this side of the fortress, there were fewer icebergs and a greater expanse of dark, swirling ocean, leading to who-knew-where. What a view. Once again, Violet thought of the trolls, living here for generations, only to be pushed out by an aggressive stranger.

The entrance appeared to have been cleaved from the lump of ice without much care. It was dark and jagged, and Violet could see the beginnings of a corridor leading into the icy mass. She couldn't think of a much less inviting place.

A fortress suggested heavy defence, but there were no guards, no locks and chains, not even a door. The location was presumably protection enough from enemies. It was possible they were the first people other than the unicorn and his kind to set foot on this island.

She turned to Nicolas and saw her own reluctance reflected in his eyes.

"I suppose we had better explore inside."

INSIDE THE FORTRESS

They walked through the doorway into the tunnelled-out corridor, leaving the yellow warmth of the sun behind them. Violet shivered. This cold, unforgiving place was just as Madam Verger had described and where she'd pictured Nicolas, huddled and broken. *Thick walls of ice; dark chambers within.* She reminded herself Nicolas was safe with her. For a moment, she paused and turned to him. She put a hand to the side of his cheek, his warmth reassuring her, although she wished for a moment she could touch his real, human face.

They continued, his hooves echoing on the icy floor as they stepped further and further into the shadows and away from the daylight. The corridor was narrow enough for her to brush the bumpy walls on either side with raised hands. They followed its straight path until they reached a sharp bend.

Violet's heart thumped, and she summoned all her courage to

walk around the corner. But it was the same: another empty, icy corridor. She kept expecting either to see the unicorn or to be plunged into total darkness, but neither happened. Pale blue light continued to filter through the ice walls. There was no sign of the Frozen Unicorn.

Violet wasn't sure where, or even if, they would find him. Had he been watching them approach across the ocean? Was he waiting for them, ready to freeze them solid as he had threatened the trolls? And what was she going to say to him? Persuade him? Threaten him? Fight him? If they were going to fight him, how would they do that without weapons? What sort of weapon would one need to fight a magical, frozen unicorn?

She remembered Madam Verger's words, spoken days ago, although it felt like months had passed.

You have the power of True Love.

Thinking it made Violet feel better, even though she didn't really know what it meant. She did feel stronger when she was with Nicolas: their love did feel like a kind of power. But how would she harness that power?

They turned another corner, slowly, tentatively, and this time it wasn't just another corridor.

They had reached a squarish chamber about the size of the entrance hall at the manor. She peeped in. In the left-hand wall was an arched opening, more ornate than the entrance to the fortress had been: carved rather than gouged. Short icicles formed a spiky, doorframe-like border. This doorway led somewhere important. Quite possibly to the Frozen Unicorn himself. She looked at Nicolas for confirmation and he nodded.

They entered the antechamber and stood close together, Violet's arm resting on Nicolas's back, her hand buried in his mane. From there, Violet could see that the arched opening led to a much bigger main room, although she couldn't see any detail, just cool blue shadows.

But almost instantly, floating out from the archway, came a voice.

"Enter," it said.

Whoever it was must have heard them. Or been watching them ever since they left the shore. Violet and Nicolas glanced at each other and the voice came again.

"Step inside. Make yourselves known."

A woman's voice: low and gravelly.

Violet widened her eyes at Nicolas, and he did the same. She hadn't been expecting a woman's voice. Everyone had referred to the unicorn as *he* or *him*. Now she thought about it, the trolls had mentioned an interpreter.

But the fact it was a woman's voice wasn't the strangest thing The strangest thing was that the voice sounded familiar.

THE FROZEN UNICORN

Violet and Nicolas exchanged a look. There was no reason to delay the inevitable; they must do as the voice commanded.

They walked in side by side, taking a few hesitant steps, but staying close to the entrance.

The room was vast: larger than Millbrook Hall, larger than any room Violet had ever seen. It was an uneven shape, but roughly circular, with the same thick, bumpy walls as the rest of the fortress, but clearer, sparkling. Violet gazed up to the high ceiling, far, far above their heads, and saw a circular hole, through which rays of bright sunlight forced their way in. When Violet had pictured a fortress, she'd never thought of a grand room like this one. She'd pictured a prison: basic and functional.

Nicolas nudged her and she followed his gaze to an arched alcove at the back of the room, which reached nearly up to the ceiling. Halfway up was an internal balcony with a spiky balustrade of upturned icicles. This balustrade became a banister, edging a staircase, which curved to the left-hand side and protruded into the room.

In the middle of the balcony stood the Frozen Unicorn.

He was just as the trolls had described him: clear as ice, majestic as a statue. She was a little unprepared for the size of him, and his sheer magnificence. He was completely see-through, with no heart, no bones, no inner workings, and yet he was living and breathing. That was surely impossible? He looked magical and powerful, as if he could do anything he wanted. He stood in profile, but turned his head towards them, watching them intently as they walked further into the room. Violet's mouth felt dry and she moved closer to Nicolas. She could feel him shaking at her side.

Nicolas glanced at Violet and tilted his head to the right-hand side of the balcony.

Violet gasped.

On her journey to the Far North, Violet had encountered so many unexpected things, she thought she would never be surprised again. A wolf with wings; clouds of fairies; a garden full of flowers in the middle of the snow. But this was the most surprising moment of all.

Nicolas had drawn her attention to a woman standing on the balcony against the wall, camouflaged against the ice. Violet knew the person, just as she'd known the voice that summoned them into the room.

She knew her, although she struggled to believe her eyes.

In some ways, she looked the same: long white dress, grey-white plait and pale eyes; but in other ways she looked different. She stood upright, holding her long, gnarled walking stick aloft like a magic staff. She looked capable and confident. She looked ... powerful.

"Madam Verger?"

CHAPTER SIXTEEN

MADAM VERGER

"Welcome, Violet," said Madam Verger, sounding as cool and calm as if Violet had walked into her cottage for a slice of apple cake. She walked behind the Frozen Unicorn, along the balcony and down the steps towards them, her staff tapping on the ice as she went.

It was her. It really was.

Violet stood motionless for a moment, gaping at Madam Verger, gaping at Nicolas, ignoring the Frozen Unicorn completely.

Although she'd known Madam Verger for most of her life, Violet couldn't recall ever having hugged her or even shaken her hand. Yet seeing her here, far from home, in this cold and unforgiving place, made Violet want to rush forward and throw her arms around her old friend. She left Nicolas's side and ran across the expanse between them, tears in her eyes.

Violet's boots skidded on the icy floor as she approached the steps. She would have got closer if it hadn't been for Nicolas, who trotted forward and stepped in front of her. A slight movement, one of his legs stretched in front of her own, but the message was clear: *stay back*. She glanced at him, confused. He was trying to warn her off. He was afraid. But afraid of what? The Frozen Unicorn, of course, but Violet had a feeling there was more to it. Surely he couldn't be afraid of Madam Verger?

As she asked herself the question, Violet glanced at Madam Verger, who stood on the bottom step, smiling. She didn't look like a prisoner. Something wasn't right.

"What are you doing here?" asked Violet, her trembling voice echoing around them. "I thought I left you back in Millbrook. You told me I must come alone. . ."

"Yes! Well done. I am delighted with how well you followed my instructions. But now you see, this is my home too. I visit as often as I can."

Her home? What was she talking about? Violet looked around,

as though expecting answers from the walls themselves. But the hard masses of ice were not forthcoming with their secrets.

"What do you think of it? Isn't it the most beautiful place you've ever seen?"

Beautiful. That was not a word Violet would ever use to describe this stark place. She thought of Elgu's hideaway in the forest, of the layers of rugs, of its cushions and smells of baking bread. So cosy and warm. She thought of the Inventor Trolls' makeshift homes out on the snowy plains. They were built with whatever was at hand, yet they were full of warmth, colour and love. No softness and comfort could be found here. No colour but white, no texture but smooth and hard.

And Madam Verger herself was just as cold and aloof.

"But I thought—"

She glanced at Nicolas, and he shook his head from side to side.

"You thought I was just the old woman who looked after the orchard? With the best recipe for apple cake, who told fascinating stories? Yes, all of that is true, but there is more besides. You are not a child any more. You must have seen there has always been more to me than apple cake and stories."

Her eyes were piercing, as if they could see Violet's thoughts, and Violet asked herself: had she known? There *had* always been something different about Madam Verger. Something Violet liked, something powerful. There had also perhaps been other clues. Her collection of curiosities. And Madam Evergreen had never trusted Madam Verger. Had Violet failed to see the truth that was right in front of her?

Madam Verger continued.

"You know me as Madam Verger, but I am also known by other names. The Orchardess, the Interpreter."

The Interpreter? The Inventor Trolls had mentioned an interpreter: someone who'd helped the Frozen Unicorn to do his bidding. Could that interpreter have been Madam Verger?

None of it made any sense at all.

"Why didn't you tell me you lived here? You could have brought me here yourself. You could have protected me – saved me the struggle of the journey—"

"No, I couldn't have done. For many reasons. I couldn't have risked my full identity being disclosed back in Millbrook."

"But why?" Violet was struggling to cope with the enormity of it all. Had Madam Verger's trips to her cousin's house really been trips to the Far North? "You lied ... for years! Since I was a little girl."

"It is surprising how the years fly by when you know what you want. A great man taught me that." She smiled thinly at the Frozen Unicorn. "If you are patient – willing to wait – then you can have anything at all."

Violet nodded slowly. All of this was a shock to her and a lot to take in, but knowing the interpreter had to be a good thing, didn't it?

"Madam Verger, I still don't fully understand what you're doing here, but will you help us? Please, explain to the Frozen Unicorn why he has to change Nicolas back."

At this, Madam Verger laughed and Nicolas reared up on his back legs, hooves clattering back down on the icy floor. Snorting, ears pinned back, he moved in front of Violet once more. And the truth suddenly dawned on her.

"You!" she cried. "The Frozen Unicorn didn't turn Nicolas into a unicorn at all. *You* did!"

THE WHOLE STORY

Violet stood, open-mouthed, staring at Madam Verger, who smiled calmly. This woman, who had been like a grandmother to her, was a stranger: the interpreter for this evil unicorn.

"You cast the spell," Violet repeated.

Nicolas nodded his head vigorously, breathing out hard through his nostrils.

She remembered how she'd run from the unicorn, fearing for her life. But there was only one unicorn in Millbrook and that was Nicolas. Which meant. . .

". . . The Frozen Unicorn wasn't even there, in Millbrook, was he? You did this for him?"

Madam Verger stepped off the bottom step, walked around Nicolas and placed a cool, bony hand on Violet's arm. Violet kept her other hand resting on Nicolas. He snorted and she could feel his muscles tensing as if he was about to run. Every muscle in her body was tense too.

"My dear girl, you must understand—" began Madam Verger, but Violet shook her arm away. It had all been a trick – a terrible trick – and she'd played right into Madam Verger's hands.

"You cast the spell . . . and yet you let me come to you the next morning and ask for your help."

Madam Verger held up her hands in front of her, palms out. "Violet, my dear. . ."

It all made so much sense now. But Violet couldn't help thinking that she should have known.

"Who are you really?" she finally asked. "And why did you do this to Nicolas?"

Madam Verger paused, as if assessing how much to share with Violet.

"If only I could have explained it to you back in Millbrook, but I feared it would have been too much to take in. . ."

"Explain now."

"Very well, I shall start with the story of how I came to be here."

Madam Verger's voice changed to storytelling mode and she started to pace back and forth across the ice, exactly as she used to in the orchard house.

"I am a woman of magic, which has not always made me a popular person. However, the stories of my youth do not concern us today. I shall begin with when I met the sorcerer. It was during the reign of King Zelos. I was already an old woman, and I was prepared to live out the rest of my days in an enchanted orchard. As it happened, things didn't end up that way."

"An orchard?" This was one thing that made sense to Violet.

"Yes, but not at Millbrook. This orchard was in the woods, a few miles from Essendor. And at that time, I had a falling out with the king, who was also a powerful sorcerer. He turned me into a bee."

"A bee?" Violet's head was swimming.

"Yes, a bee. There were many bees in the orchard, as you can imagine, and I was in a desperate situation. Anyway, the sorcerer who you now see before you in unicorn form, came to me. He had also fallen out with those in power, and had been banished from Essendor. He offered to restore me to my true form, in exchange for my servitude. I was only too happy to agree."

Violet looked up at the Frozen Unicorn. It was difficult to imagine a man somewhere behind that blank stare. "To agree to what, exactly?"

"To work for him. To use my magic alongside his, to help build his power. He was a broken man at that time, without a home, without his wand. Together, we were so much stronger. We planned to build a great castle, bigger and better than Essendor's, and a great kingdom to defeat them."

"How?"

"Those in power were able to turn into unicorns at will, and my master felt sure that if he could harness that same power then he could be a match for them. We built a great ice castle up in the clouds."

"An Ice Fortress like this one?"

"A castle – much grander. We also carved a powerful unicorn

figure from ice. In time, he learned to inhabit this unicorn form, to change back and forth, but the magic he needed was strong; it required him to dig deep within himself. In time, it became clear that his own emotions would not be enough. We found young people to provide memories to fuel his magic."

Violet glanced at Nicolas. He looked as disturbed by this as she was.

"You took people's *memories?*"

Madam Verger waved her hand dismissively. "It was something that needed to be done, for the greater good. However, it sadly all fell apart when we were betrayed by someone who worked for us. I was left for dead." Her hand crept up to the circular scar on her neck. "My master fell from the castle – a fall that would have killed an ordinary mortal. He managed to transform, but now his heart is frozen and he can no longer change back."

Madam Verger stopped pacing for a moment, and looked at Violet expectantly.

"I still don't understand what this has to do with me ... with us," she said, hand on Nicolas's flank.

"Well, you see, your sweetheart is not the only one trapped in a body that is not his own," said Madam Verger. "My master longs to be able to inhabit his human body once again. But this time, strong magic is needed. This time, only the power of True Love will turn him back."

THE OFFER

"The power of True Love?" asked Violet in disbelief. "*Our* Love?" Her cheeks reddened as she asked this in front of Nicolas.

"Yes, the power of True Love. You have proven to me how strong it is by coming here. By facing your fears and overcoming huge obstacles. Such power is unparalleled. If you give this to my master, then it will be all he needs to unfreeze his heart and regain his original form. When he has his full powers restored, he will be the most powerful man in this land. In any land! And in return, you will have anything you desire. Isn't that right, Master?"

Violet looked up to the balcony, and the Frozen Unicorn nodded slowly, ice white eyes fixed on her.

Violet closed her own eyes, thoughts whirling.

"Why didn't you ask us this back in Millbrook? Why make us come all the way here?"

She blinked her eyes open again. Madam Verger was watching her closely. "Girls and boys fall in love every day of the week. I could sense that what you and Nicolas felt was special, but we needed to test that love to see if it was true. And you have grown so much as a person, I now trust that you will understand the offer my master is making to you. You will make the right choice."

"The offer? If I understand this correctly, the Frozen Unicorn will give us anything we want for the price of our love. He will turn Nicolas back?"

Madam Verger smiled.

"Yes, that is correct, Violet. I'm so glad you understand. And, to save you pain, you and Nicolas won't remember a thing. It will be as if you'd never had feelings for each other.

"And what if we don't agree to this?"

The old woman's smile tightened. "I am sure that you will agree. It would be unwise to make an enemy of the Frozen Unicorn. You may think for a moment before you give me your answer."

CHOICES

Violet's blood felt colder than it had in the forest the night before. What would be the use of kingdoms and castles, of fine clothes and luxury? What would be the use of any of it if they gave their love away? Violet glanced at Nicolas, who looked angrier than ever, his eyes wide and rolling. Violet could see he felt exactly the same way she did. She put a hand on his neck, by his mane. Violet would never agree to that.

"Our answer is no!" She shouted it, surprising even herself.

"I know this is a shock for you, Violet, but when you have had time to take it in, you will realize what an opportunity it is."

"How can it be an opportunity for us?"

"I was always so fond of you, even as a little girl. Your parents always underestimated you. I could see you knew how much better you were than all the others. . ."

"That's not true!" interrupted Violet.

"I don't mean it as a criticism, my dear. You were better than the rest of them. You *are* better than them. Wouldn't it be wonderful if that status was realized? You could be the true princess that you are. All you have to do is help us. The unicorn standing before you is a great sorcerer and a natural ruler. He has been here for just a few years, yet see what he has created! This great fortress. . ."

"He forced people from their homes!"

At this, Madam Verger looked genuinely confused.

"Forced people from their homes? I'm afraid I don't know what you mean. . ."

"The Inventor Creator trolls. And Vyvlle in the spring garden."

Madam Verger threw back her head and laughed. "You cannot mean to say my master should have curbed his build at the request of a few trolls? It's not as if he harmed them in any way. They're still going about their trolly business as before."

"Without their homes, where they'd lived for centuries! I saw their beautiful floating houses, covered in ice. What he did was cruel and unnecessary. How foolish I was to trust you," said Violet.

Madam Verger stopped her laughter and tapped her sharp fingernails impatiently on her staff. Madam Verger was so different here. Back in Millbrook, she had a fragility about her but here, that was all gone.

"I can tell this is going to be more difficult than I thought," she said, "but I can promise you a better future, Violet. You would both stay here with me. Here, you won't just be the girl from the manor; you will be a princess, and Nicolas will be a prince. When the Frozen Unicorn has his own body back, there will be no stopping him. He will soon own the whole of the Far North, the Near North, and then he will take his power to other lands. . . You can be part of that. But the magic will not work with one unicorn and one person. We need you both to be in the same form. If you'll stay here with me, then you will have your spell of transformation."

Madam Verger was still smiling, wheedling.

So that was their choice. Unless they paid the price of their love, Nicolas would be trapped as a unicorn for ever. And it would anger the Frozen Unicorn. Maybe, until they relented, he would imprison them here. Or worse.

Violet's heart raced. It didn't feel like much of a choice, but it was their only chance to restore Nicolas. To get what they wanted, Violet must convince Madam Verger that they were cooperating. Then, once Nicolas was human again, they could find a way to escape, even if they had to put up a fight.

Violet glanced at Nicolas and he nodded. A very slight movement, but definitely a nod. She was sure he understood the plan. "Fine," she said. "We'll do it."

TRANSFORMATION

Madam Verger smiled and looked up at the Frozen Unicorn on the balcony. "Do you hear that?" she said. "These young people are being terribly obliging."

Madam Verger walked around Violet and Nicolas, circling

them slowly like a predator stalking her prey. Every few steps, she tapped her stick on the floor. Nicolas became agitated, tossing his head from side to side, and Violet turned to face him, putting one hand on each side of his face.

"It will all be well," she whispered. "Madam Verger will turn you back, but we won't stay for the next part. We will run, straight through the archway and back the way we came. We will get away from her. From the Frozen Unicorn. From everything."

Madam Verger's circle grew smaller still, and in a low voice she muttered some words Violet didn't understand. A spell. A spell of transformation, to bring Nicolas back to her. The Frozen Unicorn looked on from above, his horn glowing with a golden light.

Violet felt dizzy – very dizzy.

Nicolas would soon be back. Her Nicolas. As a person. She drew her hands away from him and took a step back. Nicolas wasn't changing. Four legs, mane, tail and horn. Had the spell failed? What if he had to stay like that for ever?

She saw her own panic reflected in his eyes. His ears were flicking back and forth, and his muscles were tense. A strange tingle began in her fingers and toes. If even she could feel the magic at work on Nicolas, that must be a good sign. She wanted to tell him that, but her mouth wouldn't do her bidding.

That dizziness again.

Madam Verger stopped circling. Violet stretched out her arms. They looked different – whiter. She'd been wearing Elgu's feathery snoncho, but the feathers had gone, replaced by a glossy white short-haired coat.

Her face was tingling all over too – her nose, her forehead, her ears. She tried putting her hands to her cheeks, but somehow they wouldn't reach. They wanted to stretch down to the icy floor and her feet wanted to stomp behind her. Strange, but at that moment it felt like the most natural thing in the world.

Nicolas's eyes were wide and he breathed hard through flared nostrils. His head jerked back and Violet stepped towards him, wanting to offer comfort. She brought her head to his and stayed like that until his breathing calmed.

Madam Verger stopped, turned her back on them, and walked towards the steps.

"There we have it. Our two lovebirds. No longer a unicorn and a human, but both the same, just as I promised."

The Frozen Unicorn, up on the balcony, neighed loudly in a laughing tone.

Both the same.

Violet stayed nose to nose with Nicolas, forehead to forehead, and looked down at their dark hooves, nearly touching on the icy floor.

Madam Verger hadn't turned Nicolas back into a person. She'd turned Violet into a unicorn.

CHAPTER SEVENTEEN

THE THIRD UNICORN

A unicorn. She was really a unicorn? She looked down at her sinewy white legs, reaching each forward in turn; they did seem to belong to her. She swung her heavy head right around, to look over her shoulder at her back half. She was all white, like Nicolas. She flicked her tail, which was long and black, but had more of a wave to it than his, like her human hair. A beautiful tail, but she didn't want it. She didn't want to be a unicorn. They'd been tricked again!

She threw back her head to shriek at Madam Verger, but the cry that emerged was not one she recognized as her own: it was more like a horse in distress. It startled her so much that she closed her mouth abruptly and stood still, heart beating wildly.

Violet? I'm so sorry for all of this.

Was it Nicolas, speaking to her? *Nicolas?*

Yes, it's me.

Now they were the same, they could understand each other. It was the first time she'd heard him speak since the night of the dance, and tears welled in her eyes. It was him, it really was him – not that she'd been in any doubt. For a moment, it made everything all right.

But Madam Verger's voice cut through her moment of happiness.

"How wonderful you are both reacquainted. Now, you have promised us your power. The Frozen Unicorn will do what needs to be done."

The Frozen Unicorn stared at them from the balcony, like an ice sculpture, watching their every move. He was a unicorn too, wasn't he? Could he understand what they were saying?

For that matter, could Madam Verger? She was able to interpret for the Frozen Unicorn, after all.

The Frozen Unicorn began to walk along the balcony towards the stairs, his hooves clacking loudly. Violet held her breath as he descended the stairs. She didn't want that evil creature anywhere near her.

The Frozen Unicorn left the steps, and came to stand by Madam Verger's side. He looked even bigger down on the ground. He moved his head as if he was speaking and Madam Verger watched him carefully. Violet couldn't understand the Frozen Unicorn and guessed he couldn't understand them either. But Madam Verger knew exactly what he was saying.

"My master says that all you have to do is touch your horns together. It won't hurt you. Your love is strong. It will be all the power my master needs."

No! Violet's plan might have failed, but whatever happened, she wasn't going to let him take their love.

Nicolas, I'm sorry. I thought if we agreed to what she wanted, then she would turn you back and we'd be able to get away.

I know. I understood. But Violet, we can still run.

Yes, yes, we will!

Violet tried to send him that thought while keeping her face as straight as possible. Madam Verger smiled and spoke softly.

"Violet, I know this is all a shock for you, but think it through. Try to understand what we are offering. Not a manor house, or a village, but a whole kingdom and maybe more. When my master has what he needs, he will turn you both back to your human selves. You are only in unicorn form in order to complete the process. Once that is done, you will be restored. You have my word. You must see, this way everybody wins."

Violet didn't believe her. Madam Verger had tricked them before. How could they believe she would turn them back this time?

Madam Verger sensed her hesitation, and her voice hardened. "Let me be clear, Violet. I'm afraid if you don't willingly give us what we are asking for, then we will take it anyway. Which, I assure you, will be a much less pleasant experience for you both."

Take it anyway? Madam Verger had said it was their choice. Another lie. What a fool she'd been. Violet had come all this way to find Nicolas. She had disobeyed her parents, travelled to a land she would never have imagined, and battled the elements. All because of Madam Verger – someone she'd trusted. Someone who spoke only lies.

But maybe Madam Verger had underestimated Violet. Violet loved Nicolas and she wasn't about to give that up.

Violet lowered her head and set her jaw.

They might think they were going to take her love away, but Violet wasn't going to make it easy for them.

FLIGHT

We have to get out now. Violet sent the thought to Nicolas. She didn't care about changing back into humans. Maybe someone back home would be able to restore them, or maybe not. At least they would be together.

Yes. We pretend to do whatever they want and then we run as fast as we can, replied Nicolas without looking in her direction.

They stood together side by side.

Madam Verger approached them palms facing up, as if they were dangerous dogs that needed placating.

"That's right, move a little closer and touch your horns together, then my master will take your power."

Violet heard the clack of ice meeting ice as the Frozen Unicorn moved nearer. She kept her eye on the archway, which was unobstructed. But Madam Verger was walking across the room towards it. All they needed to do was get out, retrace their steps and hope their icy pathway back to the shore hadn't yet melted into the sea. Surely they would be quicker than this pair – they had youth on their side.

Violet bowed her head towards Nicolas.

He did the same.

Their horns were a hand's width apart, and Violet felt it, the power between them that the Frozen Unicorn wanted.

"Well done," came Madam Verger's voice from over the other side of the room, as smooth as honey. "A little closer—"

The slow click-clack of the Frozen Unicorn's hooves grew closer.

But their horns didn't touch. At the last minute, they looked up and their eyes met.

"Now," screeched Madam Verger to the Frozen Unicorn.

Now! Violet sent the thought to Nicolas.

Violet and Nicolas surged forwards and galloped to the arched doorway, hooves chipping the icy floor. Madam Verger was suddenly there, arms stretched out, blocking their way, the drapes of her white dress faded and yellow against the walls. She held her staff in her hand and ground it into the floor, muttering under her breath as she did. Another spell?

Violet's heart beat uncontrollably, as Nicolas lowered his head and pointed his horn straight at Madam Verger.

No! Don't hurt her! Violet couldn't bear the thought of seeing Madam Verger harmed, despite all the deception.

But Nicolas kept his head lowered, eyes steely and determined. *I won't hurt her. She will move aside.*

Nicolas galloped forwards, white horn glinting as the sun's rays fell through the opening in the ceiling.

Violet shrieked (that horsey cry again). And, at the very last moment, with a final tap of her staff, Madam Verger stepped aside, with a look on her face of triumph, not defeat.

Without pausing to consider what this meant, Violet galloped after Nicolas into the antechamber.

To her horror, the exit was closing – two thick sheets of ice were sliding together like heavy curtains over the doorway. So this was Madam Verger's spell: to prevent their escape. Nicolas, ahead of Violet, would have just enough time to get through the shrinking gap, but he slowed, and turned to her.

Keep going, you can make it! Violet said.

But Nicolas shook his head. *I'm not going anywhere without you.*

The sheets of ice came together with a crack and Madam Verger's laughter rang out from the main hall.

TRAPPED

They both rushed forward to the blocked doorway. Violet checked frantically for a gap, a lever, anything to release them, but the ice had formed a thick, unbroken layer, like the walls around. There wasn't even any sign of a join.

Nicolas scraped the sharp tip of his horn along the ice. Tiny white flakes flew in the air. But Violet could see it was impossible. *There's no point trying: we'll never get out that way! I'm going to look for another exit.* She ran back into the main hall, swerving past Madam Verger, galloping around the edge, looking for anything: a trapdoor, a window. She even ran up the steps to where the Frozen Unicorn had stood, but there was no door or window anywhere. Just the circular hole high above them, through which a patch of blue sky was visible, like a bright eye gazing down on their misfortune. Violet retreated.

It was like her dreams of Nicolas. They were locked in an icy cell, with no windows and no doors. Only, unlike her dream, they were trapped with two people of magic who meant them harm and with no weapons to fight back.

"You won't find any way out, my dear. You will not escape unless we choose to release you," said Madam Verger.

Nicolas walked into the main room, head hanging heavily, as if he'd given up.

Madam Verger laughed again. "Here comes your True Love. Nicolas is a sensible boy. He knows you're beaten. And to think he could have escaped without you. True self-sacrifice – my master couldn't ask for more. Now, it is time to give him what he wants."

Nicolas stood by Violet, cheek to cheek, eyes flashing with defiance. *We will never do that, will we, Violet?*

The Frozen Unicorn walked towards them, taking his time. After all, why should he hurry when he had his prisoners exactly where he wanted them?

Madam Verger crossed paths with him, walked up the steps and stood on the balcony, looking down on them.

"You have heard quite enough from me," she said. "Now, you face my master, the Frozen Unicorn."

Nicolas turned to Violet. *We must separate. He wants us together. Let's not make things easy for him.*

As the Frozen Unicorn walked towards them, Nicolas trotted off in the other direction, over to the right-hand side of the room. But the Frozen Unicorn kept a steady line and walked towards Violet, hooves clacking loudly. Up close, he was a more intimidating presence than he'd been on the platform. He was at least a head taller than her and his horn looked sharp and deadly, like a shard of glass. His eyes, blank and cold like the rest of him, fixed on her and she looked away, despite herself.

She felt Nicolas's voice reassuring her.

Don't give him anything. He won't hurt us. He can't. He wants what we have.

Violet clenched her jaw, vowing not to give anything to this evil unicorn. But floating down from the platform came Madam Verger's voice.

"You foolish girl. You mean nothing to him. If you don't give him what he wants, my master will kill you both."

STRANGE SMOKE

The Frozen Unicorn's ice eyes fixed on Violet's, unblinking.

Then, without warning, he reared back on to his hind legs with a hideous cry that sounded like a scream. It was the first time Violet had heard him make a noise. Violet squeezed her eyes shut then opened them as he crashed back down with a clatter of hooves.

Nicolas began to gallop over, but she shook her head and warned him, *Keep back! Remember, we are stronger apart.*

The Frozen Unicorn was still again. Had he been putting on a show of power to scare her? Wafts of blue smoke were circling his legs, as though a fire had been lit beneath him. Violet checked for flames. Nothing. But then she saw the same blue smoke was circling her own legs. She had no idea what it was, but she sensed she needed to get far from its reach.

Violet backed off, in the direction of the antechamber, but the smoke followed her, as though it was stuck to her. And it was rising. It passed her thighs, tail, neck, and then began to swirl around her muzzle. She desperately looked up at Madam Verger but she called back down,

"I'm sorry, Violet, but you made the wrong choice."

The smoke filled her nostrils, but it wasn't like normal smoke. It was a magic fog, all around her, confusing her. She opened her mouth to take a gulp of air, but there was nothing but smoke.

She swung her head from side to side trying to escape it, spluttering, but there was no getting away: it was as if she was caught in a cloud.

The Frozen Unicorn watched her. Waiting. But for what?

Nicolas's voice floated across to her from the other side of the room.

Violet, are you all right?

She tried to nod, to catch his eye and tell him she would be fine, but she could no longer see him; everything was a blur. White-blue. Bluwhite. She invented that colour when she left Elgu's. She remembered it like a dream. Walking through snow. Was she caught in a snowstorm now? She couldn't remember. She tried to turn again, to escape the strange smoke, but she forgot she now had four legs. They buckled beneath her and she slumped to the floor. When she tried to right herself, she couldn't even stand.

Violet lay on her side, her cheek resting on the cold hard ice, blinking, trying to keep her eyes open. Somewhere in the blur of colour and sound she could see Nicolas's face. His eyes told her how much he wanted to save her, but she knew that was a bad idea. If he came to save her, then the Frozen Unicorn would no doubt choose that moment to take what he wanted.

She tried to warn him: *Watch out, Nicolas! Keep away!* but she still couldn't think straight. Her mind span. She had no idea if her words were reaching him as they had before. He began to gallop towards her, no longer keeping his distance. By targeting her, the Frozen Unicorn was controlling them both.

The smoke around her began to dissipate as the Frozen Unicorn turned away from her and towards Nicolas. Violet snorted and found she could think straight again. She raised her head, but she still couldn't stand: when she tried, her hooves scrabbled uselessly on the floor.

From up on the balcony, Madam Verger laughed.

"Now, Master!" she cried, pointing at Nicolas. "Just look at his face!"

Nicolas's ears were pinned back, his teeth bared and his expression fierce. She didn't know what was strongest – his love for her or his hatred for their enemy – but whatever it was, it was powerful. She could see why the Frozen Unicorn wanted this emotion.

No – keep back! warned Violet, but Nicolas didn't listen.

The Frozen Unicorn met Nicolas before he reached Violet and clashed his horn against Nicolas's like a sword. Sparks flew between them. Nicolas fought back, jabbing right and left, trying to defend himself, but also to inflict some damage on his enemy. But the Frozen Unicorn was bigger, stronger, more experienced.

The Frozen Unicorn lowered his head. At first, Violet thought he was aiming for Nicolas's face, and she cried out, making that same desperate sound. But then the deadly tip of the Frozen Unicorn's horn met Nicolas's. As he held it there, Nicolas's eyes flashed with alarm.

Madam Verger shrieked with glee. "You've done it, Master!"

A pulsing bright blue light flooded the Frozen Unicorn's body, starting in his horn and lighting up his head, neck, body, tail, legs. Then it disappeared, leaving him as transparent as before. That light, gone in seconds, recharged the Frozen Unicorn with an energy, a pulse of life, that wasn't there before.

Nicolas fell to the floor.

The Frozen Unicorn turned to look triumphantly at Violet.

His eyes were no longer frozen and blank. They were now a deep, dark blue, like the ocean she and Nicolas had crossed, and just as threatening.

CHAPTER EIGHTEEN

THE POWER

While the Frozen Unicorn's deep blue eyes were now full of colour and vibrancy, Nicolas lay crumpled on the icy floor. Like Violet, but completely still. His coat and mane were dull, greyer than before.

Nicolas, can you hear me?

There was no response.

Was Nicolas dead? He couldn't be. Violet lifted her head, desperately searching for any sign of life. His nostrils flared and his flank was rising and falling weakly. He was still breathing.

Stay with me, Nicolas.

Were her words even reaching him now? The Frozen Unicorn stood with one front hoof on Nicolas's flank. He would show no mercy, but he wanted Violet too. Madam Verger had said her master needed the power from them both. He wasn't going to rest with one.

It would be so easy to close her eyes and give up. To give in. Maybe that's what she would have done before. What was it Nicolas had said to her on the hill at Millbrook?

At some point, you're going to either have to stop falling over, or pick yourself up.

That had been a few weeks ago, but it felt like a lifetime.

And Nicolas had been right. There had always been someone to come to her assistance. Her parents, the manor servants, Nicolas himself. Even after she left Millbrook and came to the North, Nicolas had kept rescuing her. She was sure he had been the one (in unicorn form) who'd taken her to Elgu's door. When she'd been ice-skating, the fairies had helped pick her up after her fall. She never rescued herself. But who was going to help her now? Not Nicolas. Not Madam Verger. And certainly not the Frozen Unicorn.

Not only was Nicolas unable to save her, but he needed her. She couldn't continue to lie there doing nothing. She took two deep breaths, summoned all her reserves, and, on wobbly hooves, she stood up.

Violet began to walk across the room to where Nicolas lay. The Frozen Unicorn stepped off Nicolas and increased the threat, pointing his horn at Nicolas's side. All the time his eyes flashed as he goaded her to come closer.

She knew it didn't matter to the Frozen Unicorn if they were alive or dead. He had what he wanted from Nicolas now, and he wanted the same thing from her. He knew Violet couldn't stand by and watch as he inflicted hurt on her True Love. She was going to defend Nicolas as the Frozen Unicorn expected her to. He would try to take that power, that love, from her. But Violet was determined to beat the Frozen Unicorn at his own game.

Back in Millbrook, Madam Verger had assured her Violet's own power was stronger.

. . . You have a far greater power. Something that will keep you warm in the bleakest conditions, make you strong when you are weak.

And, although Madam Verger had lied to her about many things, Violet believed this to be true. She could feel it, despite the weakness in her body. She felt the strength running through her veins, in her four limbs and the horn on her head, which tingled as though it wanted to be used. All her love for Nicolas, everything she'd risked to save him, mixed with her hatred for this unicorn who was trying to take a special thing and make it his.

As she walked past the steps, she glanced up at Madam Verger. The smile on the old woman's face wavered a little.

"Be careful, Master," she called in a low voice, but the Frozen Unicorn snorted derisively at the advice. He couldn't see the strength that Violet felt, even if Madam Verger could.

Violet continued walking right over to where Nicolas lay, the Frozen Unicorn's horn pointing towards him. Up close, she could see the weak wisps of his breath in the cold air. Violet walked right up to them and pointed *her* horn at the Frozen Unicorn's body.

Get away from him. Now.

The Frozen Unicorn raised his head and stood back a couple of paces, staring at Violet. This time she met his gaze, refusing to look away. The stormy blue of his eyes angered her. That spark of life was not his – he had stolen it from Nicolas. And she was ready to fight him for it.

THE FIGHT

"That's right, Violet." Madam Verger's voice was clear but low. "Anger is good. Defend your love."

Violet blocked the old woman's words from her mind. She'd

watched the last fight and she knew what the Frozen Unicorn was going to try to do. Nicolas's mistake had been to let the point of his enemy's horn meet his own. If Violet did the same, then all her power, the love she felt for Nicolas, would flow from her horn into the Frozen Unicorn's.

She would not let this happen.

The effects of the smoke were long gone. She knew the Frozen Unicorn wouldn't use that magic again, because he needed her to be strong and fighting. He'd only used it before to lure Nicolas in. He had used her as bait and it had worked.

Nicolas's eyes flickered open.

She met his gaze. *Don't worry, I won't let him hurt you.*

Then, summoning all her strength, all her love, she jabbed at the Frozen Unicorn with her horn, one side, then the other. He was forced to abandon Nicolas to defend himself, meeting her jabs with the side of his horn.

"Don't stand for this!" Madam Verger screeched from the balcony, and the Frozen Unicorn reared back on his hind legs and roared. The deep, grating sound took Violet by surprise. He clattered back down, his hooves almost scraping Nicolas.

This angered her further.

When he reared up and back a second time, Violet was

prepared, and lunged towards him. As his front hooves began to fall back to earth and he lowered his horn to meet hers, as she'd guessed he would, Violet moved to the left.

"Watch out!" Madam Verger called to her unicorn master.

But the warning came too late. Violet lowered her head and pointed her horn not towards his horn, but to his very centre, to his frozen heart.

She concentrated all her love for Nicolas and her anger at their enemy towards the Frozen Unicorn, and it was powerful indeed. She felt a surge of this power shoot from her, and she saw it too: a violet light aiming straight and true, hitting the Frozen Unicorn in the breast.

His whole body lit up from within with an eerie light.

"No!" Violet cried. She'd inadvertently given him her power, as he'd wanted.

But he stayed, motionless, rearing up, back legs tensed, front legs held before him as if he were scrabbling at mid-air. The Frozen Unicorn was truly frozen. Rays of multicoloured light shot out of his horn, his hooves, his whole body.

Then there was a familiar sound. A high crackle of ice breaking. A fine pattern of jagged white lines spread across his static body.

Madam Verger screamed.

Violet leapt back and stood, gasping for breath.

And the Frozen Unicorn shattered into thousands of icy splinters.

THOUSANDS OF PIECES

The explosion was like nothing Violet had ever heard, as if the very roof had blasted off the Ice Fortress. If she could have put her hands over her ears then she would have done. As it was, she closed her eyes and turned her head away, hearing the tinkle of shards of ice hitting the walls and floor.

She cowered on the floor as tiny pieces of ice rained down upon her. They hit her limbs like tiny pinpricks, and tangled in her mane. Then bigger pieces started to fall. Icicles from the ceiling itself. This could be the end of everything.

But then the icy rain slowed and all she could hear was a voice screeching, "No!"

Violet blinked her eyes open. Madam Verger was inching down the steps on the other side of the room, one hand holding the spiky banister and the other clutching her raised staff. Chips of ice fell from her as she walked.

"What have you done?" the old woman cried, and Violet shook her head. She hardly knew what she'd done herself. All she knew was the Frozen Unicorn had gone. Ice was heaped up in a pile where he'd stood, and scattered widely around the room. The tiniest pieces that made her think of the broken snow globe in the Orchard House.

Violet bent and scooped up a handful, which straight away began to melt in her palm. Nothing special; just ice. How could such a terrible foe, in the end, be so fragile?

It took a moment to realize the hand holding these fragments was *her* hand – her very own human hand. She was no longer a unicorn: the spell was broken. She felt the shape of her face, and ran her gloved fingers through her hair, brushing out even more ice.

"I'm back," she said in disbelief, enjoying hearing her own voice once again. Even her old knapsack was still on her back, where it had been before she'd transformed.

All the Frozen Unicorn's magic had broken with him.

Nicolas, still lying slumped on the floor, covered in fragments of ice, had also regained his human form. Even after everything, he looked the same. The same floppy hair, the same brown eyes, just a little paler than before.

"Nicolas!" called Violet.

He smiled weakly at her and began to lean on his arms and

push himself up slowly, dodging to one side as an icicle came plummeting down from above. Violet looked up. The open circle in the roof was widening as the surrounding icicles snapped and plunged to the frozen floor. The icicles that made up the walls followed, their sharp points creating zig-zagging fissures on the floor.

Madam Verger had neared the bottom of the staircase. She waved her staff at the roof and chanted desperately, but the very steps she was standing on began to collapse. She shrieked, toppled, and slid down the last to the floor, screeching curses into the freezing air.

Without his magic to hold it together, everything the Frozen Unicorn had built was crashing down. This whole place was breaking apart, with them trapped inside.

Violet rushed to Nicolas and helped him to his feet. They stood, arms around each other, forehead to forehead and nose to nose, as they had before, but as people, not unicorns. Nicolas said nothing and nor did Violet.

Sometimes words were overrated.

CHAPTER NINETEEN

FLOATING

Time passed slowly. A howling wind blew, and crashes came from all around – some of them frighteningly close. Madam Verger was hunched on the floor, where the bottom of the staircase had been. She dropped her staff and clung to the broken banister as she might cling to the mast of a sinking ship. Violet and Nicolas clung to each other.

A great chunk of ceiling dropped from above and Madam Verger was blocked from view.

"Close your eyes," whispered Nicolas, as he stroked Violet's hair.

She closed her eyes and, despite the noise all around, felt a kind of peace. If this was the end, then at least they were together. She concentrated only on what she knew at that moment. His heartbeat. Her own breath. The scent of him.

"I saw what you did. You were so brave," he murmured.

Before she could reply, an icicle slashed past her right arm – the one missing its feathered sleeve. It sliced through the thin fabric of the tunic and she winced as the blood beaded up. Nicolas pulled her tighter. They would survive, or they wouldn't. Together.

"Remember the woods in Millbrook?" she whispered.

Nicolas nodded and she snuggled into his chest, remembering. She thought of Millbrook, of her parents, of Nicolas's family and the hall decorated for Wintertide. She thought of reflections in the millpond and the view of the village from above. She thought of Elgu's cosy home and the colour of the sky above the Inventor Trolls' tents.

When she'd run out of comforting things to think about, she remembered once again she was standing in the middle of a broken fortress with her beloved.

But by that time, the crashes were coming less often. Until all she could hear was the wind and, strangely, the waves.

Nicolas squeezed her arm gently. "Violet?"

She opened her eyes, squinting into the new brightness. She didn't look around yet – she just looked at him. Those familiar brown eyes.

"Nicolas."

They kissed softly on the lips.

He broke away and smiled.

"I like your new outfit," he said, running his hands along the feathers on her back. "It's much more fetching than the one you were wearing to greet me in the woods."

Violet thought of all the unbecoming layers she'd been wearing and managed a small laugh, then kissed him again.

She dared to look around.

The landscape had changed. The monstrosity of the Ice Fortress had gone: broken into pieces like the Frozen Unicorn. Once-deadly icicles floated on the water like flotsam from its wreckage.

It had fallen all around them, yet somehow they'd survived, floating on an iceberg that had, moments before, been part of the floor.

"I think it's all over," said Violet, taking a small step back. Nicolas caught her arm and part of the edge broke away. It was only then Violet realized how small an ice chunk they were standing on. And it was getting increasingly smaller, melting away into the sea.

"Not quite over yet then," she said, wrinkling her brow. They might have survived the fall of the Ice Fortress, but they still had to get back to land. They faced much the same predicament as they had before: multiple icebergs bobbed in the water, spaced too far apart to act as stepping stones.

Violet shielded her eyes from the sun and looked back out to shore, trying to see the route they'd taken. From the looks of things, their ice pebble path had melted. If any of it remained, it was still a long way away.

"Aren't they your friends' houses?" Nicolas drew her attention to the trolls' houses, still in the same spot they'd always been.

"Oh yes!" The blocks of ice around each of the trolls' homes had disappeared, presumably shattered like the unicorn himself. The jewel-coloured structures glistened in the sunshine – new and inviting. Another reminder the Frozen Unicorn really was gone and all his evil magic destroyed. The trolls would be able to return to their homes and life could continue here for everyone as it had before he arrived.

It could continue for Violet and Nicolas too, if only they could get back to shore.

Nicolas looked wistfully at the nearest iceberg.

"If I was still a unicorn, I could've made that jump."

Violet smiled, despite their situation. She'd been right, then, in the forest. Being a unicorn hadn't been all bad for Nicolas.

"I can't believe you're missing life as a unicorn already! Well, I for one am content to be human again and to have you back. And I'm very glad you won't be making any more dangerous jumps in the near future."

Nicolas laughed. "Without my dangerous jumps, we are somewhat stranded."

Violet managed a small laugh back, although her chest felt tight with worry. She looked all around her for inspiration – a plan. It had worked every other time, after all. Nicolas gazed out to sea and Violet looked back towards the coast. She was squinting into the bright sun, trying to assess how far out they were, when a shout came from her left.

"What have you done, you foolish girl?"

MADAM VERGER

Madam Verger.

So Violet and Nicolas weren't the only survivors. There she was, peering out from the remains of the staircase, which was floating on an iceberg similar to their own. She was some distance away, but near enough to hear, and she looked a lonely figure, her robes faded against the crisp white ice. Her hair had come loose from her usual plait and long strands were plastered across her face. A long red scratch marked her left cheek from her eye to her mouth.

"You think you will get away with this? You could have had so much. You could have been rulers of a great new kingdom, but now you will perish here in the Far North."

Violet glanced at Nicolas, who shrugged and looked away from the old woman as if she wasn't even there. She wished they had an answer, but there was none. Madam Verger was almost certainly correct.

"You'll perish too!" Violet called out. Nicolas raised his eyebrows. Yes, it was a pathetic reply, but the best she could manage.

Madam Verger laughed, the sound carrying towards them on the breeze like the sound of a seabird.

"You have no idea of my power; you never have. Foolish girl."

She spat out the last words and retreated back behind the broken banisters, peering out as if through the bars of a cage.

Nicolas whispered to Violet, "I know her power only too

well, but it doesn't seem to be able to move her off that iceberg – otherwise why isn't she laughing at us from the shore?"

Then Violet noticed something she'd thought was driftwood floating in the water near to Madam Verger's iceberg. "Isn't that her staff?"

Nicolas nodded in a small movement. "Don't draw her attention to it – she might not have seen it. Without it, she's just as powerless as us."

"True, but her iceberg is bigger," whispered Violet, panic rising within her. "How are we going to get to shore before ours melts away? And even if we do, how will we ever get home?"

As soon as she said it, she realized the solution and grinned at Nicolas.

"Madam Verger's right – I am a foolish girl! I forgot I have our ticket home right here with me."

SUMMONING HELP

Violet had been so intent on finding a way back to shore, she'd forgotten all about the blowing horn. She held it out on its leather strap and showed Nicolas.

"We don't have to get back to the mainland. We can go straight home. All I have to do is summon our ride."

Nicolas narrowed his eyes. "And what sort of ride would that be?"

"You'll see," said Violet, putting the mouthpiece to her lips. Without hesitation, she blew.

The sound that emerged from the horn was loud and haunting. It was unmistakeably a wolf's howl. Violet couldn't believe she hadn't recognized it as such on the mountainside at Wending.

Nicolas knew it straight away. "A wolf?"

Violet nodded. "A flying wolf. Candra. I just hope she can hear us all the way out here."

"*Flying* wolf. . .?"

Madam Verger laughed again from over on her iceberg. "So, that's your plan, is it, Violet?"

Violet tensed at the familiar cackle and tried to ignore her, searching the skies for giant wings.

"How long will it take?" asked Nicolas, but Violet shrugged, worried about Madam Verger's mocking laughter. It was possible the old woman had lied to her about this as well as everything else. Maybe there was no ride home.

Violet swallowed and kept looking up, watching, waiting. If much more of their iceberg disappeared, they would be plunged into the icy waters. Pushing thoughts of drowning away, she kept her gaze up.

Within minutes, she caught sight of a small dark shape in the clouds, which could easily have been mistaken for a bird. Violet knew it wasn't, though, from the slow, measured flap of its wings and the way it was heading straight for them. The shape gradually became more distinct and Candra came into sight, the beat of her wings growing louder and louder. Then a shadow fell over them as Candra flew overhead. It was as it had been in Wending, only this time Violet wasn't afraid; she was exhilarated.

Nicolas turned to Violet, open-mouthed.

"It really is a *flying* wolf!"

Violet nodded. "She brought me to the North."

"You flew on the back of a wolf?" Nicolas laughed as if he couldn't believe it, and took her by the hand. "You're amazing, Violet Reddmene."

And at that moment, Violet felt that maybe she was.

But then Madam Verger whistled and Candra's ears pricked up. She soared down and landed on Madam Verger's iceberg, where she squatted back on her hind legs, wings folded.

Madam Verger smiled widely and put a proprietorial hand at the back of her neck.

"Foolish, foolish girl," she called to Violet. "You do realize you have just summoned my transport home?"

LOYAL HOUND

Violet's face fell at the sight of Candra sitting on Madam Verger's iceberg like a loyal hound.

Madam Verger stroked the wolf's head and patted her back.

"She took you on one journey, summoned by *my* horn, and you thought she would come to you?"

Candra blinked slowly, turning her head to look at Madam Verger, then Violet and Nicolas.

"These creatures once flew around the mountains, too scared to come near to a human being. I have trained and flown with three generations of wolves, yet you really thought she'd come to you?"

Violet remembered the name band she'd removed from Candra's leg, which could have only been Madam Verger's doing. She could think of no response – she just lowered her head sadly.

"Don't worry, Violet," said Nicolas. "We'll think of something else. We've come this far together."

Another chunk of their iceberg fell into the water. Despite

Nicolas's optimism, coming up with a new plan in time felt highly unlikely to Violet.

But as she looked up, she realized Candra's gaze was now fixed on her, head cocked to one side as if she was wondering why Violet was sad. This wolf was an intelligent creature. Violet had known that on the mountainside, despite her initial fear. Candra had understood her, and Violet knew that the wolf was, on some deep level, a good creature. She'd felt the same when she'd first met Nicolas in unicorn form, and she wished she'd listened to her instincts then. Candra might initially follow horns and whistles, but Violet suspected she could make her own decisions.

Violet began speaking to Candra, very softly, so Madam Verger couldn't hear the words. She felt that Candra would understand the sentiment.

"She's not a nice person," Violet whispered, looking directly at the wolf. "Do you remember your sore leg? Would she have cared about that?"

The wolf didn't take her eyes off Violet and wriggled away from Madam Verger's stroking. Madam Verger dropped her arm to her side. At the same time, she seemed to spot something in the water nearby.

"My staff!" She pointed at the gnarled stick, floating past. "Candra, bring it to me."

"Oh no," said Nicolas, closing his eyes for a second.

Violet continued in the same low voice, ignoring Madam Verger and speaking only to Candra.

"I understand you helping her – she had me fooled too – but we're the ones who need your help now. We really, really do. Please help us. Not her."

Suddenly, the wolf took off from Madam Verger's iceberg. Her great wings opened and flapped so suddenly that the old woman was nearly knocked into the freezing ocean.

"Come back! Bring me my staff, you stupid creature!" Madam Verger screeched. She broke an icicle from the broken bannisters and threw it at the wolf, but it fell far short.

Candra didn't change course, or even look back. She'd made her decision.

"This animal is clearly a better judge of character than Madam Verger realized," said Nicolas.

There was no room to land on Nicolas and Violet's iceberg. Candra flew on to the nearest one, and with a front paw in the water on either side, paddled over so she was right next to them, then sat back on the iceberg.

Overwhelmed with relief, Violet leaned across and flung her arms around the wolf's neck in thanks. Then Nicolas and Violet crossed carefully over to Candra's iceberg, their own tiny chunk of ice breaking in two as they left it.

"How is your leg?" Violet asked the wolf.

Candra raised her paw. The skin still looked a little pink where the leather band had been, but the fur was growing back nicely. She crouched down as she had in Wending, as if inviting Violet to climb on her back.

"I'll sit in front of her wings, you sit behind," said Violet to Nicolas, assuming the same riding position as she had in Wending. It was much easier in her new, practical clothes.

Nicolas stood where he was, running one hand through his hair. "So, you actually expect me to climb on to this wolf?"

"Yes."

"And to fly home?"

"Yes, and don't take all day about it."

Nicolas took a deep breath, and climbed on to Candra's back behind Violet.

"Do they fly very high?"

She laughed. "I felt the same way the first time I flew, but I promise there's nothing to be afraid of."

"I can't believe I'm doing this," said Nicolas, and he put his hands around Violet's waist.

Within seconds of Nicolas settling into position, the great creature flapped her wings and they took off into the sky.

They circled Madam Verger's iceberg a few times. The old woman was crouched down, reaching into the water for her staff, which remained just out of reach. She stood and shouted up at them, loose hair blowing around her face.

"I am ordering you to drop those two people right now. Throw them into the ocean, and come back down and get me. At once!"

But Candra ignored the rant. She looked away from Madam Verger, put her nose down and flew off in the direction of the shore.

FLYING HOME

Whyever had Violet kept her eyes closed on her journey to the North? She'd missed out on so much. The opportunity to view the world from up above, like a bird. The joy. The excitement of it all.

In many ways, her eyes had been closed her whole life. She had been closed to new experiences, to meeting new people. She hadn't known this wonderful world was out here. She felt as though she was emerging from hibernation, just like one of Elgu's little animals. From now on, she was going to open her heart to other people and take any new experience she could.

They flew over the beach and the great mass of forest that they'd ridden through only that morning. They were following the river south. Soon, they'd reach the Inventor Creator trolls. She checked the stripes in the sky.

"It will be a pink sky again tonight!" she cried.

"And you ... like pink?" Nicolas smiled lopsidedly, missing the significance.

Violet was too busy looking at the ground below to reply. The trolls' encampment must be right below them somewhere. It was near the forest by the river. There it was! And, as she'd expected, all the trolls were flooding out from their houses, ready to gather the pure colour.

The pebbles weren't flying yet, which was good; she didn't want to frighten the wolf. The stripy-hatted troll was the first to spot them as she checked the sky. She waved a giant wave. Others noticed and soon they were all waving. Hefta and the others must have been somewhere down there but Violet couldn't tell.

"He's gone! He's really gone! You can have your homes back now!" Violet shouted as loudly as she could. At first she wasn't sure that they'd heard her, but then they all looked so excited and started to dance with celebration, and tears sprang to her eyes.

"Goodbye! Thank you!" she called, and kept waving, long after they'd disappeared from view, just in case.

Seeing the trolls triggered something within Violet and she cried for a little while. Tears of relief that they were finally heading home, and sadness she would probably never see the trolls again. She even cried a little for Madam Verger. Millbrook wouldn't feel the same without her, but she was not the person Violet had thought she was: she never had been. She wondered what would become of her.

Behind her, Nicolas sensed her sadness and held his arms around her a little tighter.

THE ACTUAL LAST FIRECONE

They landed in almost exactly the same place that Violet had left, just four days ago. The clearing on the lower slopes of Wending.

Patches of snow were dotted around, but they could see grass and leaves and earth. It was cold, but not the sort of cold that bit through her clothes and made her shiver. This must have been what Violet's world had always looked like in the winter, but it seemed different to her now. They thanked Candra, over and over, but the wolf shook away their embraces and walked off into the trees, looking back just once. Violet touched the blowing horn lightly, wondering if she would ever use it again and if Candra would come if she did. She suspected not.

Violet removed her gloves happily and thrust her bare hands deep into her pockets. There at the bottom was a familiar bumpy shape. A firecone. She took it out. It must have been there the whole time, but how? Violet cast her mind back. She'd been about to start a fire just before the scent of the spring garden had lured her in. She'd put it into her pocket, she remembered now. As she stared at it, she thought of Elgu's house, of lighting fires by the side of the frozen river, of that time she thought she'd used her last firecone. She could have frozen in the night in the forest and, all the while, this had been in her pocket.

"Are you all right, Violet?" asked Nicolas, standing at her side.

She showed him the silver pine cone.

"I found this in my pocket. What a waste!"

"Why, what is it?"

"It's a firecone: it makes fire. We could have had a roaring blaze that night out in the forest. Or I could have used it in the Ice Fortress."

"Used it how?"

"I don't know. Somehow. Like a weapon, maybe? We could have melted the fortress. Or the Frozen Unicorn himself. Or—"

"—I think you did very well without the help of any firecones, Violet."

She shuddered, remembering the sound of splintering ice. The pathetic sight of Madam Verger on that iceberg.

"I'm not sure I did *well*. I did what I had to do."

Nicolas nodded. He understood, she thought. "Anyway, I'm glad you didn't use it."

"Why?"

"Right now is the perfect time for a fire."

Violet smiled. She needed to sit and gather her thoughts. "I agree."

Nicolas took the firecone from her and rolled it around in his hand. "How do I make this thing work?"

Violet snatched it back, playfully. "Let me. You might be the Millbrook stone-skimming champion, but I'm the best Wending firecone-thrower."

She threw it hard at the ground, with her best firecone flourish, and it erupted instantly in a satisfying blaze. Her best throw yet.

"Impressive," said Nicolas, sitting down next to the fire and smiling up at her.

She joined him there, knees drawn up to her chest, feeling the comforting warmth of the fire penetrate her clothes. For a couple of minutes, neither of them said a word. Then, from down below, they heard music. A piano and people singing.

"I recognize that song," said Nicolas.

Violet strained to hear the words.

> *Embrace your loved ones; hold them near*
> *And raise a glass for Winter cheer!*

"It's Wintertide," said Violet, counting off the days on her fingers, "tomorrow!"

Nicolas smiled and they listened together, humming along to the familiar tune.

"We could go down to the inn, for food and lodgings for the night, and return to Millbrook in the morning," suggested Nicolas, after a while.

Violet shook her head. "I have a few coins, but only enough for food, not accommodation. Why don't you buy some provisions from the inn and we'll spend the night here?"

"Here on the mountain?"

"Yes! It'll be warm compared to the Far North."

Violet wasn't ready to go home yet. She wasn't sure she had the energy to provide all the necessary explanations.

"I'll stay here and tend the fire while you approach the inn. It's just a few minutes away down the hill – the first building you come to. Here, take my bag for the food."

Nicolas hesitated. "Will you be all right on your own?"

The question made Violet smile. "I should think so," she said.

With Nicolas gone, she worked on making their temporary camp as comfortable as possible. She spread her spare blankets by the fireside, singing along to the Wintertide songs. She wetted a clean handkerchief in the snow and wound it around the cut on her arm to soothe it.

Before too long, Nicolas returned with the bag stuffed full of food.

"It looks like those few coins stretched a long way," remarked Violet as she peeked inside. They had a couple of hot pies, a thick wedge of iced fruit cake, apples and a glass bottle of fresh milk.

"I believe they felt sorry for me, with no place to stay the night before Wintertide."

They sat on the blankets and tore into the pies straight away. Violet hadn't eaten a thing since the nuts and berries that morning, and the flaky pastry and rich hot filling were gloriously satisfying. They ate the cake and apples as the sun dipped below the mountains. Then, finally, they had a chance to discuss everything that had taken place over the past week.

"What happened, Nicolas? I know it was Madam Verger who turned you into a unicorn, but how? She came to your house in the village, didn't she? She left that wreath on the door?"

"No. I didn't see a wreath or anything. She must have done that when I'd gone, as a clue for you."

"How did it happen, then?"

Nicolas sighed. "It was the night of the dance. After our quarrel."

Violet lowered her eyes. "I shouldn't have got so angry—"

"—No! It was all my fault. I'm so sorry. I should have danced with you. I shouldn't have been so proud. I knew it that evening, even as you walked home. I was so angry, but angry with myself for spoiling things between us. I started for home, but then she was there, on the path."

"Madam Verger?"

"Yes. She'd overheard our quarrel, and she said she could help."

"She said the same to me!" Those shutters opening and closing. Madam Verger had been eavesdropping on the whole conversation.

Nicolas sighed again. "She invited me in and gave me a slice of cake, as she always does . . . did. She said she could fix everything."

"Madam Verger had a way of making one believe her, didn't she?"

Nicolas nodded, head down, and fiddled with his coat sleeves. "She offered me great riches – a title. She said she could make me worthy of your love."

"Oh, Nicolas." He raised his gaze and she looked him in the eyes. "Was that when she used her power to transform you?"

"Yes. She spoke of the Ice Fortress and a powerful sorcerer. I hardly knew what I was agreeing to until it was too late. Of course, she never said anything about turning me into a unicorn."

Violet could well believe it. It was exactly how Madam Verger had tricked her, after all.

"I suppose the same thing happened to all those other people. Madam Verger said they were so much older than her; they probably died years ago. But it can't have been Madam Verger taking them back then – the Frozen Unicorn must have worked alone."

Nicolas shook his head. "There were no other missing people! No prisoners. It was all lies. Madam Verger's stories were just that: stories."

All lies. For years, Madam Verger painted such a picture with her stories that they were ready to believe it all.

"And the Frozen Unicorn couldn't have brought winter to Millbrook, could he?"

"No! It just snowed, as it sometimes does. Madam Verger had been waiting for her moment and when the snow came, she seized the opportunity."

Violet nodded. The snow in Millbrook hadn't even been that deep. Madam Verger was the one who kept saying it was the worst she'd ever seen. There was so much that was only now becoming clear.

Violet watched the flames for a moment, remembering how the fairies had laughed as they danced in the smoke.

"There's one more thing I don't understand. How did Madam Verger manage to get you to the Far North?" She knew he hadn't travelled by flying wolf, and it was hard to imagine bundling a unicorn into the back of a carriage.

"I travelled there myself. On foot, or hoof, I suppose. Up mountains, across plains, over rivers. I barely stopped."

"Why?"

"To rescue you."

"But I was rescuing you!"

"I know. Madam Verger told me she'd persuaded you. I couldn't keep approaching you. I was frightened of being seen by anyone else, so while you were preparing for Wending, I was galloping as fast as I could to the Far North. To meet you."

Violet closed her eyes for a moment, catching up with this new information. When she opened them, she could see clearly.

"It was you I saw, wasn't it? Out in the snow, in the woods?"

"Yes. I'm sorry I scared you. Without my human voice, I had no way to tell you who I was. And then you hit your head. I felt terrible but I knew there was a house right nearby and I took you there."

"Thank you."

"Whose house was it? It looked so cosy, and I had a good feeling about the place, but of course you can never be sure."

Violet laughed. "Oh, it was certainly cosy. The cosiest place I've ever been. I'm so glad you took me there." The journey would have been very different without Elgu's advice and her troll-made clothing and firecones.

As the fire continued to blaze on the mountainside, she told Nicolas all about Elgu, and the River Fairies, the Inventor Creator Trolls and the spring garden. He shook his head in wonder.

"I can hardly believe what you went through, Violet. Didn't you ever want to turn back?"

"Plenty of times. Most of the time. Then I would think of you, alone and cold in the Ice Fortress, which is where I *thought* you were, and I just kept going."

Nicolas took her hand and she threaded her fingers between his. He squeezed them tightly.

"You're a very special person, Violet. But then I've always known that. To think I said you needed to get away from Millbrook, to have some adventures!"

Violet laughed. "I remember you saying that!"

She didn't say it, but he'd been right. She had needed to get away. And although at times it had been more difficult than she could have imagined, she didn't regret it. She could never regret it.

They sat for a moment, hands entwined, watching shapes dance in the fire. Then Nicolas turned to her, his expression serious.

"Do you think you have had your fill of adventure, or might you be ready to have some more?" He paused, flicked the dark lock of hair out of his eyes. "With me, I mean. After we've reassured everyone we are safe. I'd like to travel. To see things. To have adventures together."

Violet smiled and reached up to brush the lock of hair back from his forehead. "I would like that very much."

MANY YEARS LATER

IN MILLBROOK

CHAPTER TWENTY

APPLE CAKE AND STORIES

"Tell us about the snow, Mama!"

Violet smiled and unlocked the glass cabinet in the corner of the room. Madam Verger's glass cabinet, although the old curiosities were long gone. Now it was full of their own curiosities: Violet's and Nicolas's. Objects picked up from their travels in far-off lands and distant corners of the kingdom. Objects that brought back special memories. Objects that told their stories.

She selected a snow globe. Not the one she'd broken all those years ago; that was beyond repair. But a similar one, with two unicorns, rather than one, standing in a snowy scene.

Violet handed it to her son. He shook the glass sphere, and as snow fell in the tiny model world, she drew him on to her lap. Of all her children, Larch was the one who reminded her the most of Nicolas when he was a child, with the dark lock of hair that fell over his forehead. His older sister, Ember, looked more like Violet. She didn't like to sit, even for stories, and was twirling a makeshift sword around her head. Their baby sister wasn't settling for her nap, so Nicolas stood, gently rocking her with a practised motion.

"So, you want to hear about the snow. The snow in the Far North?" asked Violet.

Larch nodded seriously and tucked one curled hand under his cheek, leaving the other hand free to fiddle with the locket around his mother's neck. A single violet, pressed in glass and threaded on to a ribbon tie.

He waited for the familiar story.

"Ah, the snow was like no snow you've ever seen," said Violet with a smile. "It made everything white. The ground, the trees, even the sky was white, and the river was frozen solid."

"Was that the river you ice-skated on?" asked Ember, dropping the sword for a moment.

"Yes, with some help from the fairies."

"*Really* with fairies?" Ember joined them but remained standing.

"Yes!"

"What were their names?" asked Ember suspiciously.

"I don't know – I didn't ask! They didn't speak our language, anyway."

"Did you rescue Papa?" asked Larch.

"We rescued each other."

Nicolas smiled from over by the window, still jiggling the baby. "Your mother is being modest. She did most of the rescuing."

Larch's eyes were wide. "From the bad unicorn?"

"Yes, from the bad unicorn. He was really a bad man, who changed into a unicorn."

"Do people sometimes do that – turn into unicorns?"

Violet and Nicolas exchanged a pointed look.

"Some people do. And they say once you have that power, it never leaves you."

Larch lost interest and closed his eyes for a moment. But Ember's curiosity had been piqued.

"Was Grandmama very cross when you returned home to Millbrook?" Ember loved her Grandmama, but she could be very stern sometimes and had a lot of rules.

Violet and Nicolas exchanged smiles.

"She was mainly just pleased to see us both safely home," said Nicolas.

"Although she was a *little* cross," admitted Violet. "And she never did believe what we told her about unicorns."

"Is that why we live in our own little house and not up at the manor with Grandmama – because she was so cross?"

Violet laughed. Ember did ask unexpected questions sometimes.

"No," said Nicolas. Baby Mitty had fallen asleep in his arms, but he was pacing around the room for fear of waking her again. "Granny and Grandpa Evergreen live in the village. Grandmama and Grandpapa Reddmene live at the manor."

"So it made sense for us to meet in the middle," said Violet, with a smile.

"That's why we're now the Evermenes. Besides, someone needed to look after the orchard when the Orchardess moved on."

"Why, Ember – do you wish we lived up at the manor with Grandmama?" Nicolas asked the question gently, but Violet could tell he was worried about what the answer would be.

Ember thought for a moment. "Nah, the manor's too dark and draughty. It's good for visits—"

"—and hide and seek—" added Larch.

"—but here is much more homely—"

"—and we never run out of apple cake." Larch sat up abruptly. "May I have a slice, Mama?"

"Of course," said Violet, turning to the freshly baked cake on the low table beside her. "You can never have enough apple cake."

"Or stories," added Ember.

"Or stories," agreed Violet. She cut a large slice for everyone and continued with her winter tale.

Acknowledgements

Thanks to:

Fiz Osborne, of course!

Pete Matthews for his expert editorial eye. Liam Drane for the fantastic new and sparkly cover art. Sarah Dutton, Harriet Dunlea, Laila Dickson, Lucy Page, Tina Miller and everyone else at Scholastic for their work on the books and continuing to get the unicorns out in the world despite the challenges and changes of the past couple of years.

Louise and Jodi, aka The Streamers, for holding my hand all the way to the Far North and back. You are both wonderful writers and friends.

Simon for giving me the original Elgu nearly twenty years ago. Clara for advising on small animals in drawers. Tom for his Lego build which helped me visualise the final scenes.

Special mention to Caroline Checkley, as the joint designer of the first peacock feather snoncho.

To all my lovely readers, with thanks for staying in touch. As you know, my Dark Unicorn books often look to other fairytales for inspiration and influence. This one contains a few nods to The Snow Queen by Hans Christian Andersen, which I hope you'll enjoy.

Also available:

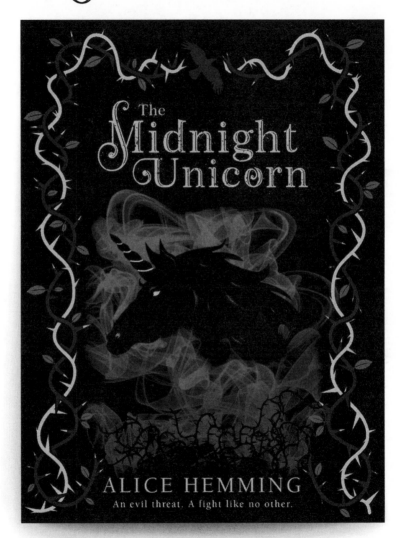

The
Darkest
Unicorn
ALICE HEMMING
Not all unicorns are good

The Cursed Unicorn

ALICE HEMMING

Would you risk everything for the people you love?

The
Blazing
Unicorn

ALICE HEMMING

An evil king, a fearsome warrior, a fight for freedom.